Firecrest

BOOKS BY

VICTOR CANNING

Firecrest

VICTOR CANNING

HEINEMANN : LONDON

William Heinemann Ltd
15 Queen Street, Mayfair, London W1X 8BE

LONDON   MELBOURNE   TORONTO
JOHANNESBURG   AUCKLAND

First published 1971
© Victor Canning 1971

SBN 434 10769 7

MADE AND PRINTED IN GREAT BRITAIN BY
MORRISON AND GIBB LTD, LONDON AND EDINBURGH

To
Daniel Richmond—with
apologies for poaching
on his fishing rights

F.—1*

The author and publisher are grateful to
Harmony Music for permission to reprint
sixteen words from "The Space Girl's Song"
by Peggy Seeger and to Essex Music Ltd for
permission to reprint six words from "Judge
Jefferies" by Chris Plail.

CHAPTER ONE

THERE WAS VERY little talk between them as Lily drove.
Earlier in the day there had been rain and the night frost now
made the road slippery in places so that most of Lily's attention
was on her driving. She had to drive because some months
earlier Harry had had his licence suspended for a year. She
smiled to herself. . . . Professor Henry Dilling, drunk in charge.
He liked his tipple now and again though he was usually very
careful about driving under the influence. But bad luck had
been waiting for him. She flexed her shoulders. It had been a
long day and a lot of driving.

Harry was whistling gently to himself. The same tune for the
last half an hour. *Que será, será.* It was buzzing in her head now
and she said, "For God's sake change the record, Harry."

He laughed and said, "Why? It's special for today. Esoteric
connection."

She didn't know what he meant, but then often she didn't
when he used difficult words. Not that she cared. He had given
her a new life. He could have his esoterics and his little secrets if
they pleased him. He had been educating her for the last three
years now, but she knew, no matter how much she tried to catch
up, that he lived on a height for ever out of her reach. Not that
she worried so long as he was good to her. And he was. He had
done a lot for her. A hell of a lot. Affection warmed her. He'd
given her a new life—and now, according to him, there was an
even better one ahead. Pots of money. She drove automatically,
capable and careful, and her mind was suddenly full of the thought
of luxuries . . . a mink coat even, expensive hotels, a villa in the

sun, herself lying by a pool in a bikini. . . . She'd have to watch her weight a bit. . . . No matter how much Harry liked it, she could do with a few pounds off . . . a little less just here and there.

On the far side of Newbury he said, "Pull up at the next crossroads." He reached over and took a small spade from the back of the car and went on, as though answering some question from her, "Give a soil analyst a few flecks of mud—and he'll tell whose back garden you've been digging. Science has over-complicated life." He reached across and cupped the palm of his hand over her knee, his fingers moulding her flesh.

When she pulled up at the crossroads he got out with the spade. She wound down the side window, lit a cigarette and watched his tall, lean form, indigo and grey under the frost-sharp starlight, disappear into the trees. She drew on her cigarette, then spread her arms and eased her body against the long drive. For all his cleverness he was a boy really . . . always getting a kick out of daft things. Making a mystery of things just for the fun of it. Billy Who, for instance. What a lot of childish nonsense that was. Still, he was her Harry. They were close, very close. Complementary. That was a word she had learned from him. Esoteric connection? What was that? A kind of love? No, that was erotic. Erotic connection. She smiled to herself. There'd always been plenty of that, and would be again before this night was over. She could sense the excitement running in him. And when he was like that, or when he'd had a few drinks, it was something you could bet on. . . . Anyway, what the hell was it all about, all this night driving and secrecy and that case of his buried God knew where in the country? If he wanted to tell her he would. If he didn't—then she would never ask. She knew better than that by now. She had driven today, following his instructions without question . . . just as she had been following his instructions for the last few years. No questions. Whatever he did was right, and for her there was gratitude and gratification because of the relief he had given her, taking her from behind the counter at Boots, no more handing out cosmetics, films and aspirins. Well, if he wanted his secrets he could have them. So long as he was kind to her he could twist her round his little finger. She didn't mind that. Kindness suited her. Let's face it, a woman had to have it.

He came back without the spade and said, "I chucked it in a pond. The water shattered like a mirror and I put up two duck." He leaned over, took her cigarette and drew on it. When he gave it back to her his hand moved up, touched her cheek and slid slowly across the warmth of her neck.

She drove on, the road becoming familiar now, trees, fields and valley shapes riding up like old friends. The white faces of known cottages and hotels marked off the miles until they were in their own village.

He got out, lifted the garage door for her, and they walked to the house with his arm round her shoulder, their breath pluming before them in the cold night air.

Inside, he poured whisky for them both. He sprawled in a chair, his feet up on another, and the excitement was clear and strong in him. He held up his glass so that the light was reflected from the crystal cuttings and the tawny swirl of the liquid. He said, "You're a big, beautiful girl and I'm going to load you with loving and luxuries."

She sipped her whisky and smiled, and she saw herself, idling in the waters of a blue-tiled pool, felt the wind in her hair as she drove an open, expensive car through the warmth of an eternal summer day, saw Harry with her, their love so strong and sure that nothing could touch or mar it.

*   *   *   *

Outside, at two o'clock in the morning, a short, fat, mildly angry man, swaddled in a top coat, padding his numbed feet on the frozen grass against the cold, saw their bedroom light go off at last. With a grunt of relief he moved away down the lane towards his car parked half a mile away. At least, he thought, he'd seen them come back, though it was a sod that he'd missed them going off. Tricky bastards. They'd done it to

3

him before. Must have moved away early in the morning. He'd have to cover the gap in his report somehow. Fudge it up, say he'd lost them in traffic. What did it matter? It wouldn't be the first time. Anyway, if it had been of any real importance the Department would have given him a couple of assistants so that he could have mounted a twenty-four-hour watch. Those two in there, warmly cuddled up in bed, and him out here, his feet like bloody slabs of tombstone marble. He blew his breath out vigorously and angrily, and wondered if he would be able to get a drink out of the night porter. Rum, he thought, a large glass of rum . . . his body suddenly ached for it.

*　　　*　　　*　　　*

Lily and Harry went to London the next day—which was a Saturday—on the train. Lily had a large suitcase with her. She was catching a plane later that morning at Heathrow. Harry went with her as far as the West London air terminal to see her off on the airport bus. He bought her some women's magazines, fussed around her, hugged and kissed her goodbye and smiled to himself at the dark glasses she was wearing because she felt they made her look like a film star. Foreign travel was still an excitement for her and when she was excited, he knew, she liked to think of herself as important. She was child and woman. As much as he could anyone, he loved her; but his strongest joy in her, he acknowledged, was that he possessed her. She was his.

After she had gone he went to a telephone booth in the main hall, dialled a London number and then asked for the Department's extension. When a familiar voice answered him, he said, "This is Dilling here. I'll be with you in an hour. I'm not bringing the stuff with me. For safekeeping I've hidden it. I know I promised to bring it, but yesterday I changed my mind. It's staying hidden until we agree on the basic financial details."

The voice at the other end said mournfully, "It was an unnecessary precaution. This is a straightforward business deal, though I must tell you that the general opinion is that your terms are far too high. We shall need a certain amount of time before a decision is made."

"You can take a reasonable amount of time. But don't forget there are other markets where I know the financial side would cause no trouble."

The voice, a little shocked, said, "For the sake of good relations, I haven't heard that remark, and please don't repeat it to anyone here. It would be most indiscreet."

Dilling said, "I shan't repeat it unless I'm forced to."

He rang off and walked to the terminal exit to find a taxi. Whatever they said, he knew there was every reason to distrust the Department until the lawyers had made the contract binding. He raised a hand to signal a taxi, thinking of Lily on her way to the airport, of Lily as he had first seen her behind the counter of Boots the Chemists in Uckfield, remembering the touch of her hand as she had passed him his change. With his mind full of her, he dropped dead from a coronary thrombosis just as the taxi pulled up beside him.

He was a little over forty-one at his death, unmarried, and with a respected reputation in his profession. It was a week before the police identified him. *The Times* gave him a third of a column obituary notice. His permanent address was a small flat in Chelsea. But although the police took some time to identify him, there were others who knew of his death within three or four hours. His estate was modest, some furniture, clothes and books and five thousand pounds held mostly on deposit at his bank. The bank also held his will. He left everything he had to Miss Lily Brenda Stevens of the Old Croft, Sparton, in the County of Berkshire. The Old Croft was a rented, furnished house, the lease of which ran out exactly one week after his death, the lease being in his name.

Lily went to Florence, to a room booked in the Hotel Excelsior. Without any immediate cause for money worries, she waited to hear from him. She heard of his death a month later through a friend she had made in Florence, but she was unaware that she had been left all that he had owned. The

5

news of his death brought tears and some real but not undue grief. She was upset that she had missed his funeral, seeing herself in smart black, a solitary grieving figure. Then, after a short time, she was content. Because of a malleable and basically shrewd character, from which commonsense was far from missing, she was happy to let time and chance with a little help from herself fashion a new direction to her life. After all it was what Harry would have wanted . . . for her not to grieve for ever, life had to go on. Love had gone from her life, of course, for the time being, but as long as she found kindness and comfort she saw no reason to complain. Things would work themselves out.

Quite a few people were looking for her, but it was a long time before she was traced. It was six months in fact and by this time Lily had moved, by way of a few other countries, to France.

*   *   *   *

The Department found her first. The Department was an offshoot of the Ministry of Defence. Its existence had never been officially acknowledged. Its functions—proliferating under the pressure of national security—were as old as organised society. Its work was discreet and indecent. Security and economy demanded that certain people and certain situations had to be handled, organised, dispatched or suppressed without the public being disturbed or distressed by any awareness of the mostly unmentionable stratagems that, in the interests of the national welfare, the Department was given an ambiguous mandate to employ. Murder, blackmail, fraud, theft and betrayal were the commonplaces of the Department. The Department existed, but its existence would have been denied. Its members and operators lived in the common society but acted outside it. Most had entered the Department aware of some of its extreme aspects and prepared to adjust themselves. None had had originally a complete understanding of it; and when this had come it was too late—for knowledge had by then brought acquiescence and even a measure of pride and self-satisfaction at being part of a body of work and action which first changed, then isolated them, and finally smoothly endowed them with an inhumanity that inwardly set them aside from all other people. The head of the Department was Sir John Maserfield.

The decoded signal giving brief details of Lily's situation and whereabouts was waiting on his desk when he came back from lunch at Scott's restaurant in Mount Street. He carried the signal to the window and read it in a shaft of sunlight. Far below the brown, polluted flood of the Thames rolled seawards and a string of black barges, like linked water beetles, fought its way upstream against the outgoing tide.

He was a shortish man, neat in a brown suit, and his movements were always abrupt, even a little finicky. Nearing sixty, he carried himself well, his face seldom expressing other than complete control of all emotion; everything about him was contained, precise and impeccable, his iron-grey moustache groomed and regimented, the fingernails of his liver-spotted hands immaculate.

He went back to his desk and pressed the bell for Coppelstone. While he waited he lit a cigarette, smoking it with brisk little flourishes, holding it away from himself between puffs as though he could not bear the thought of the smallest fleck of ash falling on his clothes. There was nothing about his composure to suggest that he was angry. But he was—at the stupidity and inefficiency that had made this search last six months. It was a disciplined anger, like all his emotions. What he felt he never showed in the office, and what he thought his speech only partly outlined. He was a compact, secret man who released little of himself to those with whom he worked.

Coppelstone came in; a big man in his late forties with thinning blond hair and a large, high-complexioned baby face. There was a small dry cut from his morning shave above his upper lip. Few mornings passed without Coppelstone cutting himself. Sir John knew why. Coppelstone went to bed well-charged with whisky every night. There was little of importance about Coppelstone which Sir John did not know.

Sir John held up the signal. "She's in St. Jean-de-Luz."

"Yes, Sir John. Just outside. She should have been traced within a week, but our French people—"

Sir John cut across the mournful voice, "Never mind that. You know what has to be done with her. Who is going to handle her?"

This last was a rhetorical question. Coppelstone knew that Sir John would have already decided who was to deal with her.

He said, "We're thin on the ground at the moment and it might be a long, tedious business."

"And it could be a fruitless one. The whole thing could be a useless fantasy—but until we know we must treat it as serious. If it turns out genuine, then we have a problem. The girl inherited Professor Dilling's estate. From our reports she's a stupid, feather-headed type of girl. But if his claim is correct then she'll be in line for hundreds of thousands of pounds." He put his cigarette carefully in an ashtray and watched the thin blue smoke curl away in the light draught from the open window. "Feather-headed doesn't mean stupid about money necessarily. We want an unencumbered asset. That means getting rid of her."

Unmoved, purely as a matter of routine, Coppelstone said, "Is that absolutely necessary?"

"You don't sit in on the finance committee, Coppelstone. If we can get something cheaply, we get it. If we can get something for nothing, then we forget cheapness. When we've got from her what we want, she'll have to go. Mind you, whoever handles her won't know that. He can just hold out the carrot of a substantial fortune."

Eight floors below, walking the streets and the river embankment, were men and women, Coppelstone thought, who had no idea of this world up here where human lives meant nothing. Momentarily he longed to be at home, isolated in his flat, pouring the first evening whisky on the road to forgetfulness.

8

He had too much on his conscience to want to be alone at night with a gallery of sharp-cut memories.

"That's a direction, Sir John?"

"Of course. If Dilling's stuff is valid, she goes, and the country's tax-payers will be saved a half a million, maybe. I agreed it with the Minister some time ago. He made the usual Christian noises at first. I thought Grimster would be the man for this." Sir John picked up his cigarette, flicked the ash neatly into the tray and then, holding it upwards like a small torch in the triangle of thumb and first two fingers, addressed the cigarette rather than Coppelstone. "Bit of a problem, Grimster. In fact, we made a mistake with him. He's basically unreliable because of it."

"He's frank about the approaches that have been made to him."

"Naturally, he's no fool. He's a first-class man, but his loyalty to this Department is in the balance. We turned a top man into a potential security risk. Our mistake, but there's no altering it."

"I don't think he'll ever do anything."

"You're wrong, Coppelstone. Give him long enough and he'll act on conjecture. It isn't a wise thing to wait until he turns against us. I'd say that he's good for one more job."

Because he liked Grimster, Coppelstone made an effort for him. "You may be reading him wrong, Sir John."

Annoyed, but not showing it, Sir John said, "No, I'm not. He's waiting for hard proof—which he'll never get. In the end he'll accept what his commonsense and knowledge of this place tell him must have been so. I like Grimster as much as you do, maybe more. Let him do this job and, when it's done and the girl's gone, then Grimster can go. Get him down to St. Jean-de-Luz right away and tell High Grange to expect both of them."

"Very good, Sir John. How far do I brief Grimster about the girl?"

"Just enough for him to operate. If he guesses what's going to happen to her eventually . . . well, he guesses. But don't

9

inform him. By the way, I left my walking stick at Scott's."
Sir John held out a cloakroom ticket to Coppelstone. "Send
someone round to collect it for me, will you?"

Coppelstone left, holding the ticket in his hand. It was a pity
about Grimster, he thought, but he was not over moved. One
went past the point of pity early in the Department. In fact
Grimster's eventual removal could be good for him. He had
always thought Sir John had Grimster marked out as his
successor. With Grimster gone he, Coppelstone, was next in
line. He looked at the ticket in his hand. . . . You had a good
lunch at Scott's—no oysters because it was August, but maybe
sole meunière with a fillet steak to follow, half a bottle of cheap
Beaune—Sir John was economical with wine—then taxied
back to the office and disposed of two lives with no more effort
than it took to send out for a forgotten walking stick. A department without charity, only a calm, inflexible dedication to a
multifaced god called security, a monster reared for the protection of the little men and women who walked the streets far
below and in whose name a thousand stupid and violent
inhumanities were practised.

On the way back to his own office, he looked into the small
room which Grimster used when he was in the building. It was
empty but on the desk was a note—*Gone to the cinema. Back five-
thirty. Girl at desk will know my seat. Ring 01. 293. 4537. J.G.*
Clamped to the corner of the table was a fly-tying vice and on
the table was a box with a clutter of materials, silk threads,
hackles and feathers, varnishes and a scattering of different
sized hooks. In the vice was a half-tied fly. Fishing meant
nothing to Coppelstone but he picked up a cape of feathers and
stroked it with one finger. Grimster, he thought, lost now in
some film fantasy that could never approach some of the
fantasies he had already endured . . . and now another waited
for him. The final fantasy which he was to share with some
blonde-haired, feather-brained girl of twenty-two, a former
Boots assistant; Dilling's girl—Dilling who had spoken to him
just a few minutes before his death—who was now the travelling

companion of a Mrs. Judith Harroway, wealthy widow with restless feet . . . so restless that they had accounted for a six months' gap in discovering the girl that Grimster would have to sweet talk and cosset, grow close to and pump dry of all information. Then with smooth expertise she would be eliminated, for there was no doubt that what Dilling had offered for sale was worth the price he had demanded. Dilling had been an odd, brilliant bird—but not one to offer specious goods. And after the girl had gone, Grimster would go.

CHAPTER TWO

THE MAID HAD shown Grimster into the lounge and when Mrs. Harroway came into the room he was standing at the large window looking out over the garden, hibiscus and oleander tangled, that sloped to the main road running from St. Jean-de-Luz to the Spanish border. Beyond the road lay a footing of low dun-coloured rocks and then the Atlantic, grey and foam-ridden under a high summer gale that now and then shook the windows with its force. He heard her entry and turned.

He was not very tall, craggily built, a cragginess that was in the face, too, furrowing and scarping it, a strong, pleasant face that smiled suddenly at her with a slow warmth that she felt could mean nothing because they had never met before and meant nothing to one another. Maybe this was professional among them. When they wanted something then everything they did and said came out with a hallmark of validity stamped on it. He had close-cut iron-grey hair and, although he couldn't be far into his forties, the grey flecking in places had turned white. His clothes were good, a small hound's tooth check suit, highly polished brown shoes, a light blue shirt and a darker blue tie. Her eye took in all the details. There was the faintest blue of obstinate stubble at the sides of his chin, though he was meticulously shaven.

He said, "Mrs. Harroway? I'm John Grimster." The voice was surprisingly deep, educated, but with a touch of some regional accent. "I think our people phoned you?"

"They did. You've come to take Lily away."

12

He smiled. "Hardly take. We'd like her help and co-operation. She stands to gain a lot by it."

Firmly, she said, "Frankly, I don't trust you people when you say someone stands to gain a lot by helping you. What you mean is that you stand to gain much more. My late husband was in politics. I know how the Government mind works. It's just a mind without a body to embarrass it with ordinary human sensations."

He nodded half agreement, thinking that she was still wide of the mark; even the mind didn't function on an ordinary human level. She was a tall woman, well-preserved, one of the young-old, not desperately fighting age, but coolly combating it with all her good sense and wealth.

He said, "We just want her free co-operation. Professor Dilling was an important man. Some of his work has been lost. Miss Stevens is probably the only one who can help us to find it. There is also the matter of his estate—which she inherits—to be cleared up. She knows about this now, I presume?"

"She does, and she's quite excited about it. Nobody's ever left her any money before. You needn't worry about her co-operation. I shall be sorry to lose her, but I feel I was going to very soon anyway. She was beginning to get restless with me. Six months is about as much as any young woman can take as companion to an old woman."

"Old?"

It was said without any shadow of false gallantry.

"I'm nearly seventy. She'll be down in a minute."

"How did you come to meet her?" Mrs. Harroway, he knew, was on the point of deciding whether she liked him or not. It was easy to tell. Somewhere along the line, probably through her husband, she had come in contact with some department like his and disliked it. He didn't care personally what decision she made. The moment he was given an assignment most of his personal feelings were stored away in a well-used depository, so much furniture and fittings to gather dust.

She said, "I met her in a hotel in Florence. We became

13

friends and I was the one who finally told her about Dilling's death. Her money was beginning to run out. There were already two or three Italian men interested in her. So, I took her under my wing as a companion." She paused and then, without change of tone, went on, "Dilling was the only man she'd ever known intimately and—I gather—he really loved and cared for her. I didn't want her second experience to be shared with some Milan manufacturer who would be fonder of his pasta and Chianti than he ever would be of her. She came with me and we travelled a lot. I don't like to be in one place long. Are you married, Mr. Grimster?"

A great buffet of wind shook the big windows, and for a moment his compact body stirred as though some of the force of the wind had entered the room.

"No, I'm not, Mrs. Harroway." That was for her, but for himself the answer was "Yes"; finally and irrevocably, married to the past and the dead, so locked in a cold love that no other human being could ever thaw him.

She moved to the door and pressed a wall bell. Half turned to him, she said, "I just want to know that she's going to be looked after. She's a silly girl in some ways, remarkably shrewd in others. Dilling tried to educate her. He taught her a lot. How to behave and how to speak in the kind of company he wanted her to keep. She's picked up some Italian and French easily, but she hasn't got a first-class mind. Reading anything but magazines bores her. So long as she is comfortable and looked after she's content to sit and day-dream. But she's good company for my kind. I had all the intellectual companionship I wanted with my late husband."

He said, "She'll be in comfort and she'll be looked after." Without any personal curiosity he waited for Lily.

Answering the summons of the bell, she came in and was introduced to him. She was a tall, very good-looking, blonde young woman with a large figure that at the moment gave her no trouble. In ten years she would be worrying about it, dieting and fighting the sudden desires for chocolates and cream desserts. She held herself well, clearly aware and proud of her figure. She'd overmade her face for this presentation. Knowing something now of Dilling he wondered whether the professor would have approved of this excess. Probably, yes. She had been his thing, part of his creation, but he would have known where to relax controls. Her face was a longish oval, the skin smooth and warm-tanned with sun beneath the makeup. Junoesque, a dish, all woman, it was hard to believe that Dilling was the only man who had had her. That might be disproved when the interrogations began. But she was a woman that no man would have been content to look at just once. Behind the chemist's counter she must have rung up many sales for unwanted aspirins and talcum powder. Hazel-green eyes, a large, firm, but far from hard mouth and, for these few moments, a change of expressions chasing one another across her face while she tried to stabilise her attitude to him and to the circumstances. He was amused as they talked to see it slowly settle to a smooth, lovely blandness as she found comfort and ease. The moment she felt at home she became herself, the relaxed odalisque waiting to be told what to do next. Her voice, beneath a not too deliberately imposed gentility, was a country voice, broad, touched with a certain throatiness which was full of an innocent sensuousness. The hand which she had held out for his grasp was soft, large and moistly warm.

When Mrs. Harroway left them, they sat down and he said, "You understand, Miss Stevens, that we want you to come absolutely of your own free will in order to help us?"

"Yes, of course. What have I got to do?"

"I'll explain all that later. We just want to talk to you about things . . . about Professor Dilling."

"Why?" The shrewdness that Mrs. Harroway had claimed moved briefly in her.

"I'll tell you later. The whole thing won't take long. A month at the very most and you'll live in a country house with everything you want."

She lit a cigarette, frowning for a moment at her badly

working lighter, and said, "It is true, is it, that Harry left me everything? That's no lie?"

"Everything. It's not much, though. Some furniture and effects, his personal stuff and about five thousand pounds."

"You call five thousand pounds not much?"

"Well, it's nice to have around."

She laughed, and it was with her whole body, shoulders and breasts moving, a natural movement that seemed to put her totally, yet innocently, on exhibition. The laughter died in her with a pleased shake of the head. She said, "Are you taking me to this country house?"

"No. I'm taking you as far as Paris. Someone else will look after you from there. But I shall join you later."

"Where is this place?"

"They'll tell you in Paris. It's in England."

"Why the secrecy?"

He grinned. "It's the way some government departments work. Professor Dilling was a very important man."

She nodded agreement and then, he guessed, because she felt it was due from her, said, "Poor Harry . . . just fancy, dropping dead like that only a few minutes after I left him, and me not knowing for weeks. I don't know what I would have done without Mrs. Harroway." Her face went grave, as though she were considering the advisability, purely for good manners, of squeezing out a tear. Then surprisingly, she grinned and said, "Probably got into trouble with one of those Italian Romeos."

Probably so, he thought. He would be interviewing her now in some summer-rented villa at Portofino or on the Lido and some overweight Italian tycoon would be proving much less understanding of affairs than had Mrs. Harroway. He could almost have wished it was that way. It would have been a pleasure to deal with the man, to frighten him ruthlessly, to threaten and hint at trouble from the local Questura.

She said, "What do I call you? Mr. Grimster all the time?"

He said, "My name is John. We could make it John and Lily, if you like."

"O.K. But it'll have to be Johnny. And are you really a . . . well, what they call a secret service agent?"

He laughed, deliberately weighting it with denial and reassurance. "Good God, no. I just work for a government department in the Ministry of Defence. A civil servant. We just want you to help us in a routine enquiry about Professor Dilling. But it's one we don't want publicised in any way. If you should meet anyone you know all you have to say is that you're going back to England, to stay in the country and settle up the details of your inheritance." She would get no chance to say it to anyone. From the moment he took her from here into his car to drive to the airport at Biarritz and the plane to Paris, she would meet no one she knew.

To his surprise, she said, "I don't really believe you, Johnny. You look as though there's something very secret about you. Where I lived with Harry in the country we had a man watching the house for the whole of a week once and Harry said he was secret service and a damned waste of money."

He said, "Anyone who wants to know something is a secret agent. The world's full of them. Chaps who snoop around in vans to check whether you have a TV licence. Inspectors who fancy you may be beating your dog or your wife. Scores of them." He smiled, and then went on, choosing his words to fit a pattern that she would recognise and welcome. "I'm a civil servant. Mostly nine until five, unless there's a special job like this—and this is the kind of job we all like to have now and then. A few weeks' stay in a luxury country house with a pretty girl so that we can ask her some questions. And don't think we're asking you to do this for nothing. You inherit everything Professor Dilling owned. Maybe we shall turn up something the lawyers don't know about, something that would mean money for you, a lot of money. Even if it doesn't you'll be paid for your trouble and will have had a pleasant month's holiday and then can come back to Mrs. Harroway if you wish."

17

"She's nice, and she's taught me a lot, travelling about. You've just got to be rude to hotel people and waiters sometimes if you want service. Sail in as though you owned the place and never let up. It works if you've got the money. Still . . . now I've got five thousand I don't know as I would want to come back. I mean I don't know *that* I would want to come back." She laughed. "Harry would have jumped me on that one. When we first met I didn't know what a split infinitive was, and, too, I used to say that things *wouldn't notice.* . . . Poor Harry. He was very patient and loving, but he was very hard to know really." She recrossed her legs, smoothed down the run of her skirt and, as she began to fiddle with her lighter and another cigarette, she went on, for the first time with a hint of coquetry, "Maybe you're like that, I think. Patient and loving—when you want—and hard to really know well."

He said, "You've just done it."

She nodded. "Split an infinitive. I know. But Harry said there wasn't a damned reason why you shouldn't if you wanted emphasis."

He smiled, knowing that she was beginning to be at home with him, knowing that, while she wouldn't give any real trouble, there was character and strength hidden by the chocolate-box face and the beautiful, bedworthy body. Looking at her legs, running in smooth, sweet curves, at the rounded thrust of her full breasts he knew that a few years ago there would have been a natural lust in him for her. Now there rested only an easy, detached design on her, a brief to break and enter her mind and memory only. He had no concern for her, except to accommodate himself to her wave-length and make a simple record of the signals that pulsed from it. Patient, loving, and hard to really know well. All that, except the loving, that had withered on the vine when Valda had been killed.

* * * *

He left her in Paris with the Embassy section, and flew alone to London. He had been a little surprised that they had wanted

18

him to go to St. Jean-de-Luz to fetch her to Paris. He could have met her at High Grange. Maybe for some reason Sir John had wanted the first leg to be an exposure, to test for other interests. He didn't know and he didn't care. You got a brief and you followed it, held strictly to it. Yours not to question why.

On his first night back Harrison turned up at his flat in time for the first whisky of the evening. Harrison he had known since a boy at Wellington; Harrison who had had the next cubicle in Combermere and couldn't even make a decent mug of cocoa, but went around with a pocket full of snares and catapults and a forbidden collapsible air gun, poaching and warring on squirrels and rabbits, laying night lines in the college lake and once taking a three-pound carp, half its side badly covered with fungus. Harrison was still poaching and laying snares. One day he would be trapped himself and knew it, though it in no way abated his cheerful dedication to deceit and chicanery. He was a fat, breathless type with a chuckling unconcern for the distant future so long as he had present money in the bank, a woman to bed with at night, and an involvement in dark activity that demanded light treading and a knowledge of the movements of every keeper. Harrison belonged to no organisation permanently. He was a free-lance, knowing all sides, and moving from one loyalty to another easily, but dedicated to nothing except his own physical indulgences and misanthropic manoeuvres; an intelligent savage at odds with the society which had caged him. Sir John knew of his friendship with Harrison, and had ordered the relationship to continue for, if Harrison felt that there were things to be got from him, there were things to be had from Harrison, too.

Harrison fixed himself a drink.

"Missed you for a couple of days, Johnny."

"Did it hurt?"

"No. How often do you check this place for bugging?"

"Never. Anything said here the world can hear."

Harrison chuckled, doubled the measure of whisky he had

given himself, and dropped his large bottom gently into an armchair. He nodded and drank and said, "You could earn a lot of money by a little co-operation."

"I don't need money."

"Revenge, perhaps?"

"If you want to be kicked out—just carry on with that line."

"It takes a lot of kicking to move me. Eighteen stone at the last score. And I know you. Revenge is in your mind like a tumour on the brain."

"Nicely put." One day Harrison would end up dead in a back alley, and Harrison knew it and was unconcerned because it seemed remote and there was a lot of money to be made and spent and women to be laid before then.

"I'll put it plainer one day. Land the proof you need about Valda's death in your lap. Then you'll come into the market. You'll want to dish them. You can gum the works up on some big deal—maybe like the important one you're on now—and then take off for parts unknown with pockets so full of loot it'll take you all your strength to climb the plane steps. Commission man Harrison says so, knows it's so. Any comments?"

"No."

Not for publication to Harrison. But he knew the man was near the truth. But the essence of truth was proof. Given proof —a very unlikely thing, for the Department was long practised in tidying up the proofs of murder—what would he do? Go in off the deep end? Consecrate himself to mischief in the fullest sense of the word, take the sword and become a master of unruly revels? God knew. Some moments could not be anticipated.

As though his thoughts had echoed clearly to Harrison, the other said, "If you knew for sure, all your training, the thousands they spent on you, would swing against them. Why not? In your heart you know they murdered Valda—"

"Shut up!" He clipped the words out without raising his voice.

"Why should I? Since Wellington you've been telling me to

shut up and I never have. Like a good boy you asked for permission to marry. They had too much invested in you to risk it in pillow talk—though if they'd understood you as I do they would have known there was no risk. So . . . why give you the flat refusal? That would have been crude. They said, yes, O.K., name the day, and before the day came they fixed her—"

"You bastard!"

Grimster jumped from his chair and his hands were around Harrison's fat neck, the pressure turned on fast and then steadying so that the man's breathing was choked. The fat, vein-lined face slowly flushed darker; and Harrison sat there without struggle, enduring it, the whisky glass in his hand untrembling and the caricature of a smile struggling through the muscles of his bloodshot face. Slowly Grimster took his hands away.

"Thanks," said Harrison. "I had a bet with myself that you would throw your glass. You did the last time. But you don't fool me. I know play-acting when I see it."

"Because we're old friends," said Grimster, "I allow you the privilege of seeing me let down my back hair from time to time."

"That, and an occasional loan are what friends are for." Harrison finished his whisky and got up to help himself to another. He toasted Grimster over it and wondered why, since this was the one man in the world he had ever liked, had admiration and understanding for, he should ride him so hard like this . . . had done ever since the day he had heard the news of Valda's death. For the money they were offering? Yes; but far from that alone. Because he loved him so much he wanted to destroy him? A lot of psychological crap. Because he was Grimster that nobody could touch, hard as iron, complete, a reproach to him because he would always be the poacher, the commission man, the fixer, the unsettled, unwanted, driven to expose the loneliness and shabbiness of others' lives and characters?

He tossed the whisky back in one draught, and said, looking

at his watch, "Must go. Got to throw my leg over a pretty little widow in an hour. A man carrying my weight mustn't miss his exercise. Any time you feel like turning your coat and picking up a sackful of roubles, yuans, pesos, dinars, dollars or whatever, give me a ring. I can show you plenty of testimonials from others who've done it, and lived happily ever after. Night, Johnny."

When he was gone Grimster reached down the side of the cushion on his chair and switched off the recorder that was hidden in the seat. In the morning he would dutifully hand the cassette to Coppelstone. By now they had a fat library of Harrisonia. He wanted them to have it. He wanted them to know what was going on. If they were innocent then there should be trust on both sides; if they weren't, one day they would let something slip out before his eyes or ears and then. . . .

He reached out for a cigar, lit it, and thought without a shade of emotional emphasis, Christ, when did it all begin?

It was the day he had been curious and old enough to ask questions about his supposedly dead father. The day at Wellington when it had become clear to him that his mother could not possibly have afforded the fees, she, a housekeeper for a wealthy farmer in Yorkshire. And, before that, nursery maid, cook, cook-housekeeper, companion in a succession of houses all over the country. The later days had brought all the proof—unknown to her—that he needed; her bureau searched, keys and locks no bar to him, the idle questions put to her over the months and the contradictions noted, the slow interrogation she never suspected and the final establishment of his bastardy. Dear Christ, why had she bothered? Bastardy was nothing to him. But for her his conception had been the big sin of her life. Even now, though he saw her infrequently, he longed sometimes to put his arm around her and say, "Forget it all." But his career had started from that, an induced need and love of breaking down a problem and of working on a person to draw out the truth unobtrusively. His own origin had been the first secret. By the time he was sixteen he knew everything except his father's name without his mother knowing he knew, imagination and a growing understanding of the way of the world bridging the few small gaps. As a nursery maid of eighteen she had been seduced by the young son of the house. She and the child were looked after; the father providing for him discreetly through his mother, some quirk of guilt or pride in the man deciding that he should go to Wellington, have good holidays, learn to fish and shoot and ride, become the proper gentleman though from the wrong side of the blanket. All his wants were cared for unobtrusively until he was twenty-one, by which time he had passed to other secrets that needed unravelling, and had found a love for the arcane and a delight in the labyrinthine. From an army commission and service he had slipped almost without a ripple into the Department and within months had taken it for his first love. For his unknown father he had no feeling, only a complete understanding. For himself he had no self-pity. The talent for that indulgence was lacking in him, not even to flicker for a moment when, within a few weeks of their marriage day to be, they had come to him with the news that Valda was dead. He destroyed every photograph he had of her, every letter, every tangible thing from and of her that he possessed. He had no need of them to keep memory awake, and for grief he substituted the iron longing for the moment of truth about her death which would release him to action. He, and he knew it, was a pleasant man, but a hard and ruthless one and he was in complete control of himself, only throwing the sop of pretended emotion now and then to Harrison for his own and departmental purposes, spurring Harrison to bring him proof if he could, living for the day when he could unleash violence with justification absolute, and so end his celibacy of mind and flesh without a care for the consequences.

John Grimster was at this moment in time the most dangerous of all animals, a man with a precisely controlled and rationalised obsession.

And Sir John Maserfield knew it and to some extent was fascinated by it because it had been produced by one of his rare departmental mistakes. It was a commonplace that none of the operators in the Department were normal. Normal men could never have operated. The demands of the Department were abnormal. Its brief was inhuman, yet considered necessary, even if never openly stated. It was there, and had to be there though there was an official conspiracy to ignore its existence, an elaborate charade enacted by everyone to mask its true functions of violence and deceit. Sir John's greatest unhappiness—disclosed to no one—was that a brilliant military career had ironically isolated and nominated him as the natural head of the Department, a ringmaster who could match ferocity, guile and suddenness of movement with any of his charges. But Grimster now was the one tiger in the ring on whom his back could only for the briefest second be turned. Yet his individual act outshone all others and would keep him in pride of place until the day came, now close, when Sir John knew that the secret, growing strain upon himself would demand relief and the tiger would have to be put down.

Meanwhile with the late August sunlight streaming through the windows high above the river, touching the silver-framed photograph of his wife and two sons on the desk, he released the edge of a smile now and then as he briefed Grimster.

He said, "Dilling had started a deal with us for a private discovery he had made. The exact nature of it is outside your brief. Physically it would consist of about twenty-odd pages of some research results of his. Personally I think they may contain nonsense. Our job is to find the papers and establish their validity or not. On his own admission he put the stuff in safe-keeping somewhere on the day before his death. Friday, 27th February, this year. The girl, Lily Stevens, was most probably with him at the time. She certainly returned with him to their Berkshire house, late on the night of that day. I don't have to

24

tell you how to operate. You've met her, so you can settle your own line. I want the usual progress reports from you. It's not a hard case, but there is a minor difficulty."

Grimster watched Sir John hold his cigarette precisely over the centre of an ashtray and neatly tap the loose tip into it.

"You mean that somebody has already had a go at her?"

The beautiful, intellectual tiger act pleased Sir John, though he did not show it. It was wicked to have mutilated this animal by mistake.

"Yes. When she was first traced, the Paris man asked her what she had been doing the day before Dilling's death. She said that she and Dilling had spent the whole day in their house, that neither of them went out. We know that that is not true. What do you make of that?"

Grimster smiled. The secret language between them was perfectly understood, soundless, just the flicker of some mental process; no acknowledgment of his deduction that someone else had talked first to her, no apology for withholding the fact from him. That was normal.

He said, "I shouldn't have thought she would have lied. If you offered her a thousand pounds to tell the truth about that day she would give it to you. Maybe it was the truth. Who did the watching?" He knew that Sir John wouldn't give him the name of the man or the men.

"We've processed him. He missed them in the morning—"

"But he fudged that one over."

"Yes. But he was there when they came back at night."

"Interesting."

"This Miss Stevens may need an upgrading in our assessment of her. You needn't rush her, but I think you'll have to get the background of her relationship with Dilling. Dig deep. She's lying. I want to know why, and I want the truth of that day. And above all, I want those papers—even though they may turn out to be useless. You can drive down today. If there's anything special you want, just let us know. The girl is all yours."

25

Sir John rose and walked to the window, looking down on the pismire shuttling of human movement interweaving along the embankment pavement, at the faint grey stippling of gulls foraging the lowtide mud below the far South Bank. Back to Grimster he said, "Coppelstone says you turned in another cassette on Harrison this morning."

"Yes. He still persists in seeing me as a likely candidate for defection or treason. You'll hear from the tape that he knows I'm on a job. I like Harrison, but he bores me at times. Particularly when I have to play up to all his insistence that Valda's death was no accident."

Sir John turned, nodded agreement, and said, "Persistence. All it needs is a hairline crack in a stone. Water and frost will do the rest. It's not a bad principle for him to work on. If his clumsy attentions become tedious, you only have to say the word."

Grimster laughed. "Let him run. He was my best friend at Wellington. I feel sentimental about him. And, anyway, one day we may want to use him." And watching Sir John at the window, an inner dialogue ran alongside the spoken one. You know, you bastard, where the truth lies about Valda. You know that this is an elaborate pantomime played between us with quick changes of masks and costumes. But one day the truth will step naked between us and then God help you if the face of truth bears the features Harrison says it has, for on that day all the dialogue and action between us will be swift and violent.

Grimster stood up. "I'll be off. It's a long drive."

Sir John came back, sat at his desk, and loosed the fraction of a smile. "Very well, Johnny. It's not the most interesting assignment. Just clear it up quickly and we'll find something more worthy of you."

Grimster moved to the door. For as long as he had worked for Sir John every interview had ended in the same way, the edge of a smile and the single use of his Christian name. Without looking back or another word he went out of the room.

26

HIGH GRANGE WAS in North Devon, about twenty miles from Barnstaple and a few miles south-east of a small village called Chittlehamholt. It was a solid, greystoned house with two upper floors. The front windows were ornamented with small, individual balconies, their rounded pillars patinaed with yellow and green lichen nourished by the mist and rain that drove across the country with the prevailing westerlies. From the outside it had a grim, prison look. Inside it was comfortable, the rooms large and gracious. It stood in two hundred acres of farm and woodland and was approached by a mile-long drive. Most of the property was surrounded by stone walls and high wire fences, but the land on the western side ran out to a high, wooded bluff that overlooked part of the River Taw some miles below the point where the River Mole ran into it. Not far from the river was the farm, occupied by a manager who ran the estate. The property was owned by the Ministry of Defence and that was as much as the local people knew about it, though in the local pubs, particularly late at night, there were various elaborate extensions of this scanty information. It had been acquired originally with the idea of making it a westerly refuge and evacuation headquarters during the Second World War largely because it had deep and extensive cellars, all of which had been steel-plated at great expense. Its original purpose long obsolete, Sir John's Department had taken it over and it was used for a variety of purposes, all of them ones in which publicity was the least welcome element. It was listed as a convalescent and training centre, yet it was seldom used as such, though the farm maintained a small stable of riding horses and there was a tennis court, swimming pool and nearly a mile of double-bank fishing rights in the Taw which below the high wooded bluff ran in a great curving oxbow shape. The fishing rights were made available—at a cheap rate—to well-vetted and high-ranking members of the Ministry of Defence and of Sir John's Department, though when these wished to fish the waters they had to stay at local hotels and the High Grange grounds were barred to them. It was an expensive white elephant, but its possession pleased Sir John who could, when his imagination was touched, be ambivalent in the spending of the taxpayers' money. Training, interrogation, secret conferences with overseas visitors and convalescence . . . these were its official uses. In cold fact, it was only very occasionally used.

Grimster liked the place. He liked the contrast between the grim exterior and the comfortable interior. He liked the rounded slopes of the stone-walled fields and the still, funereal darkness of the fir and oak woods and—because of the house's elevated position—the vast sweeps of sky, particularly when the strong winds tore and buffeted the clouds racing in from the sea. Although, apart from his time at Wellington, most of his youth had been spent in Yorkshire, he felt at home at High Grange, finding in its remoteness and high, exposed position some element of the country places where his mother had been in service.

He arrived an hour before dinner and was met by Coppelstone and the manager of High Grange, Major Cranston, R.E., long retired and missing his left eye for the last fifteen years, though it had not been lost in honourable war service but from a well-directed stone in a North African *souk* while on Sir John's business—hence this consolatory sinecure. Grimster liked Cranston. He was a small, hard, round nut of a man and, with his hair short-cropped and the black eye-patch, was a little like General Dayan to look at. He had a secretary, a Mrs. Pilch—Angela—the widow of a Colonel, who had quarters at High Grange, vetted secure and sound, and with whom— it was public knowledge—he slept every other night. He had

28

a passion for small arms and had written a book on the infantry weapons of the American Civil War. He laughed like a boiler exploding, rode to hounds, never drank, believed in physical fitness almost to the point of making it a religion and, although he was very sentimental about animals and had instituted a small graveyard for his past pets behind the tennis court, would have slit Grimster's throat without a shade of feeling if Sir John had ordered it. His father had been a clergyman. He gripped Grimster's hand as though intending to break every finger bone and said, "The river's bloody low so you won't get any good fishing, but I've no doubt Miss Stevens will prove equally diverting."

Grimster said, "Where have you put her?"

Coppelstone winked. "In the observation suite."

Grimster wasn't amused. "Was that a directive from Sir John?"

"No," said Cranston.

"Then find some excuse to move her tomorrow," said Grimster.

The observation suite, on the first floor, was bugged and each room, including the bathroom, wired on closed circuit television. Its advantages had always seemed dubious to Grimster, but he knew that it provided a great deal of amusement, sometimes prurient, in the operations and screening room behind Cranston's office.

Cranston shrugged his shoulders. "She's your baby, Johnny. What you say goes."

Going up the stairs to his room with Coppelstone, he said, "How's she taking things?"

"Like an orphan on a Sunshine Homes holiday. Feed her, amuse her, be kind to her and, I'd say, she'd settle anywhere, even in a camel-skin tent on the Steppes with a bunch of Tartars. She's a great girl with a simple innocence that's like a suit of armour. Personally, on the official side, I think she's going to give us trouble."

"Why do you say that?"

"Because she's fair bubbling to co-operate. I never trust that kind."

"She could be just a trusting type."

Coppelstone shook his head. "Nobody's that simple in this day and age."

Grimster went into the bedroom of his suite and dumped his case. Coppelstone leaned against the open door and watched him. Outside the August evening was bright with sunlight and a couple of magpies looped across the lawns in chequered flight. One for sorrow, two for joy, thought Grimster. He asked, "Is Dilling's stuff all down here?"

"In one of the store rooms on the top floor. There's a detailed inventory—down to a silver cigarette box with six limp cigarettes in it—on your desk out there."

"What make?" Grimster turned and grinned. It was an old game, the detail game, between them.

"Piccadilly, Number One. Every time I saw him, though, he never smoked. I haven't let the girl loose amongst the stuff. She's asked for it—but I told her it was here under seal until you arrived."

"She ask for anything in particular?"

They moved back into the sitting-room and Coppelstone automatically went to the sideboard and the whisky decanter. Cranston always saw that the suites were well provided.

"No—and she didn't show any surprise that it should be here. She's either a moron or blithely unconcerned about anything except herself."

Taking the whisky that was handed to him, Grimster said, "She's no moron. What did Dilling have that Sir John is itchy about—something military, political, or scientific? A formula for turning base metals into gold?"

Coppelstone grinned, sampled his whisky, feeling it lard his insides with comfort and strength, and said, "He'd finally broken through the linguistic barrier between men and dolphins and had a scheme for training them for submarine detection. Or maybe it was seals. He was vague on the point."

"For a man who drinks too much between six o'clock and midnight you're a dangerous repository for state secrets. You ought to share some of them with an old friend now and then."

Coppelstone refilled his glass. "You've got Lily Stevens. I'll keep my secrets. I'd rather it was the other way round."

"The autopsy on Dilling. No doubt that it was thrombosis?"

"No doubt. Askew did it. He's got a thing about admitting death by conventional causes, but he had to with Dilling. His ticker stopped ticking. The spring went. He'd had a minor one seven years previously."

Grimster lit a cigar, and said, "By tomorrow evening I'd like copies of *The Times* and the *Daily Telegraph* for Friday, 27th February this year."

"What for?"

"That's the day that seems to have been mislaid somewhere, isn't it?"

"Will arrange." For a moment Coppelstone's voice reverted to the official, mournful monotone. "I'm going back tonight. I'll send them down tomorrow." Then raising his glass, he went on cheerfully, "Thank God I've got a chauffeur—and a pocket flask."

Alone, Grimster wondered how much of Coppelstone's drinking was a pose. His hand might shake of a morning, but his head was seldom fuddled and there was a strength in him that could easily reject the stuff if he was on a job that demanded it. He liked him, called him his friend, but knew that the word between people in the Department was a highly conditioned one, the relationship pocked with areas of vacuum. He wondered fleetingly how it would be to have a complete and frank association with someone, to be able to relax and let the tongue and head and heart operate without guards. Like standing naked, he thought, in the middle of a busy street.

*   *   *   *

At dinner that evening there were Cranston, Angela Pilch, himself and Lily. Angela was a tall, rawboned woman of forty-odd whose conversation consisted chiefly of bringing all talk back to some area or acquaintance connected with the army

31

service of her late husband. Service abroad for so long had reduced the skin of her face to a finely wrinkled, pale, dry tan, faded the blue eyes and burnt out all softness from her long body. Grimster wondered if she talked about her dead husband in bed with Cranston.

Lily, not knowing the form, had changed into a dinner dress of pale blue velvet and for a little while she was unsure of herself, watching points and sensing the feeling of the new place and new people, but after half an hour she relaxed and accommodated herself with a natural ease. She was comfortable and being looked after and no one was unduly remarking her, making her feel out of it, and a stranger, so that she could enjoy her smoked salmon and roast duck. Harry, she knew, would have been pleased with her, at the way she was fitting in. . . . Poor Harry. . . . She was pleasantly gratified by the long way she had come since the day Harry had first walked into Boots and asked her for a cake of Imperial Leather soap. This Mrs. Pilch could be a bit of a bitch, she realised, but at the moment she was affable enough. Affable, one of Harry's words. And it didn't need any semaphore signals to tell her that there was something going between Mrs. Pilch and Major Cranston. There was nothing definite to go on in the way they talked and acted, but it was there. That eye-patch, what did it make him look like? Did he take it off when he went to bed? It was a pity about Mrs. Pilch's hair, brown, dry and brittle and looking as though she had long given up trying to do anything about it. Could be, if they got to know one another better, she would recommend a shampoo . . . something with lanoline to get the shine and life back. She was a great hogger of the conversation, though. When Johnny asked her, Lily, something about St. Jean-de-Luz she had hardly started her say when Mrs. Pilch came in with some story of herself and the dear, dead Colonel and playing golf on the course there at Chantaco. Lily knew the course because she and Mrs. Harroway had sometimes driven out there for afternoon tea, but golf was a mystery to her. Harry had once said that it was a game where otherwise

32

level-headed men well aware of their limitations tortured themselves in search of perfection. She passed up the crème brulée that followed the duck, not because she didn't like it, but because the velvet dress which she hadn't worn for a month told her that she would have to watch the old diet for a little while. Maybe the dress was a bit too much, too. Although they did you well here, there was a little bit of scruffiness about them all, except Johnny. He looked as though he had come straight out of a band box, whatever that was. She wasn't sure about him. He was pleasant and polite enough, but it was somehow as if there was something frozen up inside him and when he looked at her there was nothing in it of the kind of looks other men gave her. She wasn't sure whether that pleased her or not.

After dinner and coffee, as there was still light and warmth in the gardens, Grimster suggested that Lily might like to walk around with him. They strolled into the walled and paved ornamental garden. In the centre was a fish pond, padded with water lilies and crudely netted over the top to keep off the herons that came up from the Taw for some easy fishing.

Grimster said, "Are you settled in all right, Lily?"

"Yes, thank you, Johnny. But Major Cranston wants me to change to another suite. He says it's more comfortable and has a better view. You lot are setting out to lush me up, aren't you?"

He laughed. "Why not? We want something from you. You stand to gain as well. No point in not being frank about it." Simplicity and naïveté, he thought, are the hardest nuts to crack. But there was more than that here. Some quality, unanalysable yet, but clearly there.

She said, "I should have thought you could have found out all you want to know in half an hour from me. I've got nothing to hide—not about me and Harry. What's the big problem?"

He said, "There's no rush. Anyway, we'll make a start on it tomorrow, but first I'd like to explain something to you. I'm going to be asking you questions, about all sorts of things . . . some of them will be a bit probing and personal. I don't want

33

you to be upset when that happens. Sometimes you won't see the point of the questions, but don't worry. Just do your best. You're down here as a guest and it's your privilege to pack your bags and walk right out if you don't like it." She wasn't, but that was the way it had to seem to her.

"If you get too personal, I'll soon let you know." She laughed and moved a little ahead of him, peering through the netting at the pale shapes of the golden orfe in the pool. Her hair fell forward and he could see the faintest silvering of down on the back of her neck against the tanned skin, and the warm evening air was fronded with the scent she used, strong, rich, exotic . . . something Valda would never have used. Lily straightened up, turned to him, and said with a sudden, almost childish pride, "I really am important to you? I mean to your people and whatever this is all about?"

"You really are."

"Good, I like that. Harry used to make me feel important . . . to him. Don't you think it's a good thing to be important to somebody?"

"Of course."

She shook her head. "I don't mean important, you know, like in bed and love and all that carry-on. I mean to really be important as a person."

He said, smiling, knowing the words naïveté and simplicity were wrong for her, "Of course, I do—even though you've split an infinitive about it."

She laughed and said, "Harry and me used to have some rare old times. My, he was a one, not a bit like a professor." Over the barley field beyond the gardens a late-singing lark dropped earthwards, suddenly changing the gayness of its song to a low, plaintive cry. Lily said, "What's that bird?"

"A lark—packing it in for the day. Which is what we should be doing."

"A lark?"

"Yes." The light was fading but he saw the shine of her eyes and then was amazed as she began to recite, holding her eyes up to where the lark had been, catching at memory and her voice holding a new timbre.

> *The crow doth sing as sweetly as the lark*
> *When neither is attended, and I think*
> *The nightingale, if she should sing by day,*
> *When every goose is cackling, would be thought*
> *No better a musician than the wren.*
> *How many things by season season'd are*
> *To their right praise and true perfection!*

She finished, and smiled at him for appreciation. "Harry was a great one for poetry. I'm a very bad learner, but he knew how to teach me, though to tell the truth, Johnny, I never understood the half of it. He used—" She stopped suddenly. "You're right. It's time we went in." She crossed her hands on to her bare forearms and gave a little shiver.

He walked back to the house with her, wondering. Henry Dilling and Lily Stevens. Pygmalion and Aphrodite. He'd gone before the job was finished. Did she ever mourn him, miss him? Only now and then, probably, and that conventionally. Poor Harry. And this poetry stuff. Shakespeare. He had an odd feeling that something important had been said to him. It wasn't a new feeling. In his career he had often had it when dealing with people and had sometimes regretted later that he had not given intuition, that dark, almost palpable sense of mental contact which was so necessary in his work, more rein and spur to loose it into its full gallop.

Alone in his room, with a brandy and a cigar—since Valda had gone the brandy had appeared and he smoked more cigars than usual—he got out the Dilling file and went through it again, skipping and jumping, knowing it all by heart now, but letting his mind range free like a pointer quartering the pages, waiting on instinct to tell him when to hold and point, straining against immobility for the flushing.

Henry Martin Dilling, born 1927, the same age as himself; though Dilling was a Leo and he Taurus. Born, Formby,

35

Lancashire, and both his parents killed in the bombing of Liverpool. No brothers or sisters. Brought up by an uncle. Bright boy, scholarships, first to Manchester Grammar School (Foundation Scholar), then a Major Scholar of Clare College, Cambridge, and a First Class Honours, Part Two (Physics), and later a Denman Baynes Research Studentship and winner of the Robins Prize a year later. The bright boy's career. Some time spent in industry doing research work for the British Oxygen Company. . . . He'd read a hundred similar biographies in his time on various jobs. Various publications—on spectroscopy and multiplebeam interferometry and the microstructure of surfaces . . . diamonds, rubies, emeralds. . . . Closed worlds to most people, and to him. The feudal system had put people in closed pockets and consolidated a hierarchy, so did science now, bringing with it a new language, a new way of thought, turning ancient fantasies into facts so that the threat was lightning vivid on the horizon that one day man would destroy himself by the achievement of some final fantasy. The sibyl imagination and the old crone curiosity were slowly hunting man down. Dilling's last few years gave little to go on. He had started a small industrial research company, undercapitalised, doomed to the bankruptcy it had met six months before his death. That six months was a blank except for the day he had brought himself to the notice of the Department and had had the first of his interviews with Coppelstone. But what was he like as a man? For safety's sake he had hidden something which he was on the point of selling. He was no crank. When Dilling went to market he had something to sell. He had hidden it to protect the deal, which meant that—rightly—he didn't trust the Department. They might have pulled anything on him. (If only people knew what was done behind the scenes. Now and again it leaked and there was a row in Parliament, but it was all glossed over, had to be.) Dilling would have trusted nothing to a safe, or a bank. He would have had the intelligence to make security double sure. Briefly Grimster felt the quick rise of excitement in him. This was the kind of job he liked.

He was up at half past four the next morning. He went down
to the great hallway where a sleepy duty officer was on telephone watch and hid a yawn behind his good-morning. He
drove his car around the drive and down the farm road to the
wooded bluff over the river. He slipped into gumboots and
put up his rod, a small brook rod which would arch to its limit
if he got into a big sea trout. From the few flies he carried in
his wallet he chose a March Brown which he had tied himself,
dressed with a brown quill body and a partridge hackle with
a touch of silver twist showing in the body. He went down the
steep, treed slope of the bluff, over rocks at the bottom to the
edge of a shallow stickle which he waded easily to the other
bank. The river was low but was clear of the waist-high mist
which lay over the far fields. He had fished this stretch of water
many times and knew it well at all heights. Without much hope
for better than a trout or a few small peal, he began to fish down
the Cliff Pool from the shallow neck. The feel of a rod in his
hand, the sweet curl of the line going out brought back to him,
as it always did when he had not fished for long, the memory
of Ireland and the Blackwater where he had always been taken
once a year by his mother during his school holidays, staying
at a hotel in Fermoy and out early and late with a ghillie—
all provided, as he soon realised, by his undeclared father,
willing to make a man of all parts of him but afraid or ashamed
because of his position and family to do it with open
acknowledgment. . . .

He had a quick pluck below the neck of the pool, saw the
water boil momentarily and missed contact with the fish. Lower
down a dipper on a rock ducked and bobbed like an obsequious
dwarf waiter and a heron coming upstream saw him and
banked away over the far tall fir trees. Harrison had come to
Ireland with them two or three times. Harrison was a better
fisherman, better shot and better horseman than he, and—as
with everything he did—Harrison was ruthless, leaving laws

for those who were stupid enough to be law-abiding. In fishing he recognised no close seasons, no wet or dry fly prohibitions, would spin, prawn, worm and gaff and foul hook according to fancy, hunting without quarter because to hunt was the only really fierce joy he knew.

Half-way down the pool his fly, or maybe potted boredom, moved a salmon and it jumped high and clumsily, red flanks catching the light, and then smashed back into the water like a log. As the ripples spread out and died Grimster saw a movement high up in the trees to his right, a tic of action that just caught the corner of his eye but was enough for him. He fished on for a few casts and checked the spot unobtrusively and established all he wanted to establish, established in fact what he had felt might happen.

In the tail of the pool he hit two fish. The first ran fast downstream, then turned and came upstream quicker than he could hand the line in, jumped, and shook the hook free. The second, a few minutes later, did the same, but this time he ran back along the shallows as it came upstream, got his line in fast and kept contact, and then fought it around the pool and finally beached it. It was a nice sea trout that he judged would go about two and a half pounds.

Satisfied, he waded back across the river and went up through the wood to the tree where he had seen the movement. There was no visible sign that anyone had stood there watching, but he knew there had been someone there. He had caught the glimpse of a face and the edge of a blue shirt sleeve.

Cranston came into breakfast wearing suede desert boots, twill trousers and a blue shirt with a neckerchief at his throat. On the right sleeve of the shirt an inch below the shoulder there was the faintest green mould mark from the growth on the bark of the oak he had leant against.

What did they think he was up to? That he'd arranged a drop or a meeting with Harrison? Not yet, not ever—unless the day came when the suspicion that lived in his mind should be proven to be a truth.

CHAPTER FOUR

THEY HAD PUT her in a different suite at the south end of
the first floor. The long window of her sitting-room looked out
over its low balcony westwards to the woods above the Taw,
and beyond to the high farm fields on the other side of the
valley. This morning the sky was an unflawed blue against
which a pair of buzzards circled and spiralled lazily in the
rising air currents. It was a pleasant room, the furniture draped
in bright chintz, the carpet an oatmeal Wilton, and on the
walls were two very good reproductions of some paintings of
horses by Stubbs.

Lily had had breakfast in her room and now sat opposite
him so that her blonde hair was bright against the distant fir
trees through the window. She was wearing green slacks and a
lightweight white sweater, its rolled collar close around her
neck. She had been a little nervous at first and clearly surprised
that he had brought a tape recorder with him, but when he
recorded her voice for her and then played it back she was
delighted and made him play it twice, saying, "Honest, is that
really me? Sounds like somebody else. . . . Ever so la-di-da."
After a while he had her relaxed and realised the flattering rise
of self-importance in her. They wanted her help. She was doing
a job. She was important to them. All this warmed her ego,
he saw.

He said, "All right. Now we're ready to start, and the way
I want you to think about it is this. It's a game. A mystery
game. Like a jig-saw puzzle, perhaps, and we don't know what
the picture is going to be."

39

"I never had the patience for jig-saws," she said.

"You will for this one because when the picture is complete, you might find yourself with far more money than Dilling has already left you. The main point is this. Dilling was going to sell something to the Government. You don't have to know what it was—"

"I don't know anyway. He was close about his business stuff. Told me I wouldn't have a clue even if he tried to explain."

"That I can believe. I don't think I would either. Anyway whatever it was, he hid the drawings, or plans, or formula for it somewhere safe while the deal was being arranged. Then, unhappily, he died, and nobody knows where the stuff is hidden."

"I certainly don't."

"No. But between us we may be able to find out."

"How, Johnny?"

"I'll come to that later. The first thing I want to do is to get a picture from you of what kind of man Harry was, and what kind of life you had together."

She laughed. "Nosey, eh?" But he could see that his use of the name Harry pleased her, drew them together as though they shared a common and well-liked friend.

"Nosey—that's just it. But in a good cause. So let's fire away with some of the questions. Don't worry if they seem a bit haphazard or you can't understand why I'm asking them. In the end they'll make sense."

She stirred in her chair, reached for cigarettes and her lighter and fiddled with the lighting. Blowing cigarette smoke, she said, "Even if all this comes to nothing, Johnny—you did say I would be paid for my trouble?"

"I did."

"How much?"

He smiled. "You're a good business woman. I should say not less than a thousand, anyway."

"Goodie. All right. Fire away." Her eyes went from him to

the slowly moving tape in the machine sitting on a low table between them.

Fire away, he thought. And at random to begin with. He had to get her personally and deeply involved in this probing game, make it as important to her as it was to him. He would have to keep coming in at different angles, taking her by surprise at times, rousing her, then placating her because there were only two lines to work on: one, that she was an honest girl who would tell him all she knew but would have nothing significant to tell because she knew nothing; or, two, that for reasons unknown to him yet she knew a great deal which she was not prepared to tell. For the time being he was going to assume that the latter theory was the correct one.

He said, "Did Harry smoke much?"

"Not much. Two or three a day. But he liked to take a draw on mine sometimes. I used to say if he wanted a cigarette why didn't he have one properly."

"What kind of things did he like doing in his spare time? You know, hobbies and so on."

"Not much, really. Loaf around. He read a lot. Sometimes we'd go for walks. He knew a lot about the country, birds and flowers and things."

"What kind of books did he read?"

"Oh, just books. I don't know. Sexy paperbacks."

"Did you like him?" It was the first probe at the core of her own personality and he saw her stir with the beginning of faint indignation.

"Course I did! What a silly question. I wouldn't have been with him otherwise."

"That's all right. Sometimes I'm going to ask silly questions. Did you love him?"

She considered this, indignation gone, her sense of importance flowering. "Yes, I suppose I did. You can't tell about love, can you? I mean, I wasn't all starry-eyed or anything, but I loved him."

"Did he love you?"

41

"Of course! He was crazy about me—that's the only way to say it. He'd give me anything I wanted. Do things for me. Gosh, that was nice. It sort of made me feel I was something. Something he wanted, anyway."

"And would you have done anything for him?"

She laughed. "Of course! Except jump off the top of a cliff."

"How did you feel about his being much older than you?"

"I didn't ever have any feelings about it. He was Harry."

"Was he the first man you ever loved?"

"Yes. Oh, I'd had a thing going for a few boys—but that was nothing like it was with Harry."

"Was he the first man you ever slept with?"

To his surprise she took the question without emotion.

"Practically."

"What do you mean by that, Lily?"

"Well, you know, mucking about in the back of a car, or some park with some boy. But I never let myself go the whole way. Come to think of it, you must be about Harry's age."

"A few months older."

"Are you married or engaged, or anything?"

"No."

"No girl friends?"

He pushed an ashtray conveniently closer to her and said, "I'm the one asking the questions."

She grinned. "So you may be, but you don't get any more out of me unless you answer mine." Her words held a brief coquetry.

"No girl friends," he said. "Tell me where and how did you first meet Harry?"

It was a lead she welcomed, he felt at once; probably because it touched the one important episode in her experience, the jumping-off point to a new life and the quick blossoming of her own personality under the warmth of Dilling's love and care and consideration. All he had to do was to press the quick spur of an occasional question from then on to keep her going and the whole story came rolling out as she leaned back against her

42

chair, her eyes on the far wall, memory purling into speech, the uncomplicated lines of her life etching themselves on the rolling tape of the Grundig machine.

She had been born in the small country town of Uckfield in Sussex. Her mother was a farmer's daughter, her father a steward working mostly for the Union Castle Line. She had had a brother, younger than herself, Eric, who had been killed in an accident in Battersea Fun Fair when the family had made a holiday expedition to London. This was when she was seventeen and, after moderate schooling, was working behind the counter at Boots the Chemists in Uckfield. The brother's death had devastated both father and mother, whose marriage had become a bickering, uneasy one due to the father's long absences at sea. Small details came creeping in at times as she backtracked or jumped aside in the telling. Her best subject at school had been mathematics so the job in the shop presented little difficulty for her. When she was eighteen her mother and father had decided to emigrate to British Columbia where her mother's brother ran a fruit farm near Penticton and needed help. Lily had been given the chance of going but had opted to stay in England. Farm life held no attractions for her. So, with a girl friend, who was a hairdresser's assistant in the town —Ada Lemney—she had taken a flat and started to live independently. For a few months she had been well content. At the weekends she and Ada would get a lift to the coast and go to the cinema or skate at Brighton, and they had boy friends, but if any of them became over-eager Lily knew how to deal with them. "Once they started any serious nonsense, I put them down." Then Ada got a regular boy friend and would bring him back to the flat where he would sometimes sleep and this upset Lily because she began to feel that she was unwanted and being slowly pushed out. At this stage Harry Dilling—staying with a friend for the weekend near by (she never knew or cared who the friend was)—walked into the shop on a Saturday morning to buy a cake of soap, took one look at her and wanted her. After the weekend he had moved

43

into a local hotel and had seen her in her lunch hour and waited for her after work to walk her back to her flat. At first she had treated the whole thing as a bit of a giggle, a man much older than she was, falling for her like one of the youths around the town and, in the beginning, acting like one, walking her home, taking her to the cinema and out to dinner, but soon making it apparent that with the youthful preliminaries there was a firm resolution to get what he wanted which was her, not just her body—that came much later—but her, Lily Stevens, because he saw in her some mild potential that appealed to him and recognised in her personality some necessary complement to his own. Eventually she had been pleased, flattered and then convinced of his sincerity and had put herself into his hands and allowed herself to be led and shaped by him, accepting finally his suggestion for her to come and live with him, to be looked after, cherished and developed, as though it were not only the most natural thing in the world but something which she had been waiting for.

Grimster said, "What did you tell your parents?"

Lily shrugged her shoulders. "I wrote and said I'd become his secretary and, because of the work, lived in the same house. But they got to know the truth, of course. They had friends in the town and one or two wrote to them and told them. Mum wrote me a really awful letter. But Harry helped me answer it and, you know, after a while she just accepted things. I let her think he was my fiancé and we were going to be married."

"Did he ever say he would marry you?"

"Just the opposite. He made it clear he wouldn't. He didn't believe in anything formal like that. We just had this understanding that we were both free, that it was a contract between ourselves and either side could break it if things turned out wrong. Actually," she smiled at him, "I didn't believe that or worry about it. He was full of way-out ideas but I knew that one day he would want it all legal. . . . I mean the more and more he got to like me, the more and more he would want it to be a proper arrangement."

44

He was amused by that. Eve manipulating Adam. He went on to ask her about the house in Berkshire where they had lived. It was a furnished cottage which Dilling had rented. When he asked her to describe it she did, but only in very general terms.

He said, "Did you ever go to his London flat?"

"No. I never even went to London with him—not until that last time. He kept me in the country." She said it without any hint of rancour.

"Did any of his friends ever stay there?"

"No."

"Are you sure?"

"Course I am. There was only one bedroom to begin with. What I mean is, there was a spare room but there was no bed in it. Look, Johnny, where is all this getting us? I mean this has got nothing to do with . . . well, with what you want to know."

"It might have. Tell me—on that last morning when you went up to London, and you went off to Florence—what was the arrangement between you?"

"He said he had a big business deal on that would mean a lot of money. He got an air ticket and booked the hotel for me a week before and gave me about four hundred pounds in travellers' cheques, or maybe it was two hundred. I was to go to Florence and wait for him."

"Had you ever been abroad before?"

"Twice. Harry took me once to Paris for a long weekend. And once to Berlin."

"Berlin?"

"Yes. We stayed a couple of days at Hamburg on the way back. I liked Germany better than Paris."

"Did Harry ever say why he wanted you to wait for him abroad?"

"Well, yes, in a way. He didn't want to stay in England when his deal came off. We were going to live abroad. He talked about getting a villa somewhere. Also the lease of the cottage was almost up and he didn't want to renew it . . . so

45

it seemed like a good idea for me to go. Also I had my programme."

"What programme?"

"Of things I had to do and see in Florence. You know, pictures and galleries and buildings. Harry made a list for me. It was part of his education scheme for me." She gave the smallest of giggles. "I cheated a bit on it. I really don't go for walking round churches and staring at pictures in galleries . . . it's all so musty and dead. But there were some super shops. I got these at a place called Ferragamo's." She lifted he rlegs stiff from the floor, as though she were doing an exercise, and exhibited a pair of square-toed brown shoes with brass buckles backed by red velvet lozenges.

"You said once that a man was watching the cottage where you lived?"

"Yes."

"Did Harry tell you this?"

"Yes. He pointed him out once and said it was nothing to worry about. The people he was doing this big deal with just wanted him around for Harry's protection."

"Didn't this worry you? It might have meant Harry was in danger."

"No. Harry said it was a normal thing when you did really big business with the government."

"Did he say it was with the government?"

"I think so. Anyway, it was, wasn't it?"

"Yes. Did this man follow you around?"

"Mostly. But if we wanted to be on our own, then Harry would lose him. We used to have a good laugh over that, slipping him in traffic. Or going down to the pub for a drink and then both of us going out to the loo at the back and then taking the path across the fields to the main road where we could get a bus. He wasn't a very clever man . . . or perhaps he was just lazy."

He was both, Grimster thought. Some petty economy on Sir John's part because Sir John wasn't at that time—and perhaps wasn't even now—taking the deal seriously. Just paying lip service to it. He looked at the room clock. It was a quarter to twelve. He got up and went to the sideboard and poured a couple of glasses of sherry. Earlier Lily had waived the offer of mid-morning coffee. He handed her a glass and sat down, leaning forward and nursing his own glass between the palms of his hands. "How good would you say your memory was?"

"Fair, I suppose. Perhaps very good for some things."

"What kind of *some* things?"

"Unimportant, I suppose. Well, like at the hairdresser's— I can remember all the chatter of the assistant. They're always chatting about themselves. What their boy friend said and did and do you know who they had in last week? By the way, what's going to happen about my hair here?"

"There's a place at Chulmleigh, not far away. Or I could drive you to Barnstaple."

"I'd like that. Then we could have lunch and do some shopping. That's another thing I'm good at, things in shops and their prices. But I suppose that comes from being in a shop myself once."

Grimster sipped his sherry. So far as he could tell, and his eyes had seldom been away from her face or hands, which were always good guides to thought and emotion, this woman was being absolutely natural, her talk completely frank, unguarded, and her mood one of uncomplicated co-operation.

He said, "You've got a good memory for poetry."

She laughed. "Not really. That's a trick. I can't remember any unless you say the word."

"The word?"

"Yes, any of a lot of words. You say one and it starts it off in my mind. Like when you mentioned larks yesterday. Larks, and off I go. It's a way Harry used to teach me . . . Poor Harry. He was so good to me. He wanted so much for me and here we sit talking about him like he was some character in a play or a book. It doesn't seem right, somehow."

Listening to her, he was going over in his mind some of the

47

verse Harry might have taught her which had to be promoted in her memory by some code word.

He said, "Try a few words. Swallow, for instance?" She shook her head. "Goldfish?" Her head shook again. He fingered memory for the clichés of poetry, the cubicle at Combermere coming back, a tattered copy of the Oxford Book of English Verse spread open on the bed's grey blanket and said, "Rainbow."

She smiled, and the answer came pat, the bow of memory drawn and the arrow let fly.

> *My heart leaps up when I behold*
> *A rainbow in the sky:*
> *So was it when my life began;*
> *So is it now I am a man;*
> *So be it when I shall grow old,*
> *Or let me die!*

She laughed with pleasure as she finished and he laughed with her as the further words ran through his mind—*The Child is father of the Man; and I could wish my days to be/Bound each to each by natural piety.* There had been little of natural piety in his days.

"And you can only do it if you get the right word?"

"More or less. Some that I liked I can do whenever I want."

He finished his sherry and said, "Now tell me, you knew Harry well—what kind of place would he choose to hide something? Something not too bulky. Let's say like a brief case."

"Lord, what a question! I wouldn't have a clue. All I know is, it wouldn't be the kind of thing most people would do. Harry liked riddles and puzzles and he could do crosswords like nobody's business. He was a gadgety man, too. He used to say that when we had our own place he'd have it fixed so you could lie in bed and just press switches for the curtains to be drawn, the bath to be filled and the eggs cracked and dropped into the frying pan. . . . Still, I suppose, being a scientist or whatever, that wouldn't have been so difficult."

48

"He'd have been very clever about hiding something?"

"Dead right he would."

He paused, considering his approach, not wanting to emphasise its importance, before putting the next question.

"Let's take the last full day you spent in the cottage. The day before you went to London. Friday, 27th February this year. What did you both do?"

"You think that's the day he hid whatever this was?"

"Not necessarily, Lily. But you just run through it for me." It had to be the day. Dilling himself had said so and his observed actions, with Lily, had been established without doubt. They had slipped their tail and gone off for the whole day.

"Well, we got up late and had breakfast, and then Harry read the papers while I tidied up around. You know, the bed and doing the breakfast things."

She leaned back against the chair, head tipped a little, her eyes on the painting of a white horse by Stubbs on the far wall, and spoke easily, no sign of invention or hesitation, remembering smoothly. They'd stayed in the house all day. It was cold out with a heavy frost. She'd done her packing before lunch, leaving the case open because she had had a few blouses and some underwear to iron after lunch. They'd had a simple lunch, a bottle of white wine between them, and finished up some pieces of Brie and Cheddar cheese with a salad of endive and tomatoes, and then black coffee. After lunch . . . Here, for the first time there was some hesitation. Her head came lower, her eyes on his level, frank, smiling and her whole manner slowly charged for the first time since he had known her with a hint of intimacy, with the suggestion that they now knew one another well enough not to be embarrassed.

He said, "You went up to the bedroom?"

"Yes. I wanted to get on with my ironing, but Harry wouldn't have it. He said there was plenty of time. And when he had had wine, or an extra drink before lunch, it used to take him that way. He just wanted it and there was no stopping him. Not that I tried much."

49

They'd made love, and then Harry had gone off to sleep for an hour or more while she did her ironing and made ready to leave the next day. She took him up a cup of tea between four and five and afterwards he had bathed and changed, which he always did if their programme allowed it, at around six o'clock. The evening was spent reading, watching the television, and she had made dinner from the stuff left in the refrigerator. (Knowing they were leaving she had run their supplies down.) Tomato soup—which was Harry's favourite—fried plaice and chips—all from frozen packs—and then coffee. At eleven they went to bed. An ordinary, uneventful day.

Grimster said, "Was the man watching the house that day?"

"Harry said he was. I didn't see him. Fact, he joked about the poor man, stamping his feet in the cold out there. I remember he said that in an age of scientific miracles or something it was a primitive way of carrying on."

Not wanting to press her further now, puzzled by the contradiction of her account with the known facts, but willing to let the anomaly ride for a while in his mind, he slid away from the last full day of their life together.

"Well, that's all straightforward enough. Tell me, what kind of stuff did Harry like watching on television?"

"Anything. He'd just turn it on and stare at it. No matter what. Like he was sitting in front of a fire and warming himself. Fact, he'd drop off sound to sleep sometimes with it blaring away at him." She picked up her glass and said, "What about another of these before lunch? I never talked so much in all my life." As he went to the sideboard, she continued, "Were you really up at four this morning to go fishing?"

"Yes. Who told you?"

"The man on that telephone in the hall. My father used to go fishing sometimes. At a place called Barcombe Mills near us. It's on the River Ouse. He never caught anything worth much that I could see and our outhouse used to stink something terrible with the maggots he kept there and would forget about. I liked Dad, except when he'd had a few too many. He was a devil with women, though. But I'll say this for him, never at home. Only while he was away. What was your father like, Johnny?"

He was walking carefully towards her, carrying two glasses of sherry and the smooth progression was untouched. Long ago this kind of question had been mastered and dismissed by him.

He said, "Oh, he was just a nice ordinary chap. Nothing special about him."

She took her sherry, lifted it in a small toast to him and said, "Through the lips and past the gums look out tummy here she comes."

He laughed. "Did that come from Harry?"

"That and more. He was full of funny little sayings. Some of them pretty near the knuckle, too. But he was a nice man. My goodness he was. Poor Harry. There'll never be another like him."

He drank silently to that. Through her, he knew that he was already locked in a finely matched battle of wits with the dead man. The thought pleased him. Every word she had said about Friday, 27th February, had to be wrong. But she was no liar. He would bet on that. It was a puzzle with few clues, some intuitions, yes; and Harry had bequeathed it to him.

Lily reached a hand up to him and touched his arm. "Don't stand there looking all wooden. Sit down and tell me some things I want to know. That Mrs. Pilch, for instance. She and the Major are . . . well, like that, aren't they?"

      *   *   *   *

After lunch Grimster went down to that part of the cellars which had been turned into a revolver range and gymnasium. He signed the book for two eight-shot magazines for a Beretta automatic, noticed that it was an old, 1953 model and loosed off sixteen shots at the target, putting in eyes, a nose and a mouth with the shots and refusing to imagine any real face to the grotesque basic design. He turned down the idea of a workout in the gymnasium and went out to take a swim in the pool. Angela Pilch and Lily were sitting in cane armchairs under a coloured beach umbrella. They gave him a wave and then ignored him, chatting away and now and then laughing together. He swam a few lengths and remembered that the last time he had swum was with Valda in the ice-cold water of a Scottish loch, autumn mist drifting in the high folds of the heather-covered hills and a handful of hooded crows quartering the beach rocks, scavenging. The memory stirred him as each new one rising from the past did, and he deliberately, unemotionally, expunged it from his mind.

He went back into High Grange, drew the key of the top floor store room, picked up the inventory of Dilling's effects from his room and went on up to have a look at the stuff.

It was all laid out in a chalked off section of the large room. In the other section was a pile of chairs, tables and small desks all tabbed with Ministry of Works labels. They were used for various conferences, and that seldom for the dust was thick on them.

Dilling's stuff didn't amount to much. His flat had been a large lounge-cum-bedroom, a bathroom and a small kitchen. The kitchen stuff was in one corner, the equipment piled on to a small table. The pots and pans were clean and well-used. Dilling, he guessed, was in the habit of looking after any equipment he used. It was curious, but so far he hadn't built up any very clear picture of the man. Almost, he felt fancifully, as though the man beyond the grave were avoiding him, loath to come within reach even through the medium of Lily.

There was a low divan bed, sheets and blankets and other linen piled on it; a small, flat-topped director's desk, the cupboards and drawers empty but with the contents in two cardboard cartons on top of it; a couple of armchairs, one with a large stain on the seat cushion, drink, coffee or tea, he guessed; a three-shelved bookcase about six feet long with the books still in it; a portable typewriter which he opened, checking the ribbon—if it had been used he might have got the laboratory boys to get something from it—to find it was brand new and there was a smudge of carbon on the white metal frame where whoever had changed the ribbon had dirtied his fingers; a waste-paper basket with a hunting scene on it; two small Persian carpets of no great value; a sideboard, empty, but a carton of bottles, decanter, and glasses on top of it; a tall oak cupboard divided half and half into hanging and drawer space and full of Dilling's clothes, which—although he knew Coppelstone would have had it done—he went through meticulously to find nothing, not even an odd button or a sixpenny piece in the corner of a ticket pocket, but the clothes were clean, well-pressed and none of the shirts were frayed, and the shoes in the bottom of the cupboard had been put away clean; then there was a small coffee table on which had been set out the items which Dilling had had with him when he died, a wrist-watch with a white linen strap, a leather wallet with a few pound notes in it, some loose silver, a bunch of keys, a half-clipped cheap-day return ticket from Oxford to Paddington—had he meant to go back to their Berkshire cottage that evening?—a gold signet ring, a silk handkerchief, a knitted dark red woollen tie, a pair of cheap cuff-links, a bank cheque book used except for three cheques and none of the counterfoils filled in, a ball-point pen, and a few other odds and ends of clothing, including the jacket and trousers he had been wearing; and there gathered in an oblong space twelve feet by fifteen was all that remained of Henry Dilling, except the one thing which the Department wanted.

After his first quick glance around, Grimster started again and went through everything carefully. This had already been done and the inventory scrupulously compiled, but he liked to do it for himself. He went through the bookshelves, noting the book titles, opening each one and shaking the leaves free. He found nothing, but some of the books were annotated in the margin against passages. The remarks amused him. *So you say! For God's sake! Make up your mind—see p. 91 which states opposite!* And more than once just—*!!!!*. Grimster had the impression of irascibility when it came to reading, of intolerance with badly prepared stuff. The comments were found in fiction (of which there was not much) and in the non-fiction works which were quite catholic in range, Shakespeare, poetry—including the Oxford Book of English Verse, well thumbed—an old Badminton Library on Coursing and Falconry, some medical books including a coverless copy of The Home Doctor, but nothing scientific or in his own line.

As he finished his examination he heard someone come to the room door which he had left open. He turned to find Lily there. She wore a half-open bathing robe over a bikini and a broad-brimmed sun hat swung from her right hand.

She said, "Angela said I might find you up here. Is it all right if I come in?"

"Of course," he said. "It's all yours, literally. Would you like to be on your own here?"

She hesitated for a moment and then half-nodding said, "If you wouldn't mind, Johnny. It's a sort of a solemn moment. . . . Well, you know. Harry's things."

He handed her the key. "Lock up when you leave and let me have the key later. But, for the moment, you understand you mustn't take anything away. All right?"

"Of course."

He left her in the room and went quickly down to Cranston's office. The major was at his desk, writing a letter.

Grimster said, "Are the top floors all on closed circuit still?"

"Yes."

"Let's have the store room. Miss Stevens is in there."

They went through into the small viewing room at the back of the office and Cranston switched on the scanners, saying, "It's a bit gloomy up there. Won't be a good picture. Think she'll give you a lead?"

"I doubt it—but there's no harm in trying."

The set warmed up and Cranston pushed a selector button for the store room and the picture unfolded into a grey and white fuzz. Cranston fiddled with the definition and brought the picture up as sharp as he could.

54

"Best I can do."

The room was held in wide angle from somewhere above the entry door. Lily was standing in the middle of the chalked oblong, just looking around. The furniture and odds and ends of flat equipment would mean nothing to her, Grimster knew. She had never been there.

At his side Cranston said, "Simple shopgirl, or Mata Hari strikes again?"

Grimster gave no answer. Lily had begun to move round, just resting her fingertips on a piece of furniture now and then . . . drifting, not searching. She came to the coffee table and the pile of little things Dilling had had with him on the day of his death. She picked up the key ring, rubbed it softly in her fingers and then put it back. She was sideways to them now and her face partly hidden. She took up the wallet and then put it down, fingered the woollen tie without lifting it, and then the ball-point pen, just touching things as though some sensation flowed from them which she did not want to prolong for long. Her back was to them now and Grimster suddenly saw her shoulders slump under the beach robe and then begin to shake. Quite abruptly she turned, her face full to them, and sat on the edge of the table. In the brief moment before her hands went to her face, Grimster saw that she was crying. Then her face was hidden by her hands and she sat there, her shoulders shaking with slow sobs.

He stepped past Cranston and flicked off the set switch. Lily's grief shrank and died into the infinity of a minute silver point of light, then vanished.

Cranston, silent for a moment, fiddled with his eye-patch. Then he said quietly, "Perhaps you're right, old man. Yes, perhaps you're right."

CHAPTER FIVE

DURING THE NIGHT it began to rain, slow, heavy summer rain moving in without much wind from the west. It was still raining hard in the morning, long swathes shrouding the fields and woods.

Lily didn't appear for breakfast, though she had been down to dinner the night before showing no sign of her sudden grief. After breakfast Grimster drafted a message to Coppelstone. There had been no bank statements amongst Dilling's effects. Dilling probably tore them up as they came in. Grimster wanted copies for the last year of all statements and, if the entries were only made by cheque numbers, he wanted—if the bank still had them—all the cancelled cheques. He had found in the past that a record of a man's payments and receipts by cheque was often a broad picture of the man, and he had to get his picture of Harry much clearer than it was at the moment.

Before going up to Lily, he sat and read the copy of *The Times* for Friday, 27th February, which Coppelstone had sent down.

When he went up to Lily she was standing at the window, smoking, and watching the rain. She turned, gave him a smiling good-morning and, to his surprise, said without any preamble, "Do you know what I like about you, Johnny?"

"No."

"You always look so clean and fresh. Like dust or dirt wouldn't dare settle on you. It's funny, isn't it, how some men can be like that? At the end of the day their shirts look just as clean as when they put them on. Others—they're scruffy in an hour."

He bent down and flicked the recorder on and said, "Harry was like that, wasn't he?"

"Yes. But how would you know?"

"From his stuff upstairs. His shirts and suits and shoes."

"That's right. The moment a thing got worn or mucked up he would throw it away." She laughed. "He used to say that most people went through life carrying their rubbish with them. Sometimes he'd have three baths a day. Three! I used to tell him he'd wash himself away." She glanced at the recorder and went on, "It's another session is it?"

"Only a few questions, and then I'll take you into Barnstaple. Angela's made a hair appointment for you at the place she uses."

"Nice. But I hope they do better with me than they do with her." She sat down, crossed her legs and smoothed out the skirt of her dress. "Fire away, Mr. Inquisitor."

He said, "You've seen Harry's stuff upstairs. There's a return ticket to Oxford for the day you went to London. Did you know he intended to go back to the cottage that day?"

"No."

"He didn't mention it?"

"No. If he wanted to tell me about his plans he would, if he didn't I didn't ask."

"Why weren't there any pictures in his flat, would you think?"

"No idea. But he was pretty stuffy about art. He couldn't bear reproductions. He took down most of the ones in the cottage."

Grimster knew why there were no pictures in the flat. He had at once noticed the deficiency in the inventory and checked with Coppelstone before coming down. Harry hired two paintings a month from a gallery. At his death the current two had been reclaimed by the gallery. Harry clearly kept his flat and London life a closed book to Lily. Thinking of the copy of The Home Doctor, he said, "What was Harry like about his health?"

She chuckled. "He was the biggest fuss-ass in the world. If he had a pimple on his little toe he'd go and see a doctor about it, and he used to swig tonics as though they were lemonade. Some stuff called Metatone he used a lot."

Neat, meticulous about his person, careful to perhaps the point of anxiety about his body, dividing his life into two, one with Lily and the other in London and elsewhere . . . the picture was growing.

He said, "He had his driving licence cancelled for a year. Were you with him when it happened?"

"No. He was with a friend somewhere in Hertfordshire, I think. They got tight and Harry took a chance and got caught."

"Would you say he was a man who took chances?"

"Sometimes. Mostly he was careful. But sometimes he wouldn't care a damn."

"After he lost his licence you used to drive him?"

"Always. He wasn't going to risk being caught driving."

"Where did you learn to drive?"

"A boy friend I used to have, before I met Harry. I really can't see what all this has got to do with anything, Johnny," she said, stirring restlessly.

He smiled. "Well, it helps pass a rainy morning. The car you had at the cottage was hired, wasn't it?"

"Yes. From a local garage. He sold his when he got caught."

He moved to a different approach, saying, "How was Harry about politics? Did he ever discuss them with you?"

"Often—to put me wise about them. Politicians were all crooks, he said. In it for what they could get. He had no time for them. I must say he used to be pretty outspoken about things when he got going. He didn't have any use for the Royal Family or the Church. You should have heard him about the Archbishop of Canterbury!"

"What about England? You know, being British and patriotism?"

"You should ask that! He used to go up in the air about the way things were. He used to say patriotism was a disease. That the world should grow up and forget about nationalities. He used to make my head sing sometimes with the way he would go on. All it needed was something in the paper and away he'd go—like some fiery old colonel."

"Did he have a nickname for you?"

"No, not really. Lil or Lily was what he called me. Sometimes he'd call me Goldie or some name he'd think up."

He said, "Yesterday you said no one ever came down to the cottage to visit Harry, but from the reports of the man who was watching it we know that on Wednesday, 18th February— a week before you left—a man did visit there."

A little defensively she said, "You asked me if anyone ever *stayed* there."

"That's right, I did." Her memory for conversations was good. People in shops, the hairdresser's assistant. It was a gossip's memory, always ready to elaborate on the question asked. "Stayed" he had asked, but with Lily this would normally have been construed as "visited" as well. Something had made her put up a barrier against expanding her original answer and he guessed that whoever it had been it was someone Lily disliked.

"Well then," she said with a touch of triumph.

"Who was this man? What was his name?"

"A friend of Harry's. All I know is that he was called Billy Who."

"Who?"

She laughed at his puzzlement, and said, "Well, he came about three times in all and the first time Harry introduced him as Billy and I said 'Billy Who?' and they both laughed and Harry said, 'That's right. Billy Who.' And that's what he was from then on. It was a big joke to them, but I could tell that Harry didn't want to give his real name."

"What did you used to do when he was down there?"

"Oh, he'd usually come just before lunch. Harry and I

59

would fetch him in the car from the station. We'd have a few drinks in the pub, then eat. Afterwards we'd all go for a walk, or the two of them would and I'd stay and do things in the house, get supper ready and so on, and then later we would drive him back to the station."

"To go to London?"

"I wouldn't know. Whenever we went to the station I'd sit outside in the car."

"Did Harry insist on that?"

"No. It was just the way it was."

"Tell me what you know about him. What he was like to look at? What he and Harry andyou talked about or did together?"

"Gosh, that's a tall order."

"Try."

She did, and with prompting from him a picture emerged. He had a brief description of the man already—and hers tallied with it. A man around thirty, shortish, untidy looking, corduroy trousers, dark sweater and windbreaker, a mop of fair hair and a thin wisp of beard. He was educated, well spoken, full of laughter. "Jokey" she called it. He drank no spirits, but punished the beer, though was seldom drunk. He was mad on birds and animals. She had a feeling that his work was in some way connected with them. Once she had seen Harry give him five pounds as a contribution to the World Wildlife Fund. He was saucy, too. If Harry went out of the room he would be after her, putting his hands on her, trying to kiss her. When she complained to Harry he had laughed and said, "Oh, that's only old Billy's way. If you were to fall on your back for him he'd run a mile." He had a good voice. Sometimes on their walks he would sing and, if he'd had enough beer, the songs would be bawdy. Although he was clearly some years younger than Harry she had the feeling that they had known each other a long while, because they talked about times in Switzerland, climbing, years before, and also about holidays they had spent bird-watching somewhere, and of parties they'd been on.

But she knew nothing definite about him, not where he lived nor what he did or whether he was married or single. So far as she knew he came to visit Harry about three times and that purely as an old friend. They never talked business and didn't mind if she was in and out of the room as they talked. If they had any secrets they never hinted at them in front of her.

He said, "How was he for money? Did he seem to have plenty?"

"All I know was that he was pretty casual about it. He'd borrow a couple of quid from Harry in the pub sometimes—but he'd always offer to write a cheque for it and Harry would just roar with laughter. It was some kind of joke between them."

"Didn't you ask Harry about that?"

"No. I could always tell when Harry didn't want to be asked about something and he was so good to me that I went along with it. It's a feeling you get about respecting something someone else doesn't want to talk about. The same with Harry, for instance—he never asked me anything about things that I did before we met. You know, boy friends and whether I went to bed with them, or any kind of friends. He didn't even ask Ada's name, though he knew I shared a flat with her, until I told him."

Grimster made a mental note that somewhere among Harry's cancelled cheques there would be a good chance of one or two made out—in his real name—to Billy Who. Then, because for the first time a thin edge of uncertainty about Lily had scored his smooth assessment of her, he moved in with a small, sharp thrust of his own to unsettle her, to show her that this wasn't an idle game, to make her aware that if she were keeping things back from him then no quarter would be given.

He said, "Going back to that last day, the Friday, before you went to London. Your last full day with Harry. What would you say if I were to tell you that it couldn't have been as you said? That you and Harry went off in the car for hours? And that I could prove it?"

Calmly, without any strong reaction and without any hesitation, she said, "You mean that I was lying?"

"Yes."

She laughed. "You're crazy, Johnny. What would I lie for?" Then suddenly serious, she said, "You're not really calling me a liar, are you?"

He stood up and switched off the tape. "No, I'm not."

"I should hope not!" She let the indignation run through her voice; standing up for herself, and at the same time handing him the sharp reproof that convention demanded, all gentility gone from her voice. "I should really have to think very different about you if you thought that."

He said, "Forget it." His thrust, he felt, had come back at him. He didn't want her to be a liar and, oddly, he didn't want her to think any differently of him than she did. He liked her and part of his like demanded that she should like him, too. And that was something which was rare in him.

He said, "Come on. I'll take you into Barnstaple. We'll have lunch and then you can get your beautiful hair done."

*   *   *   *

They drove into Barnstaple, down the rain-shrouded valley of the Taw, and had lunch at the Imperial Hotel. Afterwards Grimster dropped Lily at the hairdressing salon.

While her hair was being washed and dried she relapsed into a dreamy, lazy state of mind, going over the events of the last few days. Except for a few moments in the store room when she had seen Harry's things, she had to admit that she had been happy, comfortable and pleasantly excited by all that was happening to her. It was nice, too, to be the centre of things; that tape recorder turning away and Johnny asking her questions, most of which she couldn't see the point of anyway. He was nice, too, but not in the way Harry had been. Harry, she knew, had wanted and needed her, even though he kept part of his life closed away from her. But it was a part she wouldn't have wanted or understood anyway. With Johnny there was no sign of wanting or needing her for herself. Not even a sign of making a pass at her. He was pleasant and polite, but right deep inside him there was something rock hard. . . . A woman could tell it, she told herself, just by intuition, and what was more she wouldn't mind betting that it was something to do with a woman. He wasn't engaged, or married, and he had no girl friend. Odd that. He was the kind plenty of women would go for. She shut her eyes, browsing round the thought of her wanting Johnny. It was an idea that formed easily in her mind. Since Harry had gone she had sometimes almost painfully missed their love-making and there had been moments when she had told herself that any man would do just so that she could lose herself in the kind of ecstasy that had existed between herself and Harry. Harry was the first one who had properly created it with her, but she wasn't fool enough to think that made him unique. But it being Harry who was the first had made it absolutely special . . . like the first of anything super which had been long looked forward to. There were some things between her and Harry that she wouldn't want to share with anyone. . . . Sacred, in a way, she supposed they were. Kind of out of this world. She believed Harry when he told her that she was special. She liked that. To be special. Slowly she felt an intense longing for Harry spreading in her body but with a deliberate effort of will she fought it back. It was no good crying or sighing for what was gone. Time was the great healer. And the word *time* in her mind sprung the trap of memory to release one of Harry's favourite poems so that lying there in the warm scent-and-shampoo laden air the words went through her brain, not in the way he had taught her to say them, but in a racing torrent—*Time is the feather'd thing, and, whilst I praise the sparklings of thy looks and call them rays, takes wing, leaving behind him as he flies an unperceived dimness in thine eyes. . . .* She let the lines of the whole poem pour through her mind and finished in the way that had always made Harry laugh and made her laugh silently now at the memory. *Jasper Mayne. 1604 to 1672.* And from this point, guided by no connection that she knew, she told herself that she had five thousand pounds and another thousand to come for sure, and then maybe more than that if Johnny found what they wanted, and it was all a lot of money for her, Lily Stevens of Uckfield, and she would have to ask Mrs. Harroway how to invest it, double and treble it, because Mrs. Harroway knew about money and was always talking about shares and buying this and selling that and saying that a woman with money was never neglected; which was true because while she had been with her Mrs. Harroway had turned down two or three offers of marriage by quite wealthy men, joking with Lily that what they wanted wasn't marriage but a merger and that anyway, except for one thing, men were poor fish and there was no need to marry them for it. My goodness, she was outspoken at times. Really shocking. Harry would have loved her. But sometimes she did go over the limit. After all there were some things you just didn't talk about openly, no matter what.

While Lily lazed through her memories and thoughts, Grimster parked the car and walked raincoated, hat pulled down against a rising wind, along the side of the estuary. The tide was ebbing and the flow was a rich coffee colour with the spate water from upriver. Sandpipers, oyster catchers and black-headed gulls were moving on to the flats and bars left free by the tide, and the birds made him think of Billy Who. Were birds and animals and an old friendship all he had in common with Harry? He had a feeling that they were, so far as Billy Who was concerned. But Harry? He wasn't so sure. He had a growing picture now of the man. Dilling had left a mystery. His work was hidden, and there was the riddle of the missing Friday. But if he knew Dilling, the man would have been unable to resist leaving some clue somewhere for someone. Not Lily because the clue would never have been that simple. No, it would have been left for someone like himself or Billy Who—had to be to satisfy Dilling's hubris. Whatever Harry had, he guessed, friendship or love or knowledge, he used deliberately for his own amusement or advantage. That didn't make him an unpleasant man. He gave back freely but always the balance was left in his favour. On that he was prepared to bet. He'd had Lily right under his thumb. So much so that he would lay odds that if Harry had told her to lie about something she would have lied and there would have been the devil's own job in turning her from the lie because of her love for Harry and this special loyalty she had to him, because of the way he had treated her which—except for buttering up her ego and feeding her a little superficial culture—was far more one-sided in his favour than hers. What man wouldn't want a good-looking, bedworthy, complaisant mistress on such terms? He had a suspicion that Harry hadn't been the same colour all through. The colours changed as you layered him off.

He turned, retracing his steps, and now with the seawind at his back he stopped and lit a cigar. As he puffed at it he saw a man coming towards him along the river path. With two hundred yards between them he recognised the shape and the gait. It was Harrison, wearing a flat cap and a voluminous raincoat whose skirts flapped wetly in the wind, a shabby great bird waddling towards him. He moved on to meet him and there was no surprise in him. He had long ago exhausted all the common coinage of emotion where Harrison was concerned.

When they met Harrison turned and walked back with him. His red face glowed like a misty sun and he shook his head to flick the water drops from the peak of his cap.

Harrison said, "Another twelve hours of this and the fish will run."

Grimster asked, "Where are you staying?"

"Where you had lunch, but I kept out of the way. I'm surprised they let you out with our Miss Stevens. Nice piece. I should think she'd even unthaw you. Keep you warm and active in bed."

"Our Miss Stevens?"

"More or less. You're lodging and comforting her. But we've

65

got a stake too. When I say we, of course I'm only speaking as a paid messenger. Delivery boy. Sod of a day, isn't it?"

"As a paid messenger for whom?"

Harrison laughed. "What good would it be if I told you, since what I know isn't necessarily the truth? In fact can't be because they would never trust me with it. I'm lower than the middle man in a long chain. I get paid and the name on the cheque or the type of currency tells me nothing of the truth. It could be the Egyptians, the Russians, the Americans, the South Africans or some international industrial group. All I know is that your Professor Dilling, wisely hedging his bet with your people, must have made some tentative approach to them."

"You got his name and Lily's from them?"

"Naturally. I have to know enough to work on."

"You know what he had for sale?"

"Not as much as that. Personally, old boy, I don't care a damn what it was. All I know is that it won't add to the gaiety of nations—or to their well-being." Harrison halted his steps, looking out over the flood of water sweeping under the arches of the town bridge. For a moment his face was bland with nostalgia. "Remember that first time I came to the Blackwater with you? The water was just dropping after a spate and that ghillie chap showed us how to upstream worm. I got a twenty pounder—my first fish—and you nearly lost him for me because you were so ham-fisted with the gaff? You're still ham-fisted in some ways. How's your mother these days?"

"She's old and well content."

"A condition neither of us will ever know. Perhaps, even, don't want. However, *revenons aux nos moutons*, they'll make you a handsome deal on this one. Either to spin the thing out until it's a dead duck—so that they can get on with their own home-work—or just pass along whatever stuff you pick up. You name the money or the terms you want. Your future security is guaranteed, of course. All they want is to know exactly where Dilling went on that Friday, 27th February, and what he did when he got there. There's an item in small print at the bottom

66

of the contract which says that if you go so far as to find whatever it is that Dilling hid and hand it over—then there would be a fat bonus, very, very fat."

Grimster laughed. "You're my friend and you want to destroy me. Why?"

"Don't know, old chap. Even dear old Oscar ducked that one, though he fancified the notion with nice phrases. For each man kills the thing he loves, some do it with a sword and some with a word or something. Anyway, if the Department ordered you to bump me off you'd do it. We both sold our rights in all virtues long ago. You take the Devil's shilling and he takes your soul, and you've got a good job for life—so long as it lasts. But the finger won't be put on me for a long time. I'm far too useful as a clearing house for all parties. What do you say?"

"Only that Major Cranston has probably got someone around just now who's watching us and that this meeting will be reported by whoever it is. And also by me. And you're wasting your time, as you know damned well you are. It's not me you really want. Or am I being too psychic for you when I say that?"

"Same old Johnny. No deal, then?"

"No."

"Only one thing will swing you—right?"

A small tern swooped through the rain, hovered hawklike and then dived to the water, rising almost at once with the wet gleam of a small fish showing in its bill.

Grimster was silent for a while, watching the bird and then said, as he had never openly said before, "That's something that could never come from your side. As a point of interest, why have they never tried to fake it for me?"

Harrison tossed the damp end of a cigarette away, scuffed at the wet sand with the blunt toe of his shabby suede shoe and said, "Because your nose is too good. But you never know. One day they might come up with the genuine article."

"You mean you might. You're the one who wants to package

and sell me. They've said that there's a handsome deal going if you can produce the goods."

"Could be," Harrison sighed. "Well, there it is. I'll be down here for a week or so in case you should change your mind." He turned, facing back the way they had come. "Must put in a little more exercise. Not for my body's good, you understand, but just to pass the time between eating, drinking, fornicating and scheming." He made to move away and then paused, pushing a big hand into the right pocket of his coat and pulled out an envelope. "Here, thought you might like to have this. It's not proof, of course, but I thought it might give you some idea of what Valda was really like. A sweet, innocent girl, they thought, who might make you change your ways to be worthy of her. Sweet innocence, a deadly virtue in our worlds, Johnny."

He walked away down the sand, his footprints paralleling the ones they had already made. Grimster stood, envelope in hand, watching him. Then he put the envelope in his pocket and moved on, back to Barnstaple to pick up Lily.

*　　*　　*　　*

At High Grange, Grimster gave Major Cranston a censored résumé of his meeting and conversation with Harrison so that it could be sent on to Coppelstone and Sir John. But he said nothing of the envelope which Harrison had given him. By withholding this information from Cranston solely he knew that he was conceding Harrison a small triumph; maybe, even, a small step forward in his design.

Cranston said, "This could mean that there might be a clamp down on Miss Stevens going outside this place. Somebody might try to grab her. Should we put a guard on her room at night?"

"Only if Sir John insists. I want to keep her happy and comfortable. If she smells trouble or danger she might become awkward. Personally I don't think they'll try anything. They'd like us to do the hard work for them first."

"You sound very sure."

"If you knew Harrison like I do, you'd be sure." He smiled. "He's got me marked down for a potential traitor. He's happy to wait and see. So are his people, whoever they are."

"Johnny, that's no thing to say about yourself."

"No? Come on . . ." He laughed, easing the man's embarrassment. "You know it's been said to you. You've been warned. It's no secret. Sir John has as good as said it to my face. I asked for permission to marry. After a lot of dickering around they finally gave it to me—and then Valda had an accident, and that was that. They think I've got a bee in my bonnet about it. That I think they arranged the accident."

"It's ridiculous. You can't think that."

"I'm telling you what they think I think. If I had definite proof they'd write me off. But even so, as things stand, I'm no longer one hundred per cent. You know it, they know it, and I know it. And Harrison knows it—that's why he works so hard on me. Potential traitors are rare in the market."

Cranston worked a finger under his patch, massaged his eye and then gave a sigh of disbelief.

"Johnny. It's unthinkable. Even in the Department where things can be damned tricky at times, there is a code. Our code. And there's no place for that kind of thing, or that kind of thinking. Everyone is vetted and screened again from time to time, but that's normal. Even Sir John has to go through it."

"Naturally. I was only explaining the situation to you. It's no secret. At the moment there's a question mark against me. That doesn't worry me. There are question marks against a lot of us. As you say, it's part of the code."

He went up to his room, flopped into an armchair and lit a cigar. For a moment he lay back and shut his eyes, a slow weariness dragging at his body. The one thing in the world he wanted it to be was an accident. God's hand. Nobody else's.

He sat forward after a few moments and picked up Harrison's envelope from the small table in front of him. Whatever was in it, he knew, would be no fabrication. Not between Harrison and himself. The contest they fought was in the open. Love and hate and a rough camaraderie from the moment they had first met as boys. Why? Because from birth they had both had and been aware of having some fatal flaw that was to turn them for ever from contentment, from the smooth release of banality and easy conforming?

He opened the envelope. It held a typed note from Harrison, some microfilm blowups and a couple of xeroxed documents. Harrison's note, initialled by him, read—*Did she ever tell you about this? A pity. It might have altered so much, and you would have made a great pair—professionally.*

One of the documents was a Helsinki marriage certificate registering the marriage of Valda Trinberg with one Pols Sbordensa, described as an army officer. (This was no news to Grimster for Valda had told him about the marriage.) Another document, and he recognised the form, layout and style immediately for he had seen many of them, was a report from an American C.I.A. agent detailing the secret court martial, conviction and execution of Pols Sbordensa for treasonable acts against Finland, carried out on behalf of two other countries, Sweden and Russia. (The whole of this was news to Grimster, but he was untouched by it except for a brief mental comment that it took a clever man to work for two masters.) Another document—from another C.I.A. agent—reported an abortive attempt to recruit Sbordensa's wife, who had returned to Sweden, her place of birth, and there had resumed her original nationality and name. The report indicated that Valda had rejected the facts of her husband's activities and mode of death. She believed that he had been killed in an accident on army manoeuvres. (Which was what she had always told Grimster but he was prepared, without any emotion, to accept that by the time she met him she could well have been converted to the truth.) The report concluded that at the moment her worth was not evaluated highly enough to justify the intense recruiting methods which would have to be applied. The last document, xeroxed, was a letter from a Swedish Government department to the head of the Swedish Tourist Bureau recommending her for work in the London office of the tourist bureau (where Grimster had met her) and laying out briefly the facts of her husband's death, but clearing her completely.

Grimster went to his desk and wrote a note to Sir John, enclosing the documents, but not Harrison's note, explaining that for personal reasons he preferred not to have mentioned them to Major Cranston in his report. The envelope would go up to London in the bag that left each morning. Harrison would have known that this minor disclosure about Valda would not affect him personally. Valda had been unlucky in her marriage. She had never known the real nature of his, Grimster's, work. For her he was a reasonably well placed civil servant in the Ministry of Defence.

He had not, in his note to Sir John, asked whether the Department had known the facts about Valda and her husband. He had no desire to appraise Sir John of any of his personal curiosities. It would have been a weakness if he had and a deterioration of a position which he meant to maintain until the moment when he had proof. And Harrison could never bring him that proof because Harrison dealt in the tangible: documents and copies of letters. The truth about Valda's death was not documented anywhere. It rested in the minds of Sir John and maybe two other men and the minds of men were not easily robbed.

In the hall, after he had dropped his letter in the mail bag, he met Lily. He took her into the small bar off the dining-room and ordered her a drink. She had a dry martini with a stuffed olive in it and was in a gay mood. She'd been into Barnstaple and had her hair done; she was at home around the place now, and she felt easy with all the people, and while he joked and laughed with her he knew that the time had come to start driving her hard. The honeymoon was over. He was a professional man with a job on his hands, and his pride in his own talents overrode any personal feelings or problems. Lily Stevens was a riddle that had to be solved. In some way she was still in Harry Dilling's custody. She had to be taken into his. He looked at her as she sat cocking a little finger above the martini glass—Harry wouldn't have suppressed that gentility, there would always have been an inward smile for him in that, a pleasant touch of sadism provoked by the flaw he refused to eradicate from his own creation. He had a sudden moment of intuition which told him that Harry was a man who loved oddness for its own sake. He had a jackdaw mind, too, and loved to hide things. Billy Who. Sit in the car outside the station. When he didn't want you to know something you could tell it. She'd never seen the London flat. Harry the hider. When he had something really important to hide, then it would be lodged in no ordinary hiding place. Some essential part of the mystery Harry had bequeathed to the Department, he knew, was hidden in Lily, in that beautiful bedworthy body, behind that slightly over made-up face, in that lazy, placid and dreamily aspiring mind.

CHAPTER SIX

GRIMSTER WAS UP early the next morning. It was still raining—they had had a good twenty-four hours of it now—though it had slackened to a thin drizzle. Raincoated he walked from his car through the woods and saw that the Cliff Pool was a wide, coffee-coloured flood, high up against the far meadow bank. One couldn't have waded across the tail, not even in breast waders. The river was coming out of the pool in a rough cataract so that above the noise of the water came the sound of heavy boulders and stones moving under its force. He turned left through the woods and down to the long, straight run of the upper part of the High Grange water. This piece of river was known as the Doctor's Run and was a good stretch for salmon when they were moving upstream. If the rain stopped today, then tomorrow as the river began to fall it would be worth fishing.

Grimster moved up the river, knowing that he could take a roundabout route which would bring him to his car without going back through the woods. His mind was operating along two channels. One stream of thought was concerned with planning his assault on Lily that morning, marshalling his forces for attack, assessing her weak points, debating which he should press the hardest. And while he did this along the other channel his thoughts floated free and idle, a slow summer current of memory and speculation . . . Harrison, standing yesterday on the estuary sands, bulky and damp against the rain-shrouded sky. It was true that he had nearly lost him the biggest and first fish he had ever taken out of the Blackwater

73

by his clumsy gaffing . . . this before he had learnt that swift certain stroke that drove the point home low and in the belly below the dorsal fin to keep the fish in balance. After the fish had been landed Harrison had taunted him and, with the great salmon lying close to them on the damp grass, they had come to blows. While the ghillie looked on silently assessing points, he had bloodied Harrison's nose and Harrison had knocked one of his teeth out and, later, they had both had to lie like troopers to keep the truth from his mother. Their long friendship was studded with fights of one kind and another. And now, maybe, he thought, they were locked in their last one, which was also their first one ever over a woman. Not Lily. She was nothing. A professional object. But over Valda whom Harrison had met and disliked. She was too cool and poised and immaculate for Harrison . . . "a bloody, blonde iceberg. She'll freeze you to death, old boy." She wasn't like that, but that was how she appeared to Harrison and many others. Harrison's little pile of documents was part of the fight still going on. He wanted to destroy, even after her death, any purity that remained in his memory of Valda, and he wanted to make her death and her impurity additional weapons in his hands for his attack on him, Grimster. Why did he persist? Because he wanted to see completed in him the same total rejection of all commonplace virtues, wanted them to be both entirely dead to any high decencies, dead of all virtue and charity though they still walked and talked and acted like living beings. There had been things in his, Grimster's, early background that had shaped and warped him. There were, too, in Harrison's—though he had given no more than the briefest glimpse of them when once, his family background still obscure to Grimster, he had described his mother as a bitch and his father as a drunken, broken-down Don Juan.

He turned away from the river, moving up across the slopes of the sodden field paths to his car . . . towards Lily, he thought, and this current professional problem, and after Lily, he knew so surely, to a point growing ever closer when he would have

74

to make a decision with or without absolute proof on the nature of Valda's death. And Harrison guessed that, too. Everything Harrison did was to realise that moment since he could never hasten it with real proof. Meanwhile there was Lily. With the thought of her, it suddenly occurred to him that he, with Valda, had been much like Dilling with Lily. He had walked into the Swedish Tourist Office in London to check some small point about steam passages to Stockholm. She had come from an office to the counter to help him and he had known before she even spoke that he wanted her, in a way that he had never wanted any other woman . . . a simple, powerful need never stirred in him before. For a moment, as the drizzle swept into his face, he halted, held by a rare grip of nostalgia, feeling again that moment of longing. Then, angry at the momentary weakness, he broke free, drove memory from him and walked on down the hedged path, noting the pink petals, rain- and wind-raped from the wild hedge roses, lying on the grass like damp confetti, and catching with the corner of his eye the white flick of a rabbit's scut as it moved into a patch of nettles.

In Lily's room that morning she gave him a warm welcome and held up her hands to show him a new nail varnish she had bought in Barnstaple.

"Like it, Johnny?"

He nodded and switched on the tape recorder.

She laughed. "I say. Are we in a serious mood this morning? Had a bad night?"

Taking advantage of the lead, he said, "Perhaps I am. But not because of a bad night. Because of you and Harry and this Friday, the 27th February. The whole thing is wrong somewhere and, until we have it sorted out, we'll never get anywhere."

"Well, I've told you all I know."

He said, "It isn't what you know you know. Sometimes you can know things without knowing you know them. Follow?"

"No."

"Well, never mind. Just let's attack this thing again." He

took her arm and led her to a chair. "Sit down and make yourself comfortable." When she was settled, he went on, "I want you to think about that Friday. Get your mind right back there."

"It's so long ago."

"It'll come back. Just relax and think about it, and tell me again what you remember about the day. Anything you like, and in any order you like. But if you can, try starting with getting up and let one thing go on to another. You can do that, can't you?" He gave her the warm, encouraging professional smile.

"I'll have a go."

"I'll help you with an odd question now and then."

She leaned back and closed her eyes and after a moment she began. "Well, let's see. I got up somewhere about half past seven, put on a dressing-gown and went downstairs to make some tea for Harry and me . . ."

He let her go on, flicking her a question now and then.

Lily's memory of what had been in the papers that day was a blank. She'd looked at them, yes, but she couldn't remember anything about them. But her memory for what she and Harry had eaten, and what she had done around the house was fairly full. In fact he was a little surprised at some of the small detail she could remember. She remembered all about her packing in preparation for leaving the next day, and could list the clothes she had packed. Without any hesitation this time she said they had made love in the afternoon. She went through to the evening and, because he had checked the shows in the papers, he asked her about their television watching. Harry had been watching while she fiddled around, first with dinner and then clearing it, and then she had joined him.

"Do you remember anything you saw that evening?"

"Oh, Johnny, what a question."

"Try. For instance, you've said that your set only got BBC 1 and Southern Television. There was a comedy show, all about

76

monks, called 'Oh, Brother!' on BBC 1 at five to eight. Remember that?"

He was not trying to trick her. There had been such a show.

"No. I'd have been doing the dinner things, . . . Now wait . . ." She put her hands over her eyes. ". . . yes, I do remember something." Her hands came down and she gave him a smile, pleased with herself. "I remember because we had a bit of an argument. Harry wanted to watch a thriller series on Southern at nine o'clock—but on BBC 1 there was an episode of 'The Forsyte Saga' I wanted, so he gave way to me. After that there was a 'Come Dancing' show we watched. Harry was a good dancer, you know."

And she had remembered correctly, he knew. The "Come Dancing" show had followed "The Forsyte Saga", and there had been a thriller, "Manhunt", on Southern Television at nine o'clock. But she couldn't have remembered, because the simple fact was that both of them had been out of the house at that time. The contradiction hardened something in him.

He stood up and walked to the window. The rain had stopped and a brightly washed sun was lacquering the green fields and dark conifer stands. To point the scene, a jay swooped across the lawns drawing a quick line of colour.

He turned. She was watching him, sensing his frustration, and she acknowledged it by saying, "It doesn't make sense, does it? If what your man said is true." Her voice was thin, even a little scared, he thought.

"No, it doesn't. We know that you and Harry were out of that house, certainly from around ten in the morning until at least midnight. We know this for a fact. And during that time Harry hid whatever he hid, and whatever he hid it is to your advantage as much as ours to find."

He went quickly to her, took her by the forearms and drew her up out of the chair, his face close to hers, their bodies almost touching, and he was deliberately willing fear and alarm into her. There was some power holding her back from the truth and only a greater power could free her.

She moved her body against the grip on her arms and said, "Johnny, you're hurting me."

He said, "I don't care if I'm hurting you. You've got to come clean. I like you and I want to help you. There's nothing you have to hide from me—but you are hiding something. You weren't in that house. You couldn't have done all the things you say you did. You were out with Harry, hiding something."

He took his hands off her. He saw her eyes moisten, near to tears, and then she dropped her head, hiding from him. He put out his hands, gently now, cupped her chin and raised her face to his. It was the first time that he had had any real naked physical contact with her and he felt the whole of his body briefly, before he crushed it, acknowledge the contact.

Softly, he said, "Lily, why won't you tell me the truth about that day?"

She said, "Johnny, I would, I have. That's all I know about that day. I don't remember ever being in a car with Harry and going off to hide anything. Honestly I don't." Suddenly she turned away from him, breaking the touch of his hands on her face, and cried, "Why do you keep on? I don't care if he did hide something. I don't know about it. I don't care about it, not even though it means money for me. After all . . ." she turned back to him, the tears clear in her eyes now, and said, ". . . there's more important things in life than money."

As a piece of philosophy, he thought, it was just her level, it was a cliché she turned to for comfort . . . for escape perhaps.

He said deliberately, feigning contempt, "What is it that Harry had about him that could make you his slave? Is it something so shameful that you won't even admit it to yourself? You slept with him. You were his kept woman. His thing. He treated you like a doll, a puppet, put words in your mouth, snippets of poetry. Taught you to behave in company, but let you go on making up like a tart because it amused him. He gave you a few tricks of manners, picked up some of your aitches, and had fun with you because he knew he could do what

78

he liked with you. For no reason at all he wouldn't tell you the names of his friends. Never took you to his London flat. Kept you in a country hideout to visit when he felt bored. Called and beckoned you, sent you away, made you sit like a pet poodle in his car when he saw a friend off at the station. My God, he had fun with you, cast a dirty spell over you— and do you know why? Because at heart your precious Harry didn't have the least bit of respect for you."

"Shut up, Johnny!" She came forward quickly, angry, while the tears still limned her cheeks, and smacked him across the face.

He was still for a moment. Then he said, "You're not hitting me. For the first time you know the truth. You're hitting Harry." He moved to the door and then turned and added, "You know what I want from you. The little bit you've kept back. The little bit you're either ashamed or frightened of. I know what it is now, but I'm not going to tell you because I like and respect you too much to force it out of you. When you're ready you come and tell me about it."

He went out and down to the small bar and helped himself to a large brandy and then sat down and lit a cigar, and he was thinking that the truth was always there, staring you in the face, sometimes shouting at you and you went on being deaf and blind to it until suddenly under stress it came hard and sharp out of your own mouth. Poor Harry. Bastard Harry. Apart from this little trick of Friday, 27th February, how many other little tricks had he played on her for his own private amusement? Quite a few probably, and maybe some of them in front of Billy Who and perhaps others.

*   *   *   *

Lily didn't appear for lunch. She sent a message down that she had a headache. Cranston raised an eyebrow but Grimster merely shrugged his shoulders and offered no explanation.

He was in no hurry now. He could have forced Lily on the spot, but he preferred to have it come from her when she had

79

had time to think it over and was willing to co-operate. You didn't bludgeon someone to the confessional box. They had to come of their own accord if they sought true absolution.

After lunch Grimster went up to the store room and took one of Dilling's books from the case. It was marked and worn from more than one reading. He went down to his room and settled into it. The subject matter wasn't new to him, but he had never gone into it so thoroughly before. Once something in it reminded him of an escapade carried out by himself and Harrison at Wellington. He smiled to himself, remembering the way they had rolled about, rocking with high laughter. He read on for three hours, dropping into the intense state of absorbing and recording which would imprint his mind with an exact image of each page, an acute memory of every point and example made in the book. The contradiction between what Lily *had* done and what she *said* she had done on that Friday was no longer any mystery to him, but this knowledge he knew did not by any means solve the problem. When he had finished the book, he dropped it, lit a cigar and lay back staring motionlessly at the ceiling, cigar clamped between his teeth, face set in a tight grimace, pondering the line which would have to be taken with her. There was no expert in the Department itself who could deal with it professionally. To call in an outside man would be something that Sir John wouldn't welcome because of the additional security risk. On the other hand, there might not be any need for a professional. Dilling had not been one. There was a possibility that he could do it himself. He would prefer to do it. There was now a bond between himself and Lily, the bond which had come from this break through to her, which gave him new strength, and an added intimacy with her, and these factors automatically increased his chance of success.

He went down to his car and drove down the road to the High Grange farm, had a word with the manager and then went alone into one of the old barns which was lined with two rows of battery penned hens. He spent ten minutes there as once he and Harrison had spent time in a barn on a farm near Crowthorne, a few miles from school.

Then he came out, took a spinning rod and waders from the back of the car, and went down to the river. The water was much too coloured for a fly. He went part way up the Doctor's Run and worked his way down with a large blue and silver Devon, flicking the bait out, relishing the sureness and precision of the movement, and letting the dropping flood water work it around in the current until it hung under his own bank . . . remembering the Irish ghillie who had taught him to spin, smacking at the back of his reel hand if he attempted to wind in line while the bait was working. He had one touch, brief and hard, and then the fish was off. As he looked up towards the opposite bank he saw a bulky figure coming across the wet grass. The Exeter–Barnstaple road was four hundred yards beyond the bank with the railway line lying between road and river. There was a car parked at the railway crossing gate which was always kept locked. The figure came right up to the bank, raised an arm and hand in greeting, but made no attempt to call across to him.

Grimster returned the gesture briefly. It was Harrison. Without more acknowledgment between them, Grimster fished down to the point where the river curved and ran into the Cliff Pool, without touching anything. He stopped fishing and went up through the trees towards his car without looking back at Harrison. Harrison was there, he knew, not because he was indulging in any form of psychological pressure, haunting him with his presence. He knew Harrison too well for that. Harrison was there because sitting bored in his Barnstaple hotel he had known that with the river beginning to drop if he, Grimster, were free, it was almost certain that he would go down and fish. It simply amused Harrison to check his deduction, to make sure that the old lines of intuition and communication between them were intact.

Lily didn't appear at dinner. She came to Grimster at half past eleven that evening. He was lying in bed, thinking through

81

some parts of Dilling's book, when he heard the outer door of his sitting-room open and the click of the light switch. A sliver of light angled under his bedroom door. He lay where he was, waiting. She had to do it her way, with a certain amount of drama to match the romantically coloured conventions which meant so much to her. From the moment she had left Boots to join Dilling, and on through his death and her time with Mrs. Harroway and now here, she had clearly—though she had never expressed it—seen herself as one of the main characters in a serial drama. All these things were happening to her—ordinary Lily Stevens. Good manners and a conscious desire to play her part properly forced her to conform, to shape life into the fiction it was so clearly becoming. If there were to be revelation, it should be near midnight, shade-haunted, the stage dressed right and everything appropriate to the role she had to play.

She knocked gently on his door, said his name, and then came in. He sat up in bed but did not put the light on. There was enough light coming through from the sitting-room. She was wearing a blue silk dressing-gown, open over her pyjamas. On her feet were little white leather and gold slippers, the toes turned up and fastened back in Moorish fashion. Her soft, blonde hair hung loose, freshly combed, over her neck and shoulders and, although her face was free of makeup, her lips were newly painted.

She came across to him and sat on the edge of the bed. For a moment her right hand played nervously, fingers plucking at the stuff of the bed cover, and then she said, "Johnny, I'm sorry . . ."

He said, "That's all right. There's nothing to be sorry about." He reached out and took her hand, holding it firmly as though by stopping its movement he knew that he could quieten the nervousness inside her.

She said calmly, "I had a feeling he might have done it, but I couldn't know."

"How did it all start?"

"It was a sort of joke. Something he was interested in and . . . well, he asked me if he could try on me." Her eyes went to the book which rested on Grimster's bedside table. "You've been reading about it? Isn't that one of his books?"

"Yes."

"But how could you guess? How could you know?"

How could he? Where does truth come from? Out of a patent contradiction between what she had said happened and what he knew could not have happened, and then anger and intuition working deep in him until he himself had thrown out the words against her which had given him the clue he wanted. *. . . My God, he had fun with you, cast a dirty spell over you.* . . . He glanced from her lovely, touchingly contrite face to the book at the bedside. *Hypnosis of Man and Animals,* by Ferenc András Völgyesi. Now was the time, he knew, when she needed tenderness and sympathy, or the appearance of them.

He said, "It just came to me. A hunch. The only thing it could be. Because, too, you wouldn't have held it back unless you'd felt it to be . . . well, not quite right." He smiled. "Something against nature."

She nodded. "I never liked it. Sort of spooky and . . . well . . . one didn't ought to meddle in that kind of thing. But it pleased him and he said it was all right. I didn't want to tell you about it, because I wasn't sure. And, anyway, whenever I thought about it, it was kind of like having a stranger suddenly find you naked. Do you get what I mean, Johnny?"

"Of course I do."

He slipped out of bed, still holding her hand, and said, "Let's go into the other room. We'll have a drink and you can have a cigarette, and you can tell me about it."

He put his arm around her shoulder, the movement automatic, part of the design already formed to deal with her, but at the same time he was aware that it was the first time he had put his arm around a woman since Valda and felt through silk the warmth and firmness of woman flesh.

He took her into the sitting-room, made her comfortable and

83

moved around getting the drinks and cigarettes. Valda was pushed from his mind, her place taken by the old memory of Harrison and himself, ranging away from Wellington, mischief hungry, finding a barn with a dozen cooped hens in it and Harrison—always fertile with some new ploy—showing him how to take a fowl, swing it around in the air for a few times and then press it gently on the ground and draw a chalk line away from the tip of its beak so that the bird would stay there motionless when released, hypnotised. They had hypnotised all the birds in the barn and, almost hysterical with laughter, had left them there. That afternoon he had done the same thing with a few of the birds from the farm manager's battery unit.

Lily, with a cigarette and a drink, suddenly happier, relishing the intimacy of being here, alone with him at midnight, the setting right for confidences, said, "You're not angry with me for not telling before, Johnny?"

"No, you had to come to it in your own way." He moved a small table near her so that she had a place for her drink and an ashtray for her cigarette, looking after her, deliberately relaxing her with the small palliatives of male courtesy. There was no excitement in him. He was working. She was a professional problem. He settled himself in a chair close to her, refusing the need in him for a cigar. "Tell me all about it in your own way."

She drew on her cigarette, leaned back against the chair head so that he could see the smooth, round thrust of her breasts against the pyjama silk and, above it, the faintest shadow of the bold valley that lay between them. She blew smoke and breath free with a long sigh and said, "Well, Harry . . . you know, it was the kind of thing he would be interested in. He wanted to try it. Anything new and he was after it, just for the fun of it. So he asked me if I would let him. Try it on me, that is. He said he could tell I was the type . . ."

She was, he knew from his reading of Völgyesi. She was psycho-passive. Her hand when he had first held it was warm, faintly moist. She blushed easily and there was little intellectual

84

aggressiveness or pride in her character. She liked to be wrapped up and looked after. The description in the book fitted her. *Individuals of the psycho-passive nervous constitution accept the most unlikely possibilities and adapt themselves to every prompting of the individual who is influencing them . . . they colour demands from outside with every variety of illusion. . . .*

Because she had loved Dilling, was grateful to him, she had wanted—even against some superstitious dread in herself—to please him, to do what he wanted.

Dilling had explained some of the elementary facts and principles to her and then had tried conventional methods. But at first he had had no success. As Lily described what happened, Grimster recognised some of the hypnotic techniques from Völgyesi's book; the old hand movements of Mesmer across the body without touching it, holding the subject's visual attention with a steady staring of the operator's eyes, getting her to look fixedly at some object while Harry made verbal suggestions that her eyelids were becoming heavier and heavier, making her follow slowly the movement of his finger held at the root of her nose and then slowly raised so that she had to follow it with an upturning of her eyes without moving her head, all methods—a phrase from the book came to him—*to reinforce hypnosis through a concentration of stimulus and through fatigue of certain points in the cortex with an irradiation of inhibition.* But in the end he had succeeded. Not all at once, but gradually. He held a revolving mirror on a string before her and concentrated a small beam of light on it.

She said, "It was the first thing that did anything to me. Kind of made me feel drowsy and happy . . . a sort of going off feeling, but the moment he spoke to me I'd come back. He was near it, but it was the mirror just being all silvery, I suppose, that was wrong, because when he finally got it it was as simple as pie. He was almost on the point of giving up, you know. And he was angry about it. I could always tell. He used to chew one corner of his mouth. As though he was talking to himself, not making any sound."

And then, he had tied his signet ring to a piece of string and swung it pendulum-fashion in front of her eyes, a little above them, and had told her to follow it with her eyes without any movement of her head.

She gave a little giggle at the memory and reached for her drink. "You wouldn't believe it. But I went off—bang! I didn't know I had until afterwards. I didn't remember a thing. He was like a dog with two tails. And he was all over me. I always remember the first real thing that he did that I knew about. He put me off and while I was in this—well, trance, I suppose you call it—he read out to me three pages from a book which he put back in the bookcase telling me where he had put it and then—of course, I didn't know this until afterwards—said that when he woke me up I would recite the three pages of the book—not knowing what book it was, of course—and then go and get the book from the case. And, do you know, I did. Just like he said! Mind you, though I was pleased because he was pleased, I didn't really like it. It didn't seem right, tampering around with someone like that. But he said I didn't have to worry about that, that it was used by doctors for curing people of all sorts of things, phobias and whatnot, and that if I ever had a headache, for instance, he could cure it at once. Even so I never really liked it . . . not even when I got used to it. In the end all he had to do was to hold up the ring on his hand in front of my face, no swinging string or anything, and I'd look at it for a moment and he'd say, 'Sleep, Lily. Sleep.' And I would."

Quietly Grimster asked, "Did he ever do this to you in front of other people?"

Sharply, Lily said, "Why do you ask that?"

"Because it may be important."

She hesitated and he saw the colour flush faintly across her cheeks and she partly turned her face from him.

"Yes, he did."

"With whom?"

"Just Billy Who."

86

"And you didn't like that?"

Her eyes came back to him and she said firmly, "No, I didn't. Just with Harry it was all right. But I didn't want other people there. You know, because afterwards when we were alone Harry would tell me the daft things he'd got me to do. Like, well, picking up a big book and a ruler and pretending to play a violin and making the noises with my mouth. And I didn't know a thing about it afterwards. Only once I did. He gave me two glasses of water to drink while I was like that and told me that it was whisky and I'd come to all tiddly. And I did. I was really angry with him for a bit for that. As I say, with him it was all right because I knew he'd always be there to look after me and not ask me to do anything . . . well, not ladylike. But I didn't trust him with Billy Who. He wanted to show off to him and that could have led to things."

Grimster wondered whether it had. His picture now of Harry Dilling was filling out, his true personality so little understood by her seeming to signal to him clearly. Harry had made her his thing, cossetted and trained her, and it must have delighted him that he could induce her into an hypnotic state and control her like a true puppet. While in that state she would have refused no order because she had given her trust and love to him, fearing nothing from him. Only her normal, wakeful self had finally imposed an embargo on Billy Who's presence. Harry she trusted, but not Harry with Billy Who. And, he felt, she probably had had good reason.

He said, "What ring was it? The one upstairs with all his stuff?"

"Yes. It's got those red, yellow and blue bits of enamel stuff. He always wore it."

He said, "Now let's suppose that on that Friday you actually did go off with Harry. Driving him. You went somewhere and he hid something. You might even on that day have known what it was. But when you got back he could have hypnotised you, couldn't he?"

"Yes."

87

"And while you were under he could have told you that you were to forget that day altogether, forget even the fact that he'd hypnotised you?"

To his surprise, she said thoughtfully, "I think he did. He must have done. But that would only have been to make things safe for him and for me."

"I know. But he could have told you while you were under that it had been an ordinary day like any other, made up details of what you'd done and what you'd eaten and what you'd seen on television and all the rest of it and then told you that when you came out you'd remember nothing of the true facts of that Friday?"

Lily nodded.

Grimster could imagine Dilling doing it. Planning it days before, having all the details he wanted for the fake Friday already in his mind, meals, broad conversations, television programmes checked, even the touch about making love in the afternoon. Dilling—with a big deal on his hands—didn't trust anyone, not even Fate. If he were to drop dead—then he wanted his secret to remain as a challenge. He wouldn't want it lost for ever. That wasn't in his nature. Let someone else sweat from scratch to find the clues for the discovery. That was his arrogance and it perfectly matched the quiet, smooth sadism of his mastery over Lily. As surely as the liquid in his glass was brandy, Grimster knew that until Lily had objected there must have been times when she had been put on exhibition before Billy Who. . . . Maybe some blurred, formless memory of it lingered in Lily's mind and it had been this which had held her back from telling in the first place about Dilling's practice of hypnosis on her. He could see her on exhibition before them and the swift pictures flashing through his mind made his hand tighten on his glass.

Lily, silent through his silence, now said, "What do we do about it?"

Grimster got up and moved to her. Although he didn't want it he couldn't deny the passage of a quick moment of protective tenderness. He touched the side of her face, and said, "Tonight —nothing. We'll think about it in the morning."

She stood up. The slow caress of his hand had made everything all right. He was a funny bird, hard and miles from you, you thought, but he wasn't really like that at all. He was nice, very nice. She knew she ought to have told him all this long ago; but how could you until you knew someone well enough, knew they would understand? You couldn't just blurt some things out to strangers. But now Johnny was no stranger . . . the both of them sitting here drinking in their pyjamas! They were friends . . . maybe there could even be more than friendship in the future. . . .

Before he could avoid it she put her arms round him, gave him a small hug and then stepped back, knowing she was blushing.

"Thank you, Johnny. You're ever so good to me. You really are."

CHAPTER SEVEN

THE NEXT MORNING Grimster went up to the store room
and got Dilling's ring. It was a gold ring and the coloured
enamel work was set in a gold-banded circle almost three-
quarters of an inch in diameter. Although Lily had described
it merely as a design with red, yellow and blue bits of enamel
stuff, it was no surprise to him that she had got the description
wrong. Clearly she had never examined it closely. The coloured
enamels had been worked into the shape of a bird against a blue
background. He recognised it wrongly at first as a conventional
representation of a goldcrest—a wren-like bird. Almost immediately he corrected himself, memory taking him back to the bird
books which he and Harrison had shared, thumbed and argued
over at Wellington. The craftsman who had fashioned the
enamels had, within the broad limits of his art, clearly por-
trayed a firecrest, an autumn visitor to Great Britain, for it had
the characteristic white stripe above and below the eye and a
black stripe passing through it, and carried the fiery red crest
of the male. When he held it to the window the fine enamels
caught the light, throwing back a soft, warm glow of reds,
olives, yellows and blue. He slipped it on his finger and went
to Lily's suite.

She was having her breakfast from a small table by the
window. The weather had cleared to a bright September day
and the sunlight streamed through the end window of the
sitting-room, catching the pale gold of her hair. She was wearing
her dressing-gown and pyjamas. Her feet were bare and he
noticed that she had painted her toenails the same colour as

90

her fingernails with the new colour she had bought in Barnstaple. She lay back against the chair cushions and welcomed him, a smiling, comfortable and desirable woman, a great deal of the sleek, happy, intimacy of a warm bed still about her. For a fraction of time he remembered the feeling of her skin under his hand through the silk of her pyjamas.

He said, "I've just been to get Harry's ring."

He held it out on his hand, a foot from her eyes, moving it so that the morning light caught and made the enamels glow. As she looked at it, he watched her face, wondering if it would do anything for her, even make her offer some faint shadow of the response that it used to draw from her with Harry. But she merely looked at it briefly, nodded her head and, proceeding to marmalade a piece of toast, said, "That's it, Johnny."

He sat down opposite her and said, "Do you know where he got it?"

"No."

Her strong white teeth bit into the toast and marmalade and she ate, unconcerned, a healthy, uncomplicated woman, the morning sun warm on her, the relish of food strong in her.

"He'd always had it?"

"Ever since I knew him."

"Did you know it represented some kind of bird?"

"Does it? I never looked at it closely. I mean except for when . . . well, you know. And then it was just a lot of colours to me. Harry was a great one for birds."

"It's meant to be a firecrest."

"A what?"

"Firecrest."

From her face, from the sudden immobility that took briefly but clearly the whole of her person, he knew that the word had meant something to her, jolted some part of her memory to wakefulness. The next moment she had recovered herself and was reaching out for the coffee pot to refill her cup.

"If there was another cup I'd invite you to join me, Johnny." Then she laughed. "If it was Harry sitting there I know what he would have done. He'd have tipped the sugar lumps from the bowl and used that."

Grimster smiled. "I would, too—if I wanted coffee. But I seldom drink it in the morning. Only tea. What does the word 'firecrest' mean to you?"

She turned to him slightly surprised. "Nothing. Should it?"

"I wouldn't know. But a moment ago it seemed to mean something to you. It showed in your face."

She laughed. "My goodness, you're a quick one. I wouldn't like to have done something awful and have you asking me about it. But then, I suppose, that's part of your business. You're trained to it."

He said quietly, "What did the word do to you? It might be important, Lily." His appeal to the importance of things that concerned her disarmed her as he knew it would.

"Well, it was only just for a moment. I seemed to remember something. Something about Harry . . . but if you was to offer to make me a duchess on the spot I couldn't for the life of me remember. Something just seemed to begin to come and then it went. Honest. I'd tell you if there was anything. You know that, Johnny."

"I'm sure you would."

He got up and went to the window. High above the trees by the river two buzzards were moving up lazily on a thermal spiral. Red cattle on a distant green field stood fixed in brightness like a child's painting. Turquoise-bodied dragon flies moved above the surface of the fish pool in the walled garden, and on the still air, through the half open window, he heard the clear sound of the Exeter train moving up the valley. Somewhere in Yorkshire at this moment his mother would be fiddling for her glasses, the Bible open on her table, preparing for her morning reading. The sin which had created him still kept her company, muted now, perhaps in some ways acceptable, even welcomed, giving purpose to her reading. The thought of the waste and warp of so many human lives, his own among them, suddenly present with him touched him with a longing for something unnamed, something as brief and inchoate as Lily's momentary stir of clouded response at the word "firecrest".

Without looking at Lily, he said, "Well, we've made one big step forward anyway. You did go somewhere with Harry on that Friday. And where you went and what you did is locked up inside you. How do we get it out?"

"I don't see as you can. Only Harry could do that. And he's pushing up the daisies."

He turned, surprised at her last sentence. She was lighting a cigarette and his move made not the slightest break in the flow of her actions as she snapped a lighter and held the flame to her cigarette.

He said, "I'm surprised to hear you say that."

"Say what? Oh, pushing up the daisies?"

"Yes."

"So you can be shocked." She laughed. "Well, there's no need. Harry's dead. He'd have said it himself of me the other way round. He's gone and I've got to go on. You can't live in the past. I was fond of him, loved him, yes, but you have to get over that, think of yourself if you're honest. He's pushing up the daisies and I've still got them to pick. Harry would have been the first one to agree with that." She stopped, drew hard on her cigarette and then through a veil of exhaled smoke went on without any change of tone, "Harry was the first man for me, sex and all that. I liked him and I liked it. But now he's gone that doesn't mean I don't want to be like that with someone else. It wouldn't be natural nor honest, would it?"

"No. I suppose not." From her frankness, he realised that her conception of their relationship had now altered, moving him out of the professional and into the personal orbit. Although he had no desire for it, or her, he welcomed the move because professionally it could only help him.

"There's no suppose about it. But that doesn't mean—"

"Lily, let's get back to this Friday thing. You've got something locked up inside you and you're wrong to think that Harry took the key with him. All that has to be done is for someone to put you in an hypnotic trance and then ask you what happened on that Friday."

"As easy as that?"

"I don't say it will be easy, but it can be done. Doctors can do it, professional psycho-therapists. There's nothing magic about it. It's a phenomenon which is well understood."

"So it may be, but I don't know that I'm very keen about it . . . I mean with some stranger, somebody I don't know. Anyway I don't think it would work. Certainly not with some doctor or what-have-you."

"Why not?"

"Well, it only happened between me and Harry, and only then after ages. He said to me once that most of it was a matter of having complete confidence, of being able to trust yourself with the person. Besides, isn't whatever I'm supposed to know probably a big secret, important? You wouldn't want me to blurt it all out to a stranger."

It was a thought which had been in his mind from the moment she had left him last night. The Department could get a professional medical hypnotist but he knew that Sir John would be uneasy about it. You only recruited people from outside the Department when their services could be safely isolated from the main stream of an enquiry. Lily could reveal something which might well put a security risk on any psycho-therapist or doctor, unless that person were a member of the Department. And, in any case, the force of Harry's personality was still strongly embedded in Lily's sentiments. Confidence and trust. . . . The man would have to have that.

He said, "Do you trust me? Do you have confidence in me?"

"What a question! Of course I do. You pretend to be poker-faced and cold, but really you're a nice man. You wouldn't hurt a fly."

How wrong, he thought, can you be? But at the same time a faint flush of pleasure at her words was warm in him for a moment or two.

He said, "Would you mind if I had a go?"

94

"You?" She put her cigarette down in the saucer of her coffee cup.

He smiled, "Well, it might not work. But it would keep it in the family if it did."

"But Johnny, you don't know anything about it."

"Neither did Harry once. He read a book and then experimented. Well, I've got his book and I've read it. What's more, we know it works through this—" he held up his hand with the ring on it. "That gives me a big start. It could work. And if it does I know all the questions to ask you and you know I'm on your side, that I've got your interests at heart. We want to find what Harry's hidden and buy it, and you'll get the money. We both want it to work—so why shouldn't it? If Harry could put you into trances then perhaps I—"

She interrupted him, suddenly stimulated by the trigger word "trances" and rattled off quickly, " 'And all my days are trances, and all my nightly dreams are where thy grey eye glances, and where thy footstep gleams—' "

"Lily." His voice betrayed the edge of irritation, and she relished a moment of triumph over him.

"Edgar Allan Poe. You haven't got grey eyes though, have you? Sort of slaty blue."

Ignoring the rise of this teasing spirit in her, he said bluntly, "Why shouldn't I be able to do it?"

She looked frankly, thoughtfully at him, the edges of her warm generous mouth still shadowing the teasing smile and then she said, "I think you could . . . maybe, in time. But you don't want to start now, do you? Not with me in my pyjamas!"

He said, "There's no rush. Think it over during the day. Get used to the idea. Then we might try it some time this evening. All right?"

"On one condition, Johnny." She was smiling broadly now and the coquetry in her clear.

"Yes?"

"I get stuffed up in here. You've got to take me to the cinema this afternoon. I don't care what it is. I just want to sit in a

95

cinema with a box of chocolates and—if you want to—I might even let you hold my hand."

He laughed, raised his hands in mock despair and said, "All right. If you have to be bribed."

As he moved to the door, she said, "All this long talk—and you forgot to put the tape recorder on."

"We've got beyond that stage." He went out.

* * * *

The night before when Lily had come to him and told him about the hypnotism he had deliberately not run the tape recorder because he had not wanted to disturb her mood in any way. Now he was glad he hadn't. For the moment he wanted to keep Lily to himself. Why? It was a question to which he had no satisfactory answer. Before sleeping last night he had worked it over in his mind without being able to fit any logic to it, but logic—though it was his major god—he knew was not the only process which served him. Intuition was a higher or different form of logic, and intuition had nagged him to keep what he knew for the moment to himself. After a considerable debate with himself he had decided to follow his intuition, though he knew that his discovery could not be withheld for very long from Sir John.

In the bag from London that day Coppelstone sent down a complete list of Dilling's bank payments and receipts for the last eighteen months of his life. The bank had had a standing order to pay twenty pounds a month to a William Pringle. There was no other *William* or anyone with the initial W, except two business firms, listed in the payments made by Dilling. Coppelstone, who knew what Grimster was after, had added a note—*Unless advised no, will locate Pringle and run a check.*

When Grimster told Cranston that he was taking Lily to the cinema that afternoon the Major refused permission unless Grimster got a clearance direct from the Department. Grimster phoned Coppelstone and got the clearance, but instead of going into Barnstaple where there was a chance of running into Harrison he took her to Exeter.

The film was some long, tedious and involved wartime adventure story which, to his surprise, Lily thoroughly enjoyed. He would have thought that she would have only been interested in romantic subjects or musicals. Once, at some point of tension, she shut her eyes and said, "Tell me when this bit is over. I can't bear it if he doesn't get free." She had her box of chocolates and ate most of them and once, for a period of about five minutes, she put her hand on his and held it lightly. She was like a small girl and he, an uncle, maybe, who was giving her a treat. Oddly, the feeling didn't displease him and he had to admit that within the terms of his professional assignment there had crept a considerable half-amused, half-tender feeling of responsibility for her. Despite her moments of shrewdness, her moments of almost puritan dislike of things that weren't quite right, like hypnotism, he saw that she was basically someone who, once she had given her allegiance and accepted the guarding shield of another's personality and concern, was at once malleable material on which could be stamped the impress of desires and manners fundamentally foreign to her. She had been putty in Dilling's hands. To some extent she was too in his. Idly, bored with the film, he considered the possibility of making love to her. Not because the desire was there, but as an abstract exercise carried out to sound now the extent of his own, determined celibacy. It was some moments before he realised that this was the first time since Valda's death that he had ever considered—no matter from what motive, the sudden pulse of his natural masculinity or the philosophical testing of vows and grief's slow dying—the possibility of having or loving another woman. Dispassionately he could admit that it would be easier with her than with many other women. She was everything that Valda had not been. Physically she was soft, full-fleshed, almost certainly sentimentally and romantically amorous. There would be no memory of Valda in the embrace. Valda had had the slim,

97

firm body almost of a boy which once moved by love's touch was loosed to extreme extravagance and invention. . . . For the first time he allowed himself to lift part of the curtain about his memories of Valda, no longer automatically rejecting them but running them through his mind, without pain, without emotion, without almost, he suddenly realised, any nostalgic stir in him whatsoever. The discovery made him feel a traitor and he pushed the whole speculation from his mind, the rejection passing into a short hard physical stir of his body that made Lily glance aside at him for a moment.

Driving back after the cinema, they stopped at the Fox and Hounds Hotel at Eggesford for a drink. It was an old coaching inn, now—because of its fishing rights in the River Taw—a well-known fishing hotel. Sir John stayed here when he came down for his fortnight's fishing on the High Grange water in September. Lily had a glass of sherry, rich, dark and sweet, which she liked, and he had a whisky and soda. Raising his glass to her, smiling, he saw a small frown pucker between her finely plucked eyebrows. He realised that she had noticed the firecrest ring which he was wearing.

He said, "You don't mind, do you? It's yours. You can say no if you want to."

She shook her head. "I don't mind. But why do you want to?"

"I want you to get used to seeing me with it. Just as you did with Harry. If we're going to get anywhere then in a way I've got to be like Harry for you."

At this she put her glass down on the long wooden bar top and began to laugh, her body shaking until she controlled herself, and said, "Oh, Johnny—you like Harry! You're as different as chalk and cheese."

Without knowing why, he felt a spurt of annoyance but he held it to himself. He said, "It's not going to help if you think Harry was the only one who could do it, Lily. You've got to keep in mind that you're the one, that if you've got confidence and trust in someone then you can do it for them."

She put a hand on his arm, consoled him, and said, "All

right, Johnny. You know I want to help. It was just the thought of you and Harry . . . so different."

But that evening, after dinner, in the sitting-room of her suite she was no help at all. Her little outing to the cinema had stimulated her and she had had a few drinks in the bar before dinner, and then wine with her food. She was in a giggly, flippant mood, warm and friendly towards him, her manner mirroring for the first time the closer relationship which she had built up for herself. She giggled and teased him and when pressed to be serious and to give herself to the experiment only succeeded for a few moments before the absurdity, to her, of Grimster holding the ring, first on a swinging piece of string and then on his hand before her eyes, made her break into half stifled laughter. In the end the sense of the ridiculous which she created passed to him and he gave the whole thing up for that evening. In her present mood there was no hope of his achieving anything. Later, in his own rooms before sleeping, he knew there was no forcing her. Her reaction, in fact, was to have been expected. She was embarrassed by the idea of being hypnotised and covered her embarrassment by refusing to take the trial seriously. She would come to it, he knew, but in her own time. He was sure that she was the type which Völgyesi in his book had classified as having an inherited psycho-passive nervous constitution with further acquired psycho-passive dispositions, a type which reacted admirably to the hypnotist's suggestions and was usually equally receptive to others, in fact to almost anyone. But that evening she had put up a barrier of laughter and flippancy, just as, he remembered, she had said she had to Harry the first time because deep inside her she was disapproving of what she called "mucking about with people's minds". What Harry had been through, he imagined, was what he would now have to go through. She would have to have time to get used to the idea all over again with him.

But he was wrong. He had a session with her the next morning without success, although her mood was different. He could sense her wanting to help him, wanting it too much and letting

99

that idea dominate her mind. A session in the afternoon was much the same and he was almost of a mind not to try again that day. But she herself suggested it after dinner, taking him up to her room and letting herself drop lazily into her chair, and he was almost at once successful, either because she was too tired from all the other efforts to find difficulty in abandoning herself or because, now that the novelty of the idea had gone, the process accepted, she had no inhibitions at putting herself in his hands.

The transformation, new to him, gave him a moment not of panic but of a sense of solemn responsibility at having in his hands a power for handling her and her mind for which he had no precedent. He had sat forward in his chair, facing her, his knees almost touching hers, and held the ring between the thumb and forefinger of his right hand, the enamelled bird a few inches in front of her eyes, and at once he had been aware that for the first time she was watching the ring, not the ring and himself, his face, beyond it.

He raised the ring a little higher so that it was on a level with the root of her nose and he saw her eyes follow it, her head unmoving. He raised it slowly a little higher and her eyes rolled upwards to keep it in view. As her eyes moved, he talked to her gently and soothingly. "You've got complete trust in me, Lily. You want to help me and you want to help yourself. What I want, too, you know Harry would have wanted. . . . Just relax, Lily. Let yourself go . . . slide away. . . ."

Some lines from Völgyesi's book flashed through his mind. "The fixed and upwardly converging gaze is indeed tiring and the patient is soon forced to blink. If now the 'hypnoscope' is drawn downwards, slowly and quietly, the patient's eyes will follow it and involuntarily close." This was what he saw happen with Lily. Her eyelids flickered for a moment or two and then as he slowly lowered the ring, the hypnoscope, her eyes followed it down and the lids slowly closed over them. Holding down the excitement which had risen in him, he followed the brief which Völgyesi's book had given him, speaking quietly, soothingly. At the same time he reached out and switched on the tape recorder.

"Your eyelids have become heavy, Lily. They have closed. You're relaxed. You feel fine. In a moment you'll be asleep, Lily. But you'll hear all I say and be able to speak to me."

He paused, watching her. Her body had slumped gently in the chair, her hands hung limp over the end of the arms, and her head had dropped forward a little. He reached out gently and touched her closed eyelids; there was a slight tremor in them which died away at his touch. As he withdrew his fingers, he said, "Sleep, Lily. Sleep."

She gave a little sigh and her head dropped forward farther, uncomfortably. He reached out, put the palms of his hands on either side of her face and eased her head gently back against the chair cushion. She stayed as he had put her. And then for a moment he was lost. Lily was resting there under his power, ready to listen and speak, subject to him as once she had been subject to Dilling. There was a strong movement of concern in him. There was a power in him which he had never experienced before and, curiously, something of Lily's own dislike of the phenomenon . . . somewhere deep in him, too, was a rejection of this "mucking about with the mind", a sense that he was treading a path never intended. But it was only the briefest of reactions. Locked away in Lily's memory, inaccessible even to her until hypnosis gave her an entry, were things he had to know, but for the moment—confident that if he could induce this state once he could repeat it—he felt the wisdom of not rushing her. The process with him had to become as ordinary as it had been with Dilling before he could begin to reach to the far limits of her interned memory. To rush things might destroy this new relationship. He had to learn to handle his new mastery by degrees.

He said gently, "Can you hear me, Lily?"

In a voice, lower and slower than usual, she answered at once. "Yes, I can hear you."

Remembering from Völgyesi that during hypnosis it was

helpful to keep up a continuous flow of speech and suggestion, that one sentence or question should lead smoothly to another, he began to talk to her as though they were having a normal conversation.

He said, "Who am I, Lily?"

"You're Johnny." There was no inflexion in her voice to suggest that it had been an obvious or unnecessary question.

"And you know I'm not going to do anything to hurt you or frighten you, don't you?"

"Yes, Johnny."

"Or ask you to do or say anything you wouldn't want to do?"

"Yes, Johnny."

"You won't mind if when I tell you to wake up I want you to forget everything we will have talked about?"

"No, Johnny."

He said, "You remember Harry's ring, the one with the enamelled bird design on it, Lily?"

"Yes, Johnny."

"You remember that yesterday, when I pointed out to you that it was a bird design, I said that it was of a firecrest wren?"

"Yes, Johnny."

"You remember for a moment you thought the word 'firecrest' reminded you of something?"

"Yes, I remember."

"Can you tell me now what it was? Perhaps something to do with Harry?"

Immobile, locked in hypnotic sleep, she replied in a matter-of-fact voice, "It was to do with Harry. In the cottage once."

"He mentioned 'firecrest' to you?"

"No. I was coming down the stairs from the bedroom and he was on the telephone. I wasn't paying any attention much but he was saying something about firecrest to someone."

"Why do you remember, Lily?"

"I don't know. Just 'cos it was an unusual word, I suppose."

"Did you ask Harry what it meant?"

"No. He saw me on the stairs and he waved me away. I went up the stairs."

"And you forgot all about it until now?"

"Yes, Johnny."

"But you half remembered it yesterday, didn't you?"

"I suppose I did, Johnny."

Not knowing the limits of his own power or how long she would submit to it in this new state, he was anxious not to put her under any lengthy stress, so he said, "You don't know who he was speaking to?"

"No, I don't."

"All right, Lily. In a moment I'm going to tell you to wake up and you will and you won't remember anything we've talked about. Is that clear, Lily?"

"Yes, Johnny."

"But when you do wake up I want you to do something for me and you'll do it right away, before anything else. You understand?"

"Yes, Johnny."

As she answered he was wondering whether he was right in making this move, but he felt it was important in order to give him some gauge of the direction he could exercise over her while she was in this state. In addition, too, he had to admit, there was a slight movement of pride and mild exhilaration that he had been so successful. He had a quick picture of himself and Harrison, stupid with laughter over the transfixed hens in the farmer's barn and with it a lingering disbelief in the validity of the whole process. . . . An hypnotic state was, in physical and psychic terms, wholly normal for those who had studied and practised it. He had to feel and accept this, too.

He said, "When you wake up, you'll go straight to the window overlooking the walled garden and pull the curtains back. Just that. Do you understand, Lily?"

"Yes, Johnny."

"All right, then." He put out a hand and held the loose

fingers of her right hand, and went on, "Wake up, Lily. You can open your eyes now."

He sat back, breaking his touch on her hand and as he did so her eyes opened and her head came forward slightly. For a moment she blinked her eyes, looking at him, and then without a word she got up and went across to the window and pulled back the curtains. She turned and came back to him and stood a little puzzled in front of him.

He said, "Why did you do that, Lily?"

She frowned, shook her head and then gave a little laugh, "For the life of me I don't know."

"But you want to know, don't you?"

She sat down and then said, suddenly, sharply, "Johnny, what happened?"

He stood up. "What we wanted to happen. No, no—just sit there and listen to something while I get you a drink." He leaned over the small table and ran the tape back, and then he flicked the switch to play the tape. His voice came over, reedier, backed by his faint accent which always surprised him when he heard it reproduced. *Your eyelids have become heavy, Lily. They have closed. You're relaxed. You feel fine. In a moment you'll be asleep, Lily. But you'll hear all I say and . . .*

For a moment she listened, then her eyes widened and she jumped to her feet and ran to him, putting her hands on his arms and against the sound of the tape she cried, "Johnny! Oh, Johnny, you've done it! You've done what Harry did!"

Without thought, he leaned forward and gave her a light kiss on the forehead.

CHAPTER EIGHT

BACK IN HIS own room, alone, Grimster was conscious of an elation which came far less from a professional satisfaction that he now perhaps had the key to what had happened on the missing Friday, than from a purely personal degree of satisfaction in the strange, to him at least, power which he had that night found. He could understand how it would have affected Dilling and realised that with the man's personality there would have been a strong temptation to exhibit the power —as he had done to Billy Who—and perhaps also a sadistic impulse to abuse it. There was no doubt in Grimster's mind that occasionally Dilling would have put on a comic show with Lily, and since with many forms of sadism there was inevitably an underlying sexual content, he was prepared to accept that some of the shows must have been, if only mildly, comically obscene. To have in one's gift a hypnophilic like Lily, already Dilling's puppet, must have led the man to experiment further with her, when she was hypnotised, to command and manipulate her like a true puppet, pulling any string he wished, safe in the knowledge that before he brought her back to normal consciousness he could order her to wipe out all memory of what she had been doing or saying. While it was clearly a power not to be abused there was, for the lay hypnotist anyway, a temptation to abuse it since power created its own demands. One could go too far, one could sometimes find the whole process out of control.

Völgyesi had warned against this. He picked up the man's book, visual memory making the finding of the page he wanted easy, and read, "Over the years I have met cases in my practice (fortunately not many) where lay hypnotists had put people who were extremely hypnophilic into deep hypnosis and for days neither they nor their doctors were able to rouse them. Such a loss of rapport, for instance, was shown where a shop assistant from a provincial town brought me his nephew, slung over his shoulders like a sack of potatoes; he had been in a stuporous sleep for three days. A somewhat younger General in 1926 carried in his girl friend—he had hypnotised her in bed but in the morning could not waken her." Völgyesi, himself, as a young man first experimenting with hypnosis had put a girl into a trance and had been unable to wake her, having to call in the services of a much more experienced practitioner.

A little while ago Lily had been in a state of hypnosis, but how deep it had been he had no way of knowing. That he could have made it deeper than it was he knew would have been possible by suggestion—though just how far he could command Lily's memory recall was unknown to him. In any case what he wanted from her was the memory of the missing Friday, that and that alone. He wasn't a Dilling who was handling her for his own pleasure in the power his command gave him. But as he thought about it and particularly as he recalled Lily's reaction to the discovery that he had done to her what Dilling used to do, remembering her words, "You've done what Harry did", her spontaneous movement to him, holding him, and then the light kiss he had given her, he had a feeling that in those few moments Lily had transferred many of the feelings she had had for Harry to him. He didn't want them, but if they helped him to reveal where Harry had hidden whatever it was that he had hidden, then he was prepared to accept the transfer and make that acceptance seem genuine to Lily. She had what they wanted. It was his job to get it.

The next morning he called Coppelstone on the scrambler telephone but in their conversation he said nothing about the hypnosis.

Coppelstone said, "How's it going, Johnny?"

"Fair. I think I'm beginning to get somewhere. There's been quite an interesting development. It's in my report which you'll get today. How long will it be before I get a word on William Pringle?"

"Tomorrow some time, with luck. We've got a man on it. Since you didn't want a personal approach, though, it might be a bit longer."

"Tell me—in your dealings with Dilling, particularly over the phone, did he have any special way of referring to them? Did you dream up some code name or anything like that?"

"Why?"

"It might help. But if it's not something you want to release to me—O.K."

"I can't think that it would matter if you knew. It was nothing we dreamt up. He did it for reference over the phone. Not that he phoned often. He called it 'Firecrest'."

Grimster smiled to himself. "Do you know why?"

"No." There was a pause at Coppelstone's end of the line, and then the man said, "Something tells me that it hasn't come as a surprise to you."

"No, it hasn't. Lily heard him speaking on the phone once and using the name. He waved her off."

"Does Firecrest mean anything to her?"

"Not a thing. Is Harrison still in Barnstaple?"

"Yes. He probably finds the Devon air suits him—or, more likely, he's found a willing widow. Why does he have this thing for widows?"

"He could be looking for his mother."

* * * *

Grimster went with Lily to her room after lunch. He had explained to her before lunch that he wanted to have another session with her, knowing it was wise to give her some time to think about it so that she could calm any nervousness she might still have. Now, as they sat together in her room, he had expected her perhaps to show some small sign of restlessness or disturbance. After all she knew what he wanted from her and he knew that she wanted to help him. This might have produced a degree of over excitement simply from her willingness. But, as far as he could tell, she was relaxed and easy-going, already accepting that what he had done once he could do again, a matter-of-fact, practical approach.

She said, "What are you going to ask me this time, Johnny? About that Friday?"

He said, "I might, I don't know yet. I think it's important that we get used to—" he paused, because he had been on the point of saying "playing this parlour game" but instinct told him at once that this would not be how she would regard it, so he went on, "—handling this thing between us."

She smiled and nodded, and settled herself back in her chair, pushing her legs out in front of her so that the sun through the window emboldened the nylon curves with long crescents of high lights. Then, when for a moment he neither said nor did anything, her smile broadened and she said, "Why, Johnny, you're nervous, aren't you?" She laughed. "You don't have to be. I'm ready for you. Like you said, complete trust."

"Thank you, Lily."

What she had said was true. He was nervous and he knew that he must not be. He had to have her trust and confidence, but more, he had to have confidence in himself otherwise he could never command her.

"Relax, Johnny. Harry was just the same the second time. He almost couldn't believe it would happen again. But it did. Come on, let's try."

She leaned back more, flexed then relaxed her shoulder muscles, closed her eyes and sighed with the induced comfort of her body and then opened her lids and waited for him. Her confidence overspilled to him and he suddenly felt at his ease. He held up the back of his hand to her so that she could see the ring on his finger. For a moment he saw her attention hold it, then waver, and then slowly become intent on it, the signal stimulus as Völgyesi called it, which was the link between them. Given time he knew that there might not be need even for the stimulus of the ring. He would be able to put her off with a simple command to sleep. Had Dilling he wondered ever reached that stage or attempted it? As the thought went through his mind, without any up or down movement of his hand to force her eyes to follow the ring, he saw the look on Lily's face change, the slow collapse of face muscles and then the gentle turndown of her eyelids as she slid into psychopassivity. Already on this second occasion she was accepting him and had moved willingly into the condition she knew he wanted.

He said, "Lily, you're sleepy, you're going into a deep sleep, but all the time you'll be able to hear me and answer me. You're not afraid of that, are you?"

"No, Johnny, I'm not afraid of that." The words came slowly, unemphasised.

"All right then—let's have a little talk about unimportant things to begin with. Do you remember the first time you ever met Harry?" He wanted to keep everything smooth, not to ask her any disturbing questions until—if he felt the moment was right—he could ask her about the missing Friday. It was better to go slow and gain what he wanted than to rush her in the hope of a quick solution.

Lily said, "Of course I do. When he came into the shop."

"What was he wearing, Lily?"

"Oh, a blue sweater with an open-necked shirt. White it was. Grey slacks and blue and white canvas shoes." She said it without any stir of personal emotion, no hint of amusement at the picture.

"What was your first impression of him?"

"His voice and a wink."

"Would you explain that, Lily."

"He had a nice voice, deepish so it kind of went all the way down through you. And he was cheeky with the wink when I gave him his change. He just held my fingers for the tiniest bit and winked. I had a good giggle about it afterwards with one of the other girls."

"What kind of things would you say you had a good memory for, Lily?"

"Oh, I don't know. People, some of the things they say. And places. Where I've been."

He said, "You mean if you've been somewhere only once you can pretty well remember it?"

"Yes, mostly."

"Would you remember what you were doing on any particular day, if it was an important day, say, like your birthday this year?"

"Yes, I think so."

"Where were you and what did you do on your birthday this year, Lily?"

"I was in Florence, at the Excelsior, and Mrs. Harroway took me to Pisa to see the Leaning Tower. Then we went on to the coast and had dinner at a restaurant looking over the sea and we had scampis done in some wine sauce and then some kind of fish I didn't like much. It was all boney."

"Did Mrs. Harroway give you a present?"

"Yes."

"What?"

"A green silk nightdress with black velvet ribbons threaded through the neck, arms and the skirt hem."

Smoothly, carrying her along, remembering not only Völgyesi's precept that there should be no hesitation in the way one sentence led to another but also to avoid disturbing stimuli, he moved into the area of her memory which was his only concern.

"You remember the day Harry died, don't you, Lily?"

"Yes, Johnny."

"You won't mind if I ask you a few questions of what you were doing in that period of your life?"

"No."

"You were on your way to Italy, weren't you, that day?"

"Yes."

"You had had quite a bit of packing to do for the trip, I imagine. Getting ready and all that."

"A fair bit, yes."

"Did you do it on the day before you were due to travel?"

"Most of it, yes."

"Do you remember at all when you did it? Morning, afternoon or evening?"

Without pause, Lily answered, "Through the day mostly. Some in the morning, some in the evening."

"Why didn't you pack all in one go?"

"Because I had things to do, like ironing and a bit of mending."

Keeping his voice casual, holding down his own excitement, he said, "Do you remember that day fairly well, Lily?"

"Quite well, I think."

"It was a Friday, wasn't it, Lily?"

"Yes, Johnny."

"All right then, see if you can run through the day for me. Not in every detail, of course, but the main things. Try starting from the morning and work through."

"I'll try. Well, first of all, we got up late and had breakfast, and then Harry read the papers while I tidied up around. You know, the bed and doing the breakfast things . . ."

He sat there in the same position almost as when he had first questioned her—in her conscious state—about that day, and she ran through the day in the same terms as before, the lunch and the drink they'd had with it, the love-making afterwards and Harry sleeping a while in the afternoon . . . all the details, tomato soup and fried plaice for dinner, the reading and the watching of television and, while he knew that none of it had ever happened, her voice went on, prompted now and then by him, in a slow, uncanny monotone.

When she paused, he said, "I see. Well, that's enough for the moment about that Friday. Tell me, did Harry often hypnotise you? Did he do it regularly, for instance?"

"No, not regularly. When he first learnt to do it he did it a lot. But later, only now and again."

"Now and again for what purpose? Just to amuse himself?" Something in the word "amuse" moved her, she stirred a little and he saw a fine tremble move across her eyelids.

"Just to keep his hand in, I suppose. Or if he wanted to get me to learn something . . . like poetry. And then, sometimes, if I had a bad pain."

"You mean a headache?"

"Sometimes. If I had one he'd put me off and tell me I'd wake up in five minutes and it would be gone."

"And would it?"

"Oh, yes."

"You must have been glad to have such a handy headache remover."

"Oh, yes. And for my monthly pains, too. I used to get them bad."

"Would you say that if Harry made any suggestion to you which seemed reasonable, it would have worked?"

"I should think so."

"Now listen carefully to this, Lily. That Friday we've been talking about—you know the one I mean?"

"Yes, Johnny."

"Say you and Harry had been doing something quite different from what you've told me, and say he wanted you to forget all about it, forget the day entirely, so that he could put another, one he'd made up, in its place—could he have hypnotised you and told you to wipe out the real day from your mind and only remember the one he made up for you?"

"I suppose he could have done." Her voice was flat, almost uninterested.

"All right, Lily, now I'm going to tell you something. I know that's what Harry did. He wiped out the real day and gave you another in its place. Do you believe me when I tell you that?"

"If you say so, Johnny."

As she replied he could sense no disturbance in her. She just lay against the chair, her body relaxed, the lidded eyes tilted upwards, the smooth, fresh curves of her faintly tanned cheeks touched by the afternoon sunlight. Although there was excitement in him, he kept it down, out of his voice, and moved smoothly into the next stage.

"I do say so, Lily. And now I want you to listen carefully to me. Everything I'm doing now is for your good. I want to help you. Everything I do is ultimately for your benefit. You understand that, Lily?"

"Yes, Johnny."

"Then understand this." He deliberately made his voice stronger, letting command and authority endow it. "Harry's gone, and you've got over his going. You told me so yourself. But I'm here. I've taken Harry's place. Once you were in his care and now you're in mine. You're quite happy about that, aren't you?"

"Yes, Johnny."

"Right. Now I'm going to give you an order—for your own good. The Friday you remember is the wrong one. The one Harry made up for you. Now I want you to think for a few moments. Don't rush anything. I want you to go right back deep into your memory and then, when you're ready, bring out that real Friday for us. The Friday when you went off with Harry somewhere and hid something. Take your time. Just think about it and then tell me."

He sat back a little, watching her. No part of her body moved. She lay there, almost as though she were unbreathing. He raised his left hand so that he could still see her face and also the movement of the second hand on his wrist-watch. The hand crept round a full thirty, then sixty, then ninety seconds, and Lily said nothing. He gave her five minutes, waiting through the silence and immobility which held her. Then he said, "All right, Lily. Now tell me about the *real* Friday. Where did you go and what did you do with Harry?"

Without any hesitation Lily said, "Well, first of all we got up late and had breakfast, and then Harry read the papers while I tidied up around. You know, the bed and doing the breakfast things . . ."

He sat there while she worked through all the details she had given him before, using most of the time identical words and phrases, and he heard her out, waiting and hoping for some variation since he knew that Harry might only have cut a small portion of the real day out of her memory. But his hope was fruitless. She gave him the same false day as before.

When she had finished, he said gently, "Thank you, Lily. Now rest for five minutes and then wake up."

He switched off the tape recorder and got up. He went to the window. On the lawn below Angela Pilch was setting out to take one of Cranston's dogs for a walk. Three or four house martins swooped low over the pool in the walled garden. He turned and looked at Lily, at the reposed, full, womanly figure and he wondered if Harry had ever visualised this situation. Hedged all his bets with Fate. He had that kind of mind, delighting in the labyrinthine, devising safeguards and locks against all designs on his secret, just in case. . . It had to be that way. Either he, Grimster, was not putting Lily into a deep enough sleep to allow a full approach to her mind and memory, or Harry, while he had her under hypnosis, had installed some psychic suggestion or block which he alone could remove. Had he said to her while she was under hypnosis that even if someone else could hypnotise her she would never be able to remember the true details of that Friday? If he had, then the details might be lost for ever, or would rest in her mind until someone came along who could uncover them because he would be someone to whom Lily would give herself with even more abandon and trust than she had accorded to Dilling. How the hell did he get round that one?

He moved back to the sleeping Lily and, as he did so, she stirred, her eyelids flickered for a moment and then she opened her eyes. Grimster picked up her cigarettes, handed her one and held the lighter for her. She drew the smoke, hungrily for a second, and then raised her eyes to him and said, "Well, Johnny?"

He said, "You don't remember what we've been talking about?"

"No."

"Then listen."

He went to the recorder and set the tape to play back for her. Smoking, watching the revolving cassettes, she listened without comment to the end.

At the end, he switched off the tape, and said, "Well, what do you make of that, Lily?"

She was silent for a moment and then she said, "You're sure in your mind, Johnny, that something else happened on that Friday?"

"Absolutely. You were out of the house with him for over twelve hours. When you got back he must have hypnotised you and brain-washed you. Don't get me wrong. At the time he was doing it for his and your protection. But circumstances have changed now. Harry's gone—and he's left everything that he wanted you to have hidden away and the clues to the hiding place locked up in your memory. Deep down in it somewhere. I can put you under and you give me truthful answers to all questions, except about that Friday."

She gave a little shudder of her shoulders.

"It's all a bit too spooky."

"No, it's all natural and understandable. Anyone who can sleep can be hypnotised. And most people who take the trouble can learn to hypnotise people. I was lucky with you—so was Harry—because you're an easy subject, particularly when you trust someone. But at the moment we're up against a brick wall —unless, when I put you under, I can find some way of making you disobey whatever order Harry gave you about remembering that Friday. In other words, you've got to reject Harry and accept me as the one who's really in command of you."

For a moment she smiled and said, "But I don't mind that. Harry would want it, too. He'd want me to tell you where this whatever it is is hidden so that I could have a lot of money. That's what he always was promising me."

"Nevertheless he's turned a key in a lock and thrown the key away."

Shrewdly, surprising him, she said, "You don't have to have a key to break a lock. If all I can remember now is a made-up Friday, the real one must be in my memory somewhere. Really deep down where you haven't been able to reach it yet because—"

She broke off and leaned over to knock ash from her cigarette into the tray.

"Because what?" he asked.

"I don't know." For a moment her face came up to him and he saw the shadow of some emotion quiver about her lips. "Except perhaps you don't send me off deep enough. Harry would do that sometimes. Like with my pains. He could make me sleep for twelve hours, dead out. Deep, deep, deep sleep. I remember once he made me like that and then got me to tell him things about when I was really a little girl. Things that I'd forgotten. Some things that I didn't even remember when he told me about them." She went on to tell him one or two of those remote distant childhood memories.

As she spoke he was wondering if maybe she had opened a new truth to him. There were, he knew, degrees of hypnotic sleep. So far he had only put her to sleep, suggesting no more than a normal level of sleep. Maybe he wasn't sending her deep enough to undermine whatever block Harry had set up.

He broke in on her and explained this and asked her if she felt like trying another session after dinner, when he would put her into a very deep sleep. Lily was more than willing.

But when they tried it after dinner he got the same result. Whenever he approached the question of what had happened that Friday she came out, now with almost parrot-like repetition, with the same description of the events of the day. *Well, first of all we got up late and had breakfast, and then Harry read the papers while I tidied up around.* He knew that Harry must have gone through that false day with her, that she was parroting his words and phrases and Harry had been clever enough to colour them with her style of speech. Harry had put himself in her place, speaking as she would have to speak whenever she was questioned. Annoyed by this, he realised, too, that whatever block Harry had set up, whatever lock and key guarded the truth, the device or devices would not be ordinary ones. Not with Harry. There would be nothing conventional about them.

When he brought Lily back after this session it was clear at once that she was tired, that somehow even in her deep hypnotic sleep she had been wanting to help him, working to help him but without success. She looked tired and he felt the strain in her. He fixed her a drink for a nightcap, then moved without thinking and kissed her on the side of her cheek as he said goodnight and left her.

He went back to his suite for a brandy and a cigar before bed, and found a message from Cranston saying that Sir John and Coppelstone were arriving for lunch the next day.

*   *   *   *

Lily lay in bed, tired, not far from sleep. Her fatigue at times blurred her thinking. She was thinking of Johnny and Harry but although they were two very different people in many ways they had a tendency to merge into one figure for her. Now and again she was clearly aware of this and deliberately separated them. Johnny was nice and Harry was nice, but their nicenesses were different. With Harry, she told herself, for all that he had looked after her and loved her, you could never get any idea of what went on behind him. In his head and heart. He didn't want you there. Johnny was a bit like that, but there were times when he couldn't help letting you in. Like when he lost his hardness and all that professional manner and his hand came out and touched her, or he leaned forward and kissed her goodnight. Behind the hardness there was a lot of kindness waiting. Maybe even love, but she knew that he wasn't likely to let himself go in that direction easily because Angela Pilch had now told her something of his history. Engaged to be married and then the girl, some Swede apparently, getting killed in a car accident. After that he didn't want to know about women or love. Love, maybe; but there was always the other thing . . . the thing that often came up in her like an ache, so strong sometimes that it was a physical knotting of her stomach muscles . . . the thought of it now bringing it on and making her spread and flex her legs under the covers. Wonder how he would be if she ever asked him right out about the dead girl? Change the subject, maybe. Or just give her a look and shut her up. Maybe not, maybe he was waiting for someone to come along so he could talk about it. She'd like it if it could be her. The face of Harry drifted across the image of Johnny in her mind. Harry ought to be here now. He was what she needed. Someone she could give herself to because they needed her. Not that Johnny didn't need her. He did. But in a different way. All this real or phoney Friday stuff. He had to find out about that—never mind what money might be in it for her—because it was his job. She wanted to help him and, momentarily, she was angry with Harry that he should have locked it up in her so that even she couldn't bring it out and give it to Johnny. Let's face it—there was more than a bit of nastiness in Harry at times. Like when he put her off in front of Billy Who until she put a stop to that, even though she guessed it didn't amount to much. But that wasn't the point. She just hadn't liked the idea of it, and her not knowing anything . . . just coming to and seeing them smiling. Harry didn't care what he did or said when they were together making love. He'd shocked her a lot to begin with. Not with the thing itself but with the talking about it. After all it was a private thing between two people and they didn't have to talk about it in front of other people which was what she guessed happened sometimes when Billy Who was there and Harry put her under. Though she had no proof, she was sure he did it. She only had to look at them afterwards. It wasn't proper and when you had a man and were in love there were things you couldn't even

118

tell your best friend. There were some things you just couldn't bring yourself to say. Well, not unless you really had to, like with a doctor or a parson or someone. Harry's face faded and Johnny's took its place. Poor Johnny. He wanted to know about that Friday so much, but she couldn't help him. She just couldn't. Though there was the money, of course; the money that would come to her if Johnny got what he wanted. But that only made it more difficult, really impossible. . . . Half asleep now, she felt a sudden quick turn of anger inside her against Harry. He'd love all this. He just liked complicating things. He could have done it over this business too, she guessed. She turned on her side. Drawing her knees up and holding them with her clasped hands, she slowly forced the image of Harry from her, tried to make her mind a blank and forget the long held need in her, but the blankness avoided her. Johnny's face came sliding into it. She would have to find a way, she knew. Just in case. Would have to. But how could she do it without spoiling the whole thing? That would be awful. But if Johnny wanted to know about that Friday she was almost certain that it would be the only way because that was what Harry would have done . . . what Harry would have left her with. She was pretty sure of that, knowing him. It would have been his idea of a joke against the world. Harry and Johnny. . . . Wonder what he was doing now? Sitting there with a cigar and a glass of brandy and thinking about her, Lily? More likely about his dead fiancée. Sure to be. . . . Sure to be. . . .

CHAPTER NINE

SIR JOHN AND COPPELSTONE arrived late for lunch which
was taken in the private dining-room reserved for special guests.
Only the three of them were present. Sir John—who was on
his way to a Ministry of Defence establishment farther westwards—had no desire to meet Lily. This did not surprise
Grimster. Sir John restricted to the minimum his official contacts. Lily was no more to him than a name in a file with an
attendant problem. Direct dealings with her were of no interest
to him.

After lunch, without moving from the room, Grimster played
the tapes of his various interviews with Lily and made his report
on her. Sir John heard him and the tapes through without
interruption. He sat, nursing a glass of port, a compact, self-
contained figure, neat in a ruddy brown suit of plus-fours, green
tabs to his stockings, a faint, heathery smell seeping from his
tweeds, his eyes slightly hooded against the strong sunlight that
bathed the room so that at times he seemed asleep.

When the tapes were finished and Grimster had given his
report, sticking to facts, avoiding any conjectures at this stage,
Sir John said, "There's no doubt in your mind that Dilling
hypnotised her?"

"None."

"It seems a very devious precaution for him to have taken."

"That's the kind of man he was. Anyway, I'm inclined to
think it was less a precaution than a complication that pleased
his particular sense of humour. That he had the power to wipe

120

out a real day from Miss Stevens' mind and substitute a false one was irresistible to his ego."

Sir John, his port finished, began his slow, careful process of lighting a cigarette. He said, "You had no difficulty hypnotising her. Clearly she's a suggestible type. Why is there a block the moment you approach the question of this day, the real day, do you think?"

"I think Dilling, while she was in the hypnotic state, built in some instruction to her."

"Such as?"

"He could have said that even if someone else hypnotised her she still wouldn't be able to recall the real day. Or he could have said that she would never be able to remember the real day. That it was gone for ever."

"Is that possible?"

"I don't know. I'm not authority enough on the subject. It's not suggested anywhere in Völgyesi's book. He does say that in hypno-therapy, in the case of extreme psycho-passives —which Miss Stevens is—it's advisable to give a suggestion that only a doctor can hypnotise them. This would be a safe-guard, in the patient's interests, and therefore acceptable."

"But Dilling clearly didn't say that only he could hypnotise her, because you've done it."

"But he might have said that even if someone else hypnotised her, she could only tell the truth about that day to *him*. Perhaps something like that. Or perhaps he put her to such a deep level of hypnosis that the real truth can't be got at unless she is put into the same deep state again."

"Which you've tried?"

"Yes. But I've no way of knowing how deep it was. At a guess I'd say that it wasn't as deep as Dilling could have induced."

"Why not?"

"Because there was a close emotional and physical relation-ship between them which allowed her to be easily controlled by him."

"You think that the real facts of that day are locked away for ever in her mind? That nobody can get at them?"

"No, I don't, Sir John. Even if Dilling could have produced or induced a form of amnesia about the real day, the fact remains that its details are in her mind somewhere and somebody could get at them."

"But not you?"

"It looks not. After all I'm only an amateur. Not really even that."

Sir John rested his cigarette precisely on the edge of the ashtray. "So it seems. In fact, I have a feeling that it would have been better if you had never experimented at all. You may have muddied the waters, as it were, for any expert."

It was a clear reprimand. Grimster accepted it without comment. Sir John let the stricture sink quietly and then went on, "There could be a substitute for a deep emotional and physical relationship, I suppose. A qualified practitioner—if ordinary methods failed—could I imagine use narcotics. A drugged or drunken state is, I presume, a form of hypnosis?"

"Presumably. Though I should have thought that drunkenness was a loss of control on the individual's part, not a willing handing over of control to another."

Sir John slowly raised an eyebrow, not at him or Coppelstone, but to the world at large to indicate that the qualification had little relevance. He said to Coppelstone, "Who is there that could handle it?"

Coppelstone shifted his big bulk in his chair, regretted that the port decanter was out of his reach, and said, "No one who is cleared. Once you lowered the flood gates Miss Stevens might come out with a load of information we wouldn't want floating around."

"Graphically put. And it also reveals a gap in the Department's efficiency. Why do we have to wait until a case comes up to find an expert and then have to go into all the business of vetting and clearing him? We've had this before in other spheres. We should have had on our list a consultant psychiatrist, someone who understands clinical hypnotism." He picked up his cigarette, drew on it with a birdlike, sipping motion of the mouth and then directed Coppelstone, "When you get back to London tomorrow, start looking for someone. There could be someone on the books of another branch—which would save us the vetting business—but I'd prefer it if we had our own man. And find someone without European connections. We don't want to have to clear some Pole or Hungarian. That would take for ever. I want this case resolved one way or another quickly."

At his most humble, in voice, though not in feeling, Coppelstone said, "Yes, Sir John."

Grimster said, "This could mean keeping Miss Stevens around for some time. She's not going to be content to sit around here for weeks."

Sir John said tersely, "Amuse her. She's your problem. But I want it clearly understood that you're to try no more of this hypnotism on her. We'll get an expert for that, though no doubt the whole thing will turn out to be a waste of time." He looked across at Coppelstone. "Get hold of Cranston and tell him I want my car."

Left alone with the man, Grimster waited for his own dismissal. Sir John put out a hand and gently touched one of the sharp-cut flutings on the crystal neck of the port decanter. He held the contact for a moment or two as though it were of some vital importance to him. Grimster knew at once that he was not being dismissed yet. Although their contacts had been few in all the years he had worked for him, he knew him instinctively and intuitively. He knew the ambition still in him, the self-importance that he wore coldly like a stiff, unbroken formal suit, and he knew the quiet sadism with which he pointed the workings of a devious and incredibly complex mind. Few of Sir John's thoughts were simple or frank or generous or charitable. Had they been he would have died or disappeared or have been superannuated before he ever reached his present position because the special world in which he lived would have rejected him, like the body a foreign property. His own reprimand, the order not to work on Lily any longer (which might as easily have been a commendation and a fiat to continue), scarcely touched him. With Coppelstone's going, he sensed, Sir John had devised the freedom he wanted to broach his true business.

The man's hand came away from the decanter, and he said, as though there had been no break in their conversation, "Harrison is still at Barnstaple, I understand?"

"So I'm told."

Sir John looked at him in silence for a moment, stirred a little stiffly in his chair and then said, "I've often debated with myself whether I should approach you directly about this. Even now I'm not sure that it is the right thing to do. In fact I wouldn't do it unless I had an extremely high regard and concern for you, Grimster. You know that there is no possible room for ambivalent attitudes in this Department, naturally?"

"Of course, Sir John."

"I want to talk about Miss Trinberg."

"Yes, Sir John." He was only mildly surprised that he hadn't before, but then it took Sir John a long time to come to the point of committal.

"We can be entirely frank about it. My understanding of you is that you think that for policy reasons the Department . . . well, arranged something."

"It's a possibility I considered, yes. Anyone in my position would have done."

"Quite so. And Harrison has worked on that, of course. Why should he not? If he could corrupt you it would be a feather in his cap. And if you were going to be corrupted, turn against us—it was naturally something we had to consider, and have considered. That can be no surprise to you."

"None at all, Sir John."

"Very well. Now I am going to say something to you which comes from my very high regard for you, for your capabilities and your potential. I've never mentioned it openly, but I imagine you have some idea that I should recommend you as head of the Department when I retire in a few years?"

"It's good of you to say so, Sir John."

"But that is an impossibility in the present circumstances. So long as you have the slightest conception that Miss Trinberg's death was not by accident you must appreciate the risk you have become to us—a risk, I speak frankly, which I have considered eliminating drastically. That doesn't surprise you, of course."

"No, Sir John." He smiled. "In fact I had told myself that you probably had already decided to do just that. Say, at the end of this assignment."

Sir John tapped the neck of the port decanter. "Grimster— you are too good a man to lose on the turn of a conjecture. But what am I to do? No situation remains static and the way this one is growing is dangerous so I wish it to be cleared once and for all. Miss Trinberg's death was an accident. The Department had no hand in it. This I swear to you. I know no other way of convincing you than by my word. I want you to believe me, not only because it is the truth, but because of my personal and professional feelings for you. I do not want this situation between you and the Department to develop any further. I want it wiped out. Miss Trinberg's death was nothing to do with the Department. I am not asking you to say whether you believe me or not. I've given you the truth—to protect you. If you believe it, it will become obvious to me. If you don't . . . well, Johnny, it will be stupidly tragic." The man stood up. Through the window came the sound of his car drawing up at the entrance.

Grimster said, "Thank you for all you've said, Sir John. May I say that I have always believed that Valda died accidentally—though naturally I have had my conjectures. But now I am in no doubt at all. Your word is more than enough for me."

"Then that's splendid, Johnny. Also, strictly between ourselves, I am withdrawing my order to you about Miss Stevens.

You will go on working on her as you see fit until other arrangements are made. As soon as they are we'll find you something more interesting to do."

Alone in his room after Sir John had gone, Grimster wondered why the man had come out into the open, made an appeal, sworn his word which might or might not be true? Of course he had known the Department had marked him. There seemed no motive, no point, in Sir John stating it openly . . . unless . . . unless it really *was* true, that Valda *had* died by accident. Perhaps that was an overlooked hazard in his way of life . . . nothing drastic was seen as an accident. Accidents didn't happen. Everything came from design. But accidents did happen and when they did it was hard to accept their truth. . . . He sat for a long time thinking about Valda and Sir John.

*   *   *   *

Coppelstone had brought down with him the report on Billy Who. Grimster read it in his own sitting-room after dinner. William Pringle at the moment ran a small pet shop in High Wycombe. His chief lines were cage birds and tropical fish. He was thirty-three. His mother was dead. His father was a retired clergyman living in Lincolnshire. Pringle had been educated at Oundle and then at Clare College, Cambridge. He had no private means and no fixed profession. He had been in the pet shop business for less than six months. Before that he had had a variety of jobs, some as an ordinary labourer with building and motorway contractors, and there had been a short spell as a junior master at an Essex preparatory school. He was unmarried and had no criminal record. The pet shop business was little more than solvent. Grimster could read him easily. His father had probably denied himself in order to give him his education and Pringle had come down from Cambridge without any desire to do any of the things which his father would have wished. He had moved from one job to another. There were hundreds like him, markers of the drift from families of good position and professional respectability back to the common matrix. There was only one point of interest in his brief biography. When his mother had died—five years previously—he had inherited a trust fund from which she had had the sole use of the income during her lifetime. The amount of the fund had been seven thousand pounds. Most of this sum he had invested in Dilling's electronic components company and when the company had gone bankrupt Pringle had been the chief creditor. There was no indication of how he had met Dilling or when. It was curious, Grimster thought, that—except for his monthly payment to Pringle—the debt seemed not to have worried Dilling. He had died leaving around five thousand pounds in cash, and all of it had gone to Lily. It would have been natural if Dilling had left some of it at least to Pringle. Though, of course, Pringle might have been under some obligation to Dilling before he had inherited and they could both have considered that the loss of his investment evened whatever score there had been between them. It had the ring of an odd friendship. The report had been prepared without a personal interview with Pringle. Much more would have come out if he had been questioned. Grimster doubted though whether it would have been of much help. Pringle was a fringe friend of Dilling clearly. Any firm obligations between them had either been cancelled or had never existed.

Although it was late he took the report along to Coppelstone's room to talk it over with him. Sir John had gone on to his further appointment alone. Coppelstone was returning to London in the morning. But Coppelstone was drunk and had no desire to talk about Pringle.

There were two whisky bottles, one full, the other almost empty, on the table at his elbow. He was slumped back in his armchair, his feet up on a stool. He had been drinking before and through dinner, and since dinner up here in his room. The drink had blotched his face, overheated it, but his speech, though slow, was clear enough. He welcomed Grimster, and waved his hand at the bottle in invitation for him to take a drink. Grimster refused but sat down opposite him and began to light a cigar.

"The little Napoleon," said Coppelstone, "has gone farther westwards to dispose and deploy his other minions. How did he ever work up enough common humanity to go through the mating act with his wife? It is said—mind you, only said— that he dotes on her and his two sons. The day I see him dote I'll be content to die." He reached for his glass and drank neat whisky, rolling the liquid around his mouth and wincing before he swallowed it.

"Painkiller?"

Coppelstone looked from under thick eyebrows at Grimster, and then smiled.

"We all have our pains. Even granite Grimster." In drunken mimicry of Sir John he went on, "Get my car, Coppelstone. With Miss Stevens, Grimster, you would seem to have muddied the waters for an expert. Lay off her. And no expert of mixed European descent. Too much trouble. Always unreliable, any- way. God creates and Sir John disposes. You should know what I know and have seen what I have seen." He grinned suddenly and said, "You really did it, eh?"

Grimster said, "You're bad tonight, Coppy. Why?"

"Always the little investigator, eh? It's not bad tonight. It's worse tonight and has been for a lot of nights. But my nights—owing to a sensible apportionment of departmental duties—thank God, are my own. Tell me about it—this Svengali trick. Sexual domination, the overriding commanding personality . . . you fix the eye of a fascinator on the victim and there is no refusing you—except for that stupid little Friday. And now you can't operate again. Master has said no more muddying the waters."

"Coppy, why don't you knock it off? Get to bed."

"And what will bed give me but dreams I don't want? There is no inhibiting certain areas of my cortex or is it cervix?"

"You've been doing some homework."

Coppelstone nodded. "When your reports began to come in.

Is that the ring?" He nodded to the ring on Grimster's hand.

"Yes."

"Let's see."

Grimster held up the ring, the back of his hand on the man's eye level. The movement of his hand, the momentary flash of the ring and the sight of Coppelstone's drunk-slack face triggered a sudden, fantastic hope in him. But immediately, he was thinking that it wouldn't work, couldn't work ever with this man, though since he had found his power over Lily with it he had played sometimes with the idea because whatever he did and said and thought in the waking hours was always tinged with his one desire, the need for definite knowledge to sluice through his parched, arid suspicions. Now, without any planning on his part, Coppelstone was putting himself at least in a preliminary situation for deliberate design to attempt some hold.

Grimster said casually, "She just watches it and I raise it above her eyes, telling her to follow it but not move her head and then I bring it down again quite slowly." As he spoke he brought the ring down smoothly a few inches below the level of Coppelstone's eyes which followed it, showing the familiar downturning exposure of the whites.

"Just like that?" Coppelstone reached out with one hand for his whisky glass, the rest of his body unstirring.

"That's it. Just like this. Of course, the whole point is that basically—even if an initial show of opposition is put up, perhaps for form's or pride's sake—the person really wants to go off. Wants to be entranced, wants relief. . . ." There was no excitement in him. Just the faintest hope that Coppelstone, drunk, might be responsive, that, coming here to discuss Pringle, he had been given by a twist of chance an opening that no amount of guile could have prepared. His words rode on over his thoughts. "You watch the ring. Only with the eyes. Up and then slowly down and you feel your lids getting heavier and heavier and there's a deep longing in you for sleep . . . for rest . . . for oblivion and for peace. Deep, deep sleep, such as you've never had before. . . ."

129

Coppelstone's body stirred suddenly and he said, "Absolute cock . . . absolute. . . ." But his speech died as the ring, holding his eyes, came down again and this time the lids fell with it and his head slowly tipped forward a little. His voice friendly, unaccented, Grimster went on, "Everyone wants to escape for a while through drink, through sleep, through confession. . . . You and I can understand that. We've a load of stuff we want to ease from our spirits for a while. . . ." As he spoke he saw that Coppelstone had moved into an hypnotic state . . . drifted away just as Lily had.

Without any exhilaration, no disturbance now at standing on the verge of truth, only an iron cold precision of thought sustaining him in a meticulous balance of swiftly formed design and intent, Grimster let his words come easily and monotonously. "You're asleep. You wanted to be asleep. You wanted to escape and you have escaped, and nothing can touch you now. You can hear me, can't you, Coppelstone? Even though you're sleeping, you can hear me, can't you?"

Coppelstone gave a little sigh and then said, "Yes, I can hear you."

"That's good. Very good. Because there are lots of things you want to tell me. Lots of things you've got bottled up inside you that you want to get rid of. Isn't that so?" He reached out as he spoke and took the whisky glass gently from Coppelstone's hand and put it on the tray. Then he put the palm of his right hand against Coppelstone's forward tilted head and eased it gently against the back of the chair. "That's better, isn't it? Much better?"

"Yes, that's better."

"Then just relax and be comfortable. This is the best sleep of your life and when you wake up you're going to forget that it had anything to do with me or the ring. You're not going to remember anything except that I came in to talk to you and have a drink and that you dropped off to sleep in your chair and when you woke I was gone. Is that clear, Coppy?"

Without hesitation the man said in the unaccented manner

which he was now used to hearing from Lily, the voice flat, automatic, divorced from emotion, "Yes, that's clear."

"Good. So don't let's rush things. Let's first make sure that you really are ready to co-operate with me. Put your right arm and hand straight out in front of you." He was too hard bitten in this service not to have at once known that maybe what had seemed like a fluke of chance to him had also been a designed opening that Coppelstone for some reason of his own, or from some departmental instruction, had been ordered to seek, and was now acting with easy deceit. Although he had never made the test before the details of Völgyesi's book were there in his mind to be drawn on. "Turn the palm of your hand upwards, Coppy." The man turned his palm upwards. Coppelstone he knew could simulate drunkenness if the need called for it, could even operate in a drunken state if that had been his design, but not even Coppelstone, he knew, could feign hypnotic-catalepsy. "Now, when I tell you, I want you to try to let your arm drop down, but you'll find you won't be able to do so. Your arm will be stiff. You won't be able to move it. Do you understand that?"

"Yes."

"All right. Drop your arm."

Coppelstone's arm remained rigid. For a moment there was a faint muscular quiver through his whole body. Then he said, almost plaintively, "I can't."

Soothingly, Grimster said, "It's nothing to worry about. Only a simple demonstration." As he spoke Grimster reached out to the table and took from it the round tray which held the glass jug of water, the two whisky bottles and the glasses. "Hold this tray on your palm. You can do it easily. You won't drop it. You can balance it without trouble." He placed the tray on Coppelstone's hand, balancing it so that it rested firmly, and said, "There. Now you're holding it easily. It's heavy but you can support it, can't you?"

"Yes, I can."

"Your arm is stiff, absolutely rigid, isn't it?"

131

"Yes."

"You can't move it, can you?"

"No."

"And you won't be able to until I tell you you can. You understand that, don't you?"

"Yes."

"All right. Now try to drop it."

He watched Coppelstone closely. There was no movement in his arm, not even a quiver of muscles now, but for a few seconds the left side of his face showed the flicker of deep muscle effort.

"I can't," said Coppelstone.

"All right. Don't try any more. Just hold it like that." Even at this stage Coppelstone might be fooling him. He was strong enough to support the tray easily, but after a few minutes even he would find the strain too much. Grimster meant to make that test . . . God knew he had seen plenty of demonstrations by the Department in giving deceit all the appearance of truth. From his reading of Coppelstone he was no easy psycho-passive like Lily. He was intelligent, naturally cynical, wary, the last person to succumb easily to hypnosis. He was the type who would almost have to want to be hypnotised before he could abdicate control over himself. He watched the level surface of the water in the jug. It showed only the faintest movement. He said, "You're doing very well. You're doing it because you've got confidence in me, because you want to help me. That's true, isn't it?"

"Yes, it's true."

"You want to help me."

"Yes, I want to help you."

"Who am I?"

"You're Grimster."

"That's right. I'm Grimster. And you're Coppelstone, my friend. And now I'm going to ask you some questions and I want you to answer them. You don't mind doing that, do you?"

"No."

132

"Good. And understand you won't be able to remember any of this when you wake up. Tell me, have you a line to Harrison?"

Without hesitation Coppelstone said, "Yes."

"A departmental line, or your own line?"

"My own."

"How long have you had it?"

"About a month."

"Do you think that Sir John knows?"

"No."

"Why did you do it?"

"It's not easy to say. I think . . . I think because it seemed a way out."

"A way out from what?"

"From things."

"Have you passed Harrison stuff about Miss Stevens?"

"Yes."

"Since when?"

"In the last two weeks."

"Who is Harrison working for?"

"I don't know."

"At a guess who would you think?"

"The Americans. Or the Russians. Possibly, too, a private consortium who would sell to the highest bidder."

"What was it that Dilling was offering for sale?"

"It's very technical in detail."

"Give me a general idea. He must have got that far to have had the Department interested, mustn't he?"

"Yes. It was some new development of the laser beam principle which could be applied to military work. Particularly for the infantry."

"He died before he disclosed the full technical details?"

"Yes."

Grimster reached out and lifted the heavy tray from Coppelstone's palm and put it on the table. There was no doubt in his mind now that Coppelstone was genuinely hypnotised. He said, "All right, you can lower your arm now."

Coppelstone's arm dropped to his side. The man was his now absolutely, but although there was only one thing he vitally wanted from him he knew that for his own protection and for the satisfaction of his instincts as a professional there were also peripheral areas of information which it would be to his advantage to explore. Just as he had not rushed Lily for details of the lost Friday, he now held back from asking immediately about Valda, about the truth of Sir John's statement. Coppelstone was lying back in the chair, a huge, fleshy repository of information, open to pillage.

He said, "The stuff that Dilling hid—would it have been his research papers? The technical details of this discovery of his?"

"So he said."

"Why did he hide them—because he didn't trust you and Sir John?"

"That's right."

"If you could have arranged for their theft you would?"

"Naturally. Arrangements were being made. It would have saved us money. That's what the Department is for. Blackmail, robbery and murder—"

"All right, Coppy. Take it slowly. What kind of deal is Miss Stevens going to get if the papers are recovered? They are her property, aren't they?"

"Yes, they're her property."

"How is Sir John going to deal with that?"

"The moment we get them she'll go."

"Conveniently, accidentally?" There was no surprise in him as he spoke. The thought had been a phantom, suppressed at the back of his mind right from the beginning of this case because he knew Sir John and his insistence on economy, knew his credo that you only paid when you were forced to pay.

"Yes."

"Well, we know that kind of thing is easily arranged, don't we?"

"Yes."

134

"You and Sir John and I have arranged the same thing before many times, haven't we?"

"Yes."

"All right. Now don't be upset by the next question. We're friends, we've known each other a long time. All I'm interested in is the truth. I'm not going to be upset and there's no need for you to be when you answer. Did Sir John arrange a convenient accident for Valda Trinberg?"

"Yes, he did."

"The car accident was rigged?"

"Yes."

"How?"

"She was forced off the road, over the drop by one of our men."

It was no surprise to Grimster that only a few hours earlier Sir John had lied to him about Valda's death. Sir John would use any stratagem which served him to resolve a situation his way. Sir John had had Valda killed. . . . He could see her driving, winding her way down the steep hillside to the loch far below and the other car coming down fast behind her—a car that had never been traced—and swerving to bump her, to send the car slowly cartwheeling over a three-hundred-foot fall. Without emotion, even as he went on talking, he knew that if he could find the man's name he would kill him and if the name were withheld he would kill Sir John. Sir John, name or no name, he would kill.

He said, "Who was the man?"

Coppelstone, voice flat, the man no more than an answering service, said, "I don't know. Someone Sir John briefed from the European division. I think he's dead now."

Or never to be traced, Grimster knew. But it was unimportant. Sir John would go.

"Sir John thought if we married there'd always be a security risk? That I wouldn't be able to keep the truth from her?"

"Yes."

"Others married. Why was he so much against my doing so?"

135

"Because you were special."

"In what way?"

"He had you lined up to take his place, I think. He didn't want you cluttered up, sharing your life with someone else instead of the Department wholly."

"Has he ever considered that he made a mistake?"

"Yes. He admits it now."

"Just admits? No regrets?"

"Regret, too—that he turned you into a bad risk."

The next question flowed from him automatically, born of his knowledge of Sir John. He knew the Department and its ways and was only giving life again to one of the many phantoms that glided through the mists of his mind amongst a crowd of familiars.

"What does he intend to do about that?"

"Arrange another convenient accident when your job is done."

Coppelstone stirred a little, his body perhaps moving to some inner distress of the spirit.

Grimster said, "All right. That's enough talk. You're tired, very tired and you're sleeping deeply. Just go on sleeping. It's what you want, isn't it, a long, deep sleep?"

"Yes."

"Good. Sleep for half an hour. Then still in your sleep you'll get up, go into the bedroom and undress and get into bed, and you'll go on sleeping until the morning. You understand?"

"Yes."

"And when you wake up, you'll remember nothing of what's happened or of what you have said to me. Nothing. Is that clear?"

"Yes."

"In the morning you'll remember only that you got very drunk, that I was here for a while, and when I left you went off drunk to bed. Now sleep, sleep deep, and when the time comes go off to bed."

Coppelstone's head rolled a little to one side and his breath, thick in his throat, made a soft slurring sound. Grimster reached for the whisky bottle and a glass and poured himself a drink. He sat opposite the man nursing his glass. No matter what the weight of his other thoughts and deliberately controlled emotions, an habitual safety factor still presided over his mind. Coppelstone was no fool. When he woke in the morning, although he would remember nothing, his mind would be active, even suspicious. Given the smallest lead he might be led to suspect what could have happened. That was why it was important that there should be two used whisky glasses on the tray and at least a couple of cigar butts stubbed out in the ashtray. They had sat and drunk and Coppelstone had slumped off into slumber and he, Grimster, had left him.

He looked at his watch. It was just past midnight. He sat, his eyes on the sleeping Coppelstone, his brain frozen from any thought pursuit. What he had known all along might be true, was true. Body and mind were almost rigid with anti-climax. There were things to be thought, and things to be done, but for this still, midnight period there was a cold comfort in physical and mental isolation. He sat, drank and smoked, and after half an hour Coppelstone stirred in the chair opposite him and then, his eyes closed, lifted himself slowly from it and moved, swaying a little, across to his bedroom door. He went in, leaving the door half open. There were the sounds of a light switch and Coppelstone's body noises as he undressed, shoes clattering to the floor and, a little later, the thump of his dropping on to the bed.

Grimster walked to the bedroom door. The main ceiling light was on. Coppelstone lay on the bed, arms and torso naked, a cover drawn partly over him. He began to snore gently.

Grimster went out, leaving the door half open and the light on. He paused by the table to stub out his cigar in the ashtray.

He went back to his own suite. It was nearly one o'clock. He passed through into his bedroom and began to undress, moving between bathroom and bedroom, and as he did so the traces of scent in the air came slowly through to him and without any high interest or surprise he recognised the scent and knew that not so long ago Lily had been in the room. But the momentary thought of her was nothing but the flick of a leaf's movement in the wind across a Highland road as he saw the car smash through crude wooden safety barriers and turn nose down and begin the long slow cartwheeling to the heather and granite slopes below.

CHAPTER TEN

HE DIDN'T SLEEP. He lay on his bed with the window
curtains pulled back and watched the slow wheel of the stars
and heard the call now and then of the small brown owls that
hunted the hedgerows and the dark line of clipped yews around
the tennis court. There was no real thought in him, only a
frozen state of mind and body which he was content to accept.
At the moment there was no need for action or thought. That
would come in the not far future. He knew now what he had
always suspected. There was no surprise, no anger, no grief.

He lay and watched the night sky pale and swell with limpid,
nacreous light and then he got up and pulled on a sweater and
old trousers and went down through the house. The attendant
on the door desk looked up with sleep-smudged eyes and
nodded.

He went out to his car and he knew that, when he came back,
he would really be coming back, to himself and all that he had
to do. He knew it would be like that and there was no hurry
in him.

He drove down the road and past the farm and on to the
gateway that gave entry to the dark wood above the Cliff
Pool. With the growing light small parties of rooks were flying
low and purposefully from their night roosts towards the high
fields and their foraging. A woodpigeon sailed loftily up from
a pine, clapped its wings and dropped fast and curving on the
rising morning breeze as it saw him.

Mechanically he opened the back of the car and pulled on
his waders and began to set up his rod. The rod was an old

139

Hardy's "Pope". Beautiful, cherished. Handled right it would hold and kill a twenty-pound salmon in fast water. He walked down through the trees, dead leaves, pine needles and moss slippery under his feet, and he knew exactly how he would find the river, dropping fast at the end of the spate, clearing to that pale amber colour that demanded a fly to swim, subtle, delicately working across and down the current. Where the path came out at the tail of the pool, he stepped into the river and waded across, the water almost lipping the tops of his waders, and then made his way upstream, swathing through the dew-heavy grass five yards back from the pool. A kingfisher went downstream, cooling its fiery breast in the spray low above the rocky runout of the pool. Across the fields to his right the railway embankment was hidden by mist. As he passed at the back of the fishing hut he saw the mist-spangled spiders' webs under the eaves glitter as the light strengthened. He was aware of himself and the growing day around him, but the awareness held no pain, no pleasure, no purpose. He was just using time and action until the true moment came for direction and intent.

As he came back to the river a heron that had been fishing the head of the pool rose and slid with slow wing beats away across the water and into the meadow mist, greyness closing on greyness. He went down into the water where the heron had been, moved in quietly, felt the coldness move through the rubber of his waders, and then he stood there quietly and watched the river smoothing into the top of the pool, spreading and coiling and slackening in its run. On the far side under the great oaks the granite rocks were hung with fern and moss that distilled the morning mist in slow drops. Beneath, in the cool depths he knew there were fish. Taking the battered tin box from his pocket he selected a fly and tied it to his cast. It was a small silver-bodied Dusty Miller that he had made himself. The rising morning breeze had strengthened and there was a faint ripple on the pool's surface. He knew the pool in flood and he knew it in drought. As he fished it was not the dark, disturbed surface that he saw, but the bottom of the pool, each gravelled scoop, each ribbed outrun of strataed rock, each boulder and rise and fall of the rough bottom. He fished and the feeling of fishing gave him a little inner life, a slow enjoyment touching his coldness as he cast and watched the slow curl of the line. As the fly sank he nursed it, and held it as it came round below him into the shallower water where more often than not the take came. He watched the pool, he watched his line, and he watched the place where he knew his fly was working. At once he was aware of everything around him and also of the smallest detail. It was as though his body were full of eyes, his fingers on rod and line slowly waking with almost electric sensation.

He was halfway down the pool and almost opposite the fishing hut when he heard and saw Harrison. The man came round the side of the hut, his heavy tread clear above the constant noise of the river. Grimster turned his head for a moment. Harrison stood on the bank three feet above him. He was wearing a dirty old raincoat, gum boots sleek with grass dew, and an old tweed hat with the brim turned up. His face was large and red, the broad heavy chin dark with the past day's stubble still. He had a cigarette in his left hand and in his right hand there was a gun of some kind. Grimster saw all this and turned his eyes back to the water, working rod and line automatically to bring his fly swimming across the idle pull of the pool's current.

Harrison said, "Good morning, Johnny."

Without turning Grimster nodded.

Harrison stood and watched him and with each fresh cast Grimster made and with each step he took downstream, Harrison stepped ahead of him. Although there was no fear in him and little curiosity, he knew that Harrison had come to kill him. But as certainly as he knew it he knew also that Harrison could not kill him. Not on this day.

Harrison said, "What have you got on?"

For the first time Grimster spoke. He said, "A Dusty Miller."

Harrison drew on his cigarette, then crushed the glowing end in his fingers and tossed it away. He said, "If I were sentimental I'd say this was as good a time, place and pursuit as any. Personally I hope it happens to me in bed. Apoplexy following the orgasm."

Grimster felt the stiffness of a smile touch his face. Harrison who was coming to kill was bringing life back.

"How did you know I would be here?"

Harrison chuckled. "You had to be one morning. I've come for the last three."

"Each time with a gun?" He wasn't moving now. He covered the same piece of water three times, lengthening his line a little with each cast.

"Each time with a gun. Orders. Nothing personal."

"What is it you want from me?"

"Does it matter? Does curiosity still live even though you'll be dead in a few moments?"

"That doesn't sound like you."

"The early morning makes me pompous, Johnny. I apologise."

Not from fear, nor from a desire to gain time, but still, as some warmth of inner life began to creep back, unable to put logic to this moment and, because of his nature, instantly searching for it, prepared to pretend some weakness to get it, he said, feigning sincerity, "I'm in a position now to do a deal."

"Valda?"

Grimster nodded, his eyes on the water. The surface boiled slowly and then the movement was gone. A fish had come short to his fly. He let the fly come round with the swing of the current, held it and worked it gently, hoping to bring the fish back or attract another.

"Interesting, but irrelevant now," said Harrison, and then added in a different tone, "You moved one then. When I was here yesterday there were half a dozen fish moving. Fresh run some of them looked."

Grimster retrieved his line, swept it back and cast. As the line went out and fell he jerked his wrist and arm instinctively and put an upstream bend in it so that the fly would work

142

smoothly and naturally downstream and across without being dragged by the pull of the current on the line.

"So you've come to kill me."

"Inter alia—yes."

Harrison would give him no more than that, he knew. But little as it was, it was something to work on.

He said calmly, "You'd better get on with it." He was wondering whether Harrison had the instinct and will in his right hand to do it. They were brothers of a kind and brother could kill brother, but—and for a certainty this obtained between them—there had to be an excusing, expiatory ritual. It came.

Harrison said, "I'm happy for you to fish that cast out. Only when one thing ends should another begin."

On the water Grimster saw the upstream bow of his line slowly pull straight in the flow and then check slightly. No sudden knock, no hard pull. He dropped his rod point, giving more line and saw now the downstream bow begin to shape and he knew that out there, three or four feet down, a salmon held his fly gently in its mouth. He gave more line, increasing the downstream bow, waiting for the drag of the pool's current on the line to pull the fly down to the scissors of the fish's jaw. In a few seconds he would swing the rod sideways and drive the hook home deep, if the fish had not already hooked itself. Behind him he knew that Harrison would have seen the line check, would be watching the growing downstream bend in the line. To confirm it Harrison said from his left, a momentary movement seen in the corner of his eye, "You're into one, Johnny. As a farewell gift I'll let you take it. I owe you more but it's all I can afford."

Grimster moved his rod firmly, deliberately and at an angle, and he felt at once the weight and the resistance. The feel of the line through his fingers as he took all slackness out of it told him that the hook was well home. For a few moments the fish made no movement at all.

Behind him Harrison said, "Land him, Johnny. My farewell gift. The Fates are in a dramatic mood this morning."

143

The salmon moved suddenly, a fast hard run straight up the pool, taking loose line over his fingers and through the rod rings, making the silk sing and the top of the rod bow from the easy, nursing pressure he put on by gently braking the line. At the top of the pool the fish jumped. A sudden silver explosion, dazzling against the dark shadowed rocks and bracken below the trees. The fish smacked back to the water on its side, spray and foam spouting, trying to shake the hook. Grimster kept contact with it and moved back and out of the water, pulling in the slackening line fast with his left hand as the salmon turned and ran down the pool, jumped twice, and then went deep, boring towards the runout.

Standing now on the little beach below the low grassy bank, Grimster held the fish and then moved down to get below it, holding firm so that the salmon could not make the fast, broken water of the runout and race away downstream to break him.

Harrison now was upstream and a little behind him and, as the growing side strain of the line made the fish swing across the current and then move into a short run up the pool, Harrison said, "A clean fish. Fifteen pounds maybe. Don't spin it out, Johnny. Kill him fast. I've a busy day ahead."

Upstream the fish jumped again and then bored deep and the tug and thrust of its anger at the hook in its mouth moved through Grimster's arms and shoulders like a fast blood pulse. For a moment he was tempted to work the fish easily, to give it freedom to run downstream, down and out of the pool, with him following it in the fast water. Harrison had made his promise, his farewell gift, and would be honourable. He had only to follow out into the wide torrent, let the rod go, and then swim and scramble for the far bank. There was a fifty-fifty chance he might make it. But he moved upstream, keeping the pressure of the arched rod on the fish, walking it up, until he was standing on the head of the little beach again.

The fish suddenly turned and moved towards him fast, gaining the freedom of fast slackening line and then, before he could gather it and make new contact, the salmon turned and raced hard obliquely across the pool. The slack whipped out and fresh line screeched from off the reel. Under the far rocks it jumped high and Grimster slightly dipped the rod-tip to avoid a break. A few seconds later he knew that it had been the last real fury in the fish. He gained line, mastering the salmon now, and saw it come to the surface far out and roll twice on its side before it went under.

Close to him, Harrison said, "Tiring. But don't trust him. He's a big boy."

Grimster worked the fish. It made two or three more short runs but he knew now that if the hook held he was the master, and the knowledge was all warmth in him. He was alive and he knew his powers and he was sorry for Harrison and the only uncertainty in him was whether he should kill Harrison or let him go. He had killed often before, under orders, and there was now no feeling in it. But now the warmth in him craved for real killing and he knew he would have to wait and see whether the cold mandate given to him last night ran to Harrison who would have already shot him by now if the fish out there had not turned, lazily, bored, and mouthed the wet shape of the Dusty Miller, taking it out of the dim memory of the way, as a salmon parr in this same stream, maybe this same pool, it had taken the rising nymphs and the caddis grubs in their stony cases on the stream's bed.

Twelve feet from him the fish surfaced and rolled, tired, exhaustion claiming it. Grimster stepped into the water and swung the fish above him, bringing the rod across. He let the salmon hang in a foot of water, watched it, broad back black stippled, silver flanked, seeing the fly lodged tight in the scissors of its jaws, seeing the long hooked under jaw of the cock fish. He drew it into the shallow water at the beach edge and it struggled once or twice so that, with the pressure of the rod's strain, it almost beached itself.

Above him, Harrison said, "Well done, Johnny. What better way could you want to go out?"

Holding the rod away from him, slack line in his left hand,

looped, ready to slip free if the fish found the strength to turn from the beach and make a run, Grimster stepped outside it and with the tip of his right foot jerked the salmon clear on to the dry shingle of the beach. Having no net or gaff he reached down and grabbed it around the thick wrist of its tail, lifting it, the heavy body of the fish arching and twisting, but firmly held. He raised it for Harrison to see; Harrison standing a yard from him and two feet above him on the bank, the fishing hut behind him, an empty whisky bottle standing on the lid of the store box at its side, the fishing hut itself made from an old Great Western railway carriage . . . every detail of Harrison and the world around him was etched sharply in his mind. For the first time he made real conversation with the man, ignoring the gun that was levelled at him, and said, "You're wrong. About twelve pounds. Not long in the river, but no sea-lice. Remember your first salmon in the Blackwater, and the fight we had?"

Harrison nodded and his right hand moved down half an inch and sideways three so that the fish Grimster held gave no cover to his body, and Grimster knew that Harrison would fire within the next five seconds, fire without the grace of another word, and knowing this and knowing the certainty in him of not dying . . . not on this day . . . he suddenly unflexed the right-angled bend of his arm by which he was taking the strain of the salmon's weight and slung the fish sideways at Harrison's bulk, dropping the rod and slack line from his left hand as he did so.

Harrison fired as the fish seemed to hang in the now sun-dappled air between them. Grimster felt the fast clip of air against his cheek as the bullet passed him, later to know that it had gone right through the salmon's thick body, angled deep down below the dorsal fin, striking the backbone and emerging on an inch's deflection which was enough to make it miss him. The salmon hit Harrison breast high as he fired again, the shot going skywards as his bulky body staggered backwards.

Grimster jumped the low bank and kicked the gun from

146

Harrison's hand as the man went backwards to the ground. As Harrison rolled to his side to come up, he kicked again, hard and deep into the flabby stomach. On the wet grass the salmon suddenly moved, quivered and bowed its great body, jerked, and then was still except for a fine trembling of the great tail fin.

Grimster picked up the gun, warm and contented, sensible of a new freedom of the spirit. Valda was truly dead now. All that remained were her obsequies, and the settling of her true estate. For the first time in years he was at liberty to be himself, not a ghost in a wakeful world.

Harrison groaned and slowly sat up. His hat had fallen off and absently he reached out and put it on. He spat and grunted, wheezed for breath and finally said, "Christ. . . ."

Grimster held the gun on him and said, "Stand up and turn your back to me."

Slowly, without query, Harrison did as he was told. Grimster stepped close, put the gun into his back and felt around his body, feeling pockets, patting at the warm raincoated bulk. Then still close, the gun's pressure hard against the other's spine, Grimster said, "Now do me another favour and explain why you were ordered to kill me—inter alia."

Breath still laboured, Harrison said flatly, "You know I can't, Johnny."

"If you don't I might kill you. There'd be no trouble tidying up."

"Then you must do it. I was going to do it to you." Then, flippancy breaking into the sincerity, the cold knowledge of himself, he added, "Hell, if you'd kicked me six inches lower you'd have got my courting tackle and ruined me for life."

"Inter alia," said Grimster.

"No, Johnny. Not even for you—or for myself. If you're going to do it O.K. I let you have your salmon. Perhaps I rate a cigarette?"

Grimster stepped back from him and Harrison turned slowly and then felt in his coat pocket for cigarettes and matches. He lit a cigarette, looked down at the salmon, the hook in the struggle now pulled clear of its mouth, and then at the rod which lay on the beach and said, "The old 'Pope'. Handed down from father to son in the best families. So it was true about Valda?"

"You've always known it was."

"Guessed—no more. But you've only just had proof." He shrugged his shoulders and made a small move away, "So—what have I got to fear from you? I'd have killed you, but you don't want me. You want to keep it fresh and clean, nicely burnished for the right one. That's not me. You're a killer all right, Johnny—but you've got a sentimental fixation now about priorities. Work from the top down, eh? I'm well down the list."

Harrison turned and walked away, ducking under the low hawthorn by the fishing hut, moving out into the long field grass, ignoring the path, marking a ragged swathe through the standing pasture, and Grimster let him go, watching him move across to the far railway line, seeing him clamber over the white gate that was always kept locked to keep cattle off the line, and finally disappear down the slope on the far side. And he had no feeling, not about Harrison. No feeling at all. He turned and threw the gun out into the pool and then began to collect up his rod and line. He slipped a twisted handkerchief through the gills and out of the mouth of the fish so that he could carry it. He waded back over the river, and walked up through the woods to his car.

Sitting in the car, he took the firecrest ring off his finger. Nobody wanted to kill him yet just for the satisfaction of having him dead, not even Harrison's people. Harrison had wanted him dead to take something from him. Inter alia . . . Harrison would be regretting that now.

He began to examine the ring carefully.

*　　*　　*　　*

Coppelstone was down to breakfast, a small shaving nick on

148

the side of his chin the only sign of his night's drinking. No one else was at the table. Angela Pilch and Lily seldom came down for breakfast, preferring to have it in their rooms. Cranston was still in his office.

So far as Grimster could tell Coppelstone was his normal self. No memory of their true session remained.

Grimster said, "You should feel like hell this morning."

Coppelstone smiled. "I should every morning, but I never do. Sorry I passed out on you, but I'm not used to company normally. I hear you got a fish this morning?"

"A twelve pounder, fairly clean run. By favour of Harrison."

"Harrison?"

Without mentioning Valda, Grimster told him what had happened, and finished, "Why should Harrison want to kill me?"

"No idea. You want us to do anything about him?"

"That's up to Sir John when he hears. For myself, I know he may try again so I shall be ready." He leaned back and toyed with his coffee spoon. "The trouble with this Department is that it has a trick of complicating the simple and obvious."

"It's full of tricks. Nasty ones. It's become its own authority, Satanic, though Sir John regards himself more as the Pope. The ends justify the means, all sins carry their own absolution and the P.M. and his cabinet in Downing Street would hit the roof if they knew half of the things that went on. They never will, of course. They don't want to. We're the department of dirty means—means to save money, trick the industrious and talented, and protect and cherish that legendary beast we call national security. The Department could have been honest with Dilling, examined his discovery and paid him a fair price. If the Department were like that you and I wouldn't be sitting here now—and Sir John would have had to be content with being a country J.P., working off his sadism on traffic offenders and the odd child rapist. The trouble with government departments, particularly those concerned with defence and security, is that they become autonomous, create a divinity for themselves and withdraw from life as the man in the street knows it. But of course you know this."

"It's good to hear it restated sometimes. Will Sir John be taking his usual two weeks down here this year?"

"Yes. Beginning of next month. Why?"

"Because if we get this Dilling thing cleared up in time, I'd like to come back for a week's fishing—and I don't want to be here when he comes."

He sat there, easy and calm, not a different man, but a differently ballasted man, riding high with the buoyancy of a long carried load removed from him. There were other small things to do first, but ahead lay the pleasure of knowing that he was going to kill the man. Down here held an appositeness. Down here he had learnt the truth about Valda. In his mind's eye he had already picked the spot, the time of day, and the method. The thought of it was curiously as innocent and relished as the longing for morning to come on Christmas day to discover a promised gift. His mother had always been good with presents, never disappointing him.

After breakfast he went up to Lily's suite. She was sitting by the window reading the *Daily Mail*. She gave him a smiling good-morning, and then said, "Your boss was here yesterday?"

"Briefly, yes."

"He didn't want to see me?"

"No. Disappointed?"

"It would have been polite."

"I agree."

She gave him a quick look, and said, "What's happened to you?"

"Nothing."

"Yes it has. You've got a fat grin all over your face, Johnny. I like it. But why—nobody's said anything funny. Or did you get a nice surprise?"

"No. But I think I just missed one."

"Oh, what was that?"

"You came to my room late last night, didn't you?"

150

"Johnny!" She blushed quickly and turned her face from him to hide it.

"Didn't you?"

"Of course I didn't. What kind of woman do you think I am?" She turned back to him. "But if I had would you have minded?"

Because he knew her now, knew that the simple desire for a man by itself would have never made her come to him, there was a curiosity in him to know the real reason. It had to be a good one to have pushed her to the act. He also guessed that it was not a reason which she would discuss here and now with him. He would have to wait her time again.

He said, "No, I wouldn't have minded."

"Johnny!" She laughed and it was high and forced, covering her embarrassment, covering more than that, some design he knew that she would not easily relinquish. She got up and came close to him and said, "What *has* happened to you?"

"I don't know. Maybe because I had a good morning and caught a fish."

"You've caught something more than a fish. You've caught something that's warmed you up. You think a woman can't tell? I can see I'll have to watch my step with you now." She faced him, a little wrinkle of a frown over her eyes, and then went on, "No, I know what it is."

"Yes?"

"You've made up your mind about something, haven't you?"

"Perhaps."

With a shrewdness that didn't surprise him, she said, "About living in the past? About life . . . like, you know, it's got to go on?"

He put out a hand and just touched her arm, and he said, "Do you trust me?"

"You know I do."

"In the way you did Harry?"

"How do you mean?" She was genuinely puzzled now. "You are in a funny mood this morning, aren't you?"

151

"What I mean is, if I told you to do something—except jump off a cliff—because it was for your own good you'd do it, and not ask questions?"

She hesitated for a while and then said, "Yes, I suppose I would. If you really meant it. But I don't understand, Johnny. What's in your mind all of a sudden?"

"I'm not sure myself at the moment. I've just got a feeling about something. About something we might have to do. I just want to be sure that you'd go along with me."

"Well, of course I would if you said it was the right thing to do. Has something gone wrong?"

He smiled, not professionally now. He liked her and wanted to help her. More than that, out of a perverseness which arose from his own decision to kill Sir John, he also needed to thwart the man before he killed him. He now wanted for Lily all those things which Dilling had promised her. He wanted to find whatever it was that Dilling had hidden and make the deal for the dead man. But not on the terms that the Department had laid down, that the moment the discovery was made Lily should go so that due economy could be made. A cold calculation by Sir John which would have consigned all her vigour and beauty and simplicity to oblivion before her time. She should be able to go on and become overplump, marry, and be soundly ploughed and seeded in bed by some appreciative man, have children and smack their heads for bad behaviour, and love and cherish them, take the wealth that Dilling would have given her and be generous or spendthrift with it and eventually go in the fullness of such time as God allotted to her. God, not Sir John Maserfield. There was a warmth in him now, it was true; and a patience beyond any he had known before. There was no hurry in him to finish with Sir John. The man would always be there, waiting for him. But first he had to secure for Lily what Dilling had wished her to have. It was a debt which he, Grimster, now owed to her because without Dilling's death, without Lily's presence in this house, he would never have known the truth about Valda. To ensure Lily's safety and happiness was a debt of honour he had to pay before he would be free of all obligations except the final one which he owed to Valda who had been killed because of him.

He said, "No, nothing's gone wrong. Everything is going well."

She said practically, "But there's still that missing day."

Moving to the door he said over his shoulder, "I think we're going to be able to handle that one between us." He didn't look back. He didn't want her to see his face, and he knew that she didn't want him to see hers. His fingers on the door handle, he added, "I've got to go off with Coppelstone on a trip today. I shan't be back until late tonight, past midnight some time."

CHAPTER ELEVEN

COPPELSTONE WAS GOING back by train from Exeter. Over breakfast that morning Grimster had said that he would drive him to the station before lunch. But instead of taking him to Exeter, he took him to the station at Taunton. When Coppelstone asked him why, he said, "It works in better with my movements. I'll let you have a report later."

Coppelstone smiled, and before he left him to go into the station said, "Inter alia—is that it?"

"Yes."

"Harrison made a mistake there. He'll know it, too. You may find the bird flown."

"It's a chance I'll take."

With Coppelstone safely on the train, though he might get off anywhere and telephone, it was still a chance he was willing to take. That Coppelstone had a line to Harrison was unimportant to him; that Coppelstone was now a traitor gave him no surprise, no anxiety and no desire to condemn. Other men in the service had taken the same route as Coppelstone; some lasted, most didn't—but they did it generally because it was the last spurt in them of a twisted virtue, a silent, dangerous protest, a wish for absolution through self-destruction.

From Taunton Grimster drove to High Wycombe. There was a lot of traffic on the main roads and it took him three and a half hours, but he was not worried about time. There was an unhurried, fatalistic feeling in him which he had known before, something close to a sensation of absolute certainty that things would, today at least, go his way. Harrison should have killed him quickly, without any grace and without any talk. Harrison had made a mistake—and Harrison should have known better because both he and Harrison knew that life and death were always balanced on the shaking fulcrum of a mistake.

He came down the steep hill into High Wycombe, the town sprawling up and down both sides of the narrow river valley, and he found William Pringle's pet shop in a side street running off the main road that curved through the town. It had two bow windows, small paned, with a door between them. Across the top of the windows ran the legend—Pringle's Petquarium. The word made him wince. Both windows were full of animal and fish supplies. A cardboard strip hanging inside the door read—Open. There was a woman in the shop buying dog food. Grimster stood at the doorway and watched as the man serving her scooped out hound meal from a sack and weighed it for her. The woman was the only customer.

When she came out, Grimster went in. He closed the door behind him, slipped the catch on the lock and turned the cardboard slip so that it read—Closed—to the outside world.

The place was bright with neon strips and from the concealed lighting in the rows of tropical fish tanks that lined one wall in double tiers. From a cage on the opposite side of the shop a guinea pig gave a sudden happy whistling and in another cage a grey rabbit chewed sullenly on a limp piece of cabbage leaf. The place smelled faintly of animal urine and meal dust, but it was clean and everything tidily arranged.

William Pringle, still holding the meal scoop in his hand, looked at Grimster with mild curiosity. He was just as Lily had described him, unruly fair hair and a wispy untidy beard. He wore a red, open-necked shirt, green corduroy trousers, sandals, and there was a black working apron tied around his waist. His blue eyes were frank, unafraid.

He said, "If you've come for the till, you aren't going to get enough for a good meal."

Grimster said, "I just wanted a little privacy. Do we talk

here or have you got a back room?" He handed Pringle his regulation identification card from the Ministry.

Pringle glanced at it, made his own mental connections, shrugged his shoulders and then flipped the scoop back into the sack of hound meal.

"This way, Mr. Grimster. I was just going to make a cup of tea. Interested?"

"Thank you."

He followed Pringle into the room at the back of the shop. A big roll-top desk took up most of the space. There were two chairs, a small floor bookstand, and a sink under the window with boards each side that held a small gas stove, a gas ring and various pieces of cooking equipment. A camp bed, the covers neatly folded, ran down one wall and one corner had been curtained over to make a wardrobe. It was neat but crowded. Pringle motioned to him to sit down while he went to the window and began to fill a kettle. The lower half of the window was open. Outside was a small yard with crates and animal cages lining each wall. On the outer window sill a wide bird table had been fixed.

Grimster said, "This is an official enquiry. If you are in any doubt you can ring the Ministry and check that I am what my card says I am."

Pringle, back to him, said, "There's no need. I believe you." His voice was good, well modulated, educated and deep. It would have graced his father's pulpit.

Grimster said, "I want to ask you some questions about the late Harry Dilling."

Pringle lit the gas ring and put the kettle on it. "Go ahead." He crumbled a piece of bread in his hand and tossed the pieces on to the bird table. A few sparrows and a chaffinch flew to the table to take them.

"He was a great friend of yours?"

"Yes."

Pringle sat down and offered Grimster a cigarette. Grimster shook his head. Pringle lit a cigarette and added, "The best

156

I ever had." He smiled, "Mad bugger Harry. But brilliant."

"What was the financial arrangement between you'?"

"Financial arrangement?"

"You know what I mean. How much did you put into his business?"

"Oh, I see. Somewhere around six thousand."

"Who found the rest?"

"Harry."

"When he went bankrupt you lost the lot?"

"Sadly, yes."

"That must have worried Harry."

"Not that you would have noticed. He was sensible of it—but not worried."

"Did he make any arrangement about it?"

"Yes, he did."

"I'd like to know what."

Pringle shrugged his shoulders and reached out to the desk. He pulled a drawer open and took out an envelope which he handed to Grimster and said, "That's a photostat of the document. The original is with my solicitor." He smiled. "At least, it's with *a* solicitor."

Grimster pulled the photostat of the document from the envelope and began to read it. It wasn't a long document but it had been properly drawn up. He read it twice and Pringle sat and watched him. It was an assignment from Dilling to Pringle of a one-seventh share in all the rights, capital or royalties, which might accrue from the sale or lease of Dilling's inventions, discoveries or technical processes over the whole of his lifetime, these rights to continue after his death in perpetuity to Pringle, who would have the right to bequeath them in his turn to whomsoever he wished.

The kettle began to whistle and Pringle got up to make the tea.

Grimster said, "This is dated after his bankruptcy."

"That's so. Apart from a small monthly payment, it was the

only way he could think of that might eventually get me my money back. I told him not to bother about it, but he did. At times he could be extraordinarily punctilious. Not often, but when he was there was no shaking him. I didn't care a damn about the money really. It came easy—and it went."

"Did he ever talk to you about the project he was hoping to sell to our Ministry?"

"Only in the vaguest way."

"Have you any idea what it was?"

"No. Though I guessed it must be something in his line of country."

"Did he ever refer to it by name?"

"Oh, yes. Firecrest he called it."

"Why?"

"Search me. Harry just picked a word, I suppose." He brought a cup of tea to Grimster in a large white mug with a picture of a trumpeting African elephant on it. "If that's not strong enough, say so. I'll put in another tea bag." He held a bowl for Grimster to take sugar lumps with his fingers.

"Did you know that Dilling hid all the relevant papers about this project somewhere shortly before his death?"

"Yes. He told me."

"When?"

"The day he died."

"At what time?"

"Around four o'clock in the morning. He phoned me up here for a chat."

"Was that usual?"

"With Harry, yes. If he couldn't sleep he'd phone me sometimes and we'd chat. This time he just said that he didn't trust the Ministry to give him a fair deal so he'd taken the precaution of hiding his stuff."

"But he didn't say where?"

"No."

"I've a feeling that that's not a strictly honest answer."

"We're all entitled to our feelings." It was said pleasantly, but for the first time there was in his words a strength and purpose that flowed from the gentle rise of antagonism.

Grimster decided to ignore it. He said, "Were you with Harry when he was caught for drunken driving?"

"Yes."

"It was between Luton and Leighton Buzzard, wasn't it?"

"Yes."

"What were you both doing in that part of the country?"

"Harry was staying the weekend with me. It was one of my bad periods just before I had this place. I was working for a fencing and road building contractor near Bletchley." He paused, sipped at his own mug of tea, the mug pictured with a row of pink flamingoes. "Mr. Grimster, why don't you come directly to the point of your visit?"

"Do you know what it is?"

"Of course I do. You want to know to whom I've sold that assignment of Harry's. How much I got for it and so on."

"If you say so. Anyway, who did you sell it to?"

"That's my business."

"How much did you get for it?"

"I'm happy to say quite a lot of money. Far, far more than Harry owed me."

"What else did you sell?"

"Nothing."

"Mr. Pringle, let's be very sensible. At the moment we're dealing in a civilised way with one another. I ask you a question and you give me an answer. But if you refuse to give me the answers I know you can give, it would be a simple matter for me to take you in to the Ministry and make you give the answers. You no doubt know that we can be very unpleasant in our methods when we wish."

"I'm sure you can. When you sup with the devil use a long spoon."

"That sounds like Dilling."

159

"It was. That's why he hid his stuff."

"All right, Mr. Pringle—now let me have some answers without fuss. Apart from the assignment—which at the moment is valueless—you sold something else. Something which was really worth a lot of money. What was it?"

For a moment Pringle hesitated. Through the open window behind him came the sound of a pack of sparrows quarrelling in the yard. A blue-tit flew down to a swinging bag of bird food above the table and began to feed. The debate within Pringle resolved itself, and he said, "Knowledge."

"Go on."

"Harry was no fool. He hid his papers so that your people couldn't get at them while the preliminary dealing was being done. He didn't overlook the possibility that he might be run over or have something happen to him. He had a great responsibility to Lily and an obligation to me. He didn't want his stuff to disappear for ever. So when he phoned me early on the morning of his death, he told me how I could find them if anything went wrong."

"He told you where he'd hidden them?"

"That wasn't Harry's way. He told me how I could find out where they were. It was that knowledge, Mr. Grimster, that I sold with the assignment."

Grimster said, "You know you did a foolish thing, don't you? Or perhaps you don't. Perhaps you don't know the kind of people you've dealt with. The moment you've helped them, really helped them by working out where the hiding place is— they'll kill you. You're an honest man, Pringle—but you've only sold them a one-seventh part. They wouldn't be content with that. They want Lily's six-sevenths as well. She'd never get it and you would know it and cause trouble—unless they put you out of the way. You would, wouldn't you? You're fond of Lily."

"Yes, I like her very much. And, of course, she must have her six-sevenths. They've agreed to that."

Grimster shook his head. "You may be good with animals,

Pringle. But you know nothing about the human animal. Right now you're in bad trouble. You're committed to them and if you help them they'll kill you eventually."

"You're trying to scare me."

"I *am* scaring you because you know it's the truth. Look—" Grimster held up his hand, the back towards Pringle so that the sun through the window caught the enamelling of the fire-crest ring. "Early this morning they tried to kill me. Inter alia, they said—which was a mistake. They tried to kill me, not because they wanted me dead but because they wanted something I had. The only thing I could have had, Pringle, was this ring. You know this ring, though you've very carefully not given it a glance since I came in. You've been with Harry when he put Lily off with it and made her do ridiculous things for you both. When Harry phoned you he said, I'm sure, if things go wrong get hold of the ring and you'll be able to work it out. He wouldn't have said much more I don't think. Harry liked to be mysterious and oblique."

"That's just what he did say."

"But you understood."

"Of course. I gave Harry the ring years ago. I found it in an antique shop in Edinburgh. The gold band which holds the enamel plaque on top unscrews and there's a little cavity behind."

"I know, Pringle. I discovered that for myself this morning. But what was there is no longer there. I took it out. But I want an explanation of what I found means. You can give it to me, and you're going to give it to me because it's the only way you can save your bacon. You're going to tell me what it means and then you're going to get the hell out of this country as fast as you can. Don't bother about this shop and the animals—just phone the nearest branch of the Royal Society for the Prevention of Cruelty to Animals and drop it in their lap. Drop everything and get to Heathrow as fast as you can. Travel fast and far, and then stay. In six months they'll forget about you. I know them. By then you'll be unimportant and written out of their minds. But for the next couple of weeks they'll be after you. Do I make myself clear?"

"Clear and not very comforting, Mr. Grimster." Pringle stood up, holding his mug, and went on, "Like some more tea?"

"No. And don't try to fool me. You're in trouble. Help me and I'll give you all the help I can to get away somewhere safe, names, places and foreign currency to tide you over."

Pringle stood at the sink board, filling his mug, his back to Grimster, his broad frame blocking most of the window on to the yard. As he held the teapot over the mug there was a sudden scurry from the feeding sparrows and other birds around the low bird table, a rush of wings and small alarm calls, and suddenly Grimster knew the alarm was meant for him. The birds outside knew Pringle. They came to him, not flew from him when he appeared. But now they were dispersing in a rush of wings and with their flight the broad back of Pringle suddenly jerked down and he crouched, body and knees bent, so that the half-open window was clear. As Grimster threw himself sideways from his chair, he saw the dark shape of a man outside. A man who had come at some signal Pringle had given, at some signal previously arranged because Harrison had been clever enough to realise his mistake, quick enough to know that he had given too much away and must work fast to recover the advantage which had temporarily been taken from him. The shot the man fired hit the wall behind Grimster's chair on the line and at the level his head had occupied a few seconds earlier.

Grimster rolled towards the door, and, as his right arm came up free on the first turn over, he threw his elephant mug at the top half of the window frame. The glass smashed and cascaded down to the sink and window sill. The man fired again. The bullet hit the skirting board alongside the door as Grimster rose, jerked the door open, and ran through.

He went out into the side street and walked slowly down to the main road, brushing floor dust from his clothes, tidying himself up, and adjusting his shirt cuffs and tie. There was a smear of dirt on one cuff and the sight of it made him smile as he remembered something Lily had once said about his appearance. He walked to the park where he had left his car. There was no point in staying around. The man at the window had not been Harrison. There was nothing he could do about Pringle now. They would take him away and hold him safely in the hope that he could be used later. If they couldn't they might eventually let him go—though they'd probably see their money back first—or they might just get rid of him. Was it Harrison, he wondered, who had first had the idea of approaching Pringle? Whoever it was, it had to be someone who had understood Dilling's character. Under no circumstances was Dilling going to over-tempt fate when he hid his papers. That was a character trait which had become apparent to him, Grimster, late. Somewhere or other—and certainly not in Lily's mind—Dilling would have left a definite clue, not for anyone to read but for someone like Pringle who knew his mind and his history and his way of thinking. But Pringle now was blocked from Grimster for good and the neatly folded piece of thin paper which he had found within the ring cavity was meaningless. It was safe now in another hiding place, but as he started to drive back it was clear in his mind.

Unfolded, the paper was about four inches square. At the top of it, written in a small neat hand were the words—*Que será será*. At the bottom in a small circle was what looked like a crudely drawn, childish almost, worm or caterpillar, its back arched up in a loop, its head thickened to a small blob. Between the top inscription and the arched worm at the bottom was a neatly drawn sketch map with curving double lines for roads or paths and little groups of small, blacked-in circles for what could have been trees. In the centre of the plan was a pair of two small circles. On the base line of the trees an equilateral triangle with dotted sides had been constructed, the base line inscribed "30 ins". At the apex of the dotted triangle was a red-inked cross. On the left-hand edge of the plan was another, and bigger, cross, slightly sloping and with the upright of the cross marked top and bottom as the compass points North and South. To the west of the triangulation, contained in the curve of a double line, was an irregularly shaped area cross-hatched with thin ink lines. When he had first looked at the paper Grimster had known that the sketch plan by itself would tell him nothing. The words *Que será será* and the crudely drawn worm were the real clues. Pringle would probably have read them at once, but Pringle was now barred to him. Anything he was going to get he would have to get from Lily. Whether that was possible he didn't know, but he did know that when he got back Lily would be waiting for him.

*   *   *   *

Some time soon he was going to kill Sir John. The decision carried no moral or ethical problem. It was, too, oddly divorced from love for or loyalty to Valda. She was long gone now. Torn right out of his life. The murder of Sir John would be the final obsequy and then he would owe nothing to anyone, and be left demanding nothing for himself. This which was happening now—returning late, he moved into his bedroom— had to be, because without it some ritual part of the killing of Sir John would be missing. The man had given him this assignment, and through this assignment had brought him to the truth he had long suspected. It seemed to him, therefore, that the assignment must be completed diligently step by step and finally closed with the killing of its instigator. Not only did the logic have to be sparse and tidy, but all emotion attached to it had to follow the same bare lines. Lily was now an integral part of the design, a player like him in the play. While they acted, they accurately shadowed life, simulated with near sincerity all necessary emotions, spoke words which had almost instant truth and conviction, knowing that the moment they stepped off the boards action and speech would have become dead things. Without knowing why—or perhaps inventing some sentimental half-truth for reason—she was as compelled as he was to dedicate herself to this part of the final ritual.

There was no lamp on in the room, but the light from the sitting-room behind him showed him the bed. She was lying with her back to him, fair hair just visible on the pillow. He knew that she was not asleep. He knew, too, that she would not turn or make any movement, would give him no word, but would lie there waiting for him to join her. He knew now what for some time he had suspected, knowing Dilling, guessing the safeguard he had put about his secret, knowing, too, that she had either known or guessed the safeguard too, but would never have been able to bring herself to name it—that also was part of Dilling's mastery. He had left her a fortune and a key to it which she could not use unless she indulged in self-delusion. She lay there now because she had finally come to understand her true feeling for Dilling and how his had been for her. She must know now that she hated Dilling. Grimster was sorry for her, even angry for her, but for himself there was nothing; though when he moved into bed with her he knew they would both play their part and go on playing it in the days to follow because the understanding between them was complete.

He went into the bathroom, moving as he did every night to the moment for bed, and he made no change in anything he did, knowing she would expect none.

He got into bed and he lay there for a moment or two in the dark room, not touching her, but sensing the tremble in her body as she lay with her back to him. Not since Valda had he been in bed with a woman. The thought carried no anguish. Valda was gone. He reached out after a while and turned Lily to him. He felt her body still shaking and he put his arms around her and held her. The warmth of her body moved into his. He put up a hand and touched the smoothness of her neck and let it rest there. Slowly he felt the tremor of her body quieten and die and he settled her body more comfortably against his and then, lying together, no words needed between them, they slowly drifted off to sleep.

It was early morning when he woke and knew that Lily was awake too. They made love and, since this was the high point of pretence in the play they shared, the pretence acquired its own validity, drawing it from them so that there was only a narrow shading between truth and reality. Each body moved with its own inner deceit and passion, and then each mind sensed the slow crumbling of design before the almost total onrush of a shared ecstasy, sweeping in like a flood tide and then slowly receding.

As they lay together afterwards, Lily put out a hand and switched on the bedside lamp. Her eyes, shadowed and misty, were on him and there was no barrier between them.

She said, "Johnny, my love. Do it now."

He leaned above her, the lamp light full on her face, and he raised his hand with the firecrest ring on it, and saw her eyes hold his for a moment, saw the slow movement of a smile move her mouth, and then her eyes come back to the ring and follow it as he began to talk to her, moving her into sleep, smoothing her way into the depths where Dilling—in the aftermath of passion—had locked away his secret, and then double-locked it by telling her that she would never remember that true Friday until another man should take her in love and then question her.

Quietly he said, "You're asleep, Lily, but you can hear what I'm saying, can't you?"

"Yes, Johnny, darling." Her voice was low, relaxed, shaded with a feeling that he had not heard before.

He said, "Sleep deep, Lily. Deep, deep, but stay with me. You feel good, don't you, Lily?"

"Yes, Johnny." The words finished with a small sigh and her head rolled gently a little sideways on the pillow. For a moment the sight of her face, of the half parted lips, touched him with a tenderness that made the muscles of his shoulders shudder.

"As good as you used to when Harry did it this way?"

"Yes, Johnny."

"Do you remember the last time it was this way with him, Lily?"

166

"Yes, Johnny."

"When was that, Lily?"

"The night we came back from the long drive."

"You took the long drive on the Friday, the day before you went to London to go to Italy, didn't you?"

"Yes, Johnny."

"Do you remember that day well, Lily?"

"Yes, Johnny."

"What time did you leave the house, Lily?"

"Early, before it was really light."

"Do you remember more or less all the details of that day? What you did or where you went?"

"Yes, Johnny."

"Could you take me to the places you went to, Lily?"

"Yes, Johnny."

"When you wake up, Lily, you're going to remember all about that day. Do you understand that? You're going to remember that Friday and you're going to take me back to all the places you remember and tell me all about that day. Is that clear, Lily?"

"Yes, Johnny."

"There's no doubt in your mind, is there?"

"No, Johnny."

"You want to tell me, don't you, Lily?"

"Yes, Johnny."

"All right, Lily. In a few minutes you will wake up and you'll feel happy and glad about what you've done tonight."

He bent forward and kissed her lips lightly and then he reached out and switched off the bedside lamp. He moved from her and lay back in the darkness listening to the sound of her slow breathing. After a few minutes the sound changed and he felt her body stir. He put out a hand and found hers.

Out of the darkness, almost remote in sound her voice came. "Did it work, Johnny?"

"It worked, Lily."

She was silent for a while and then she said slowly, each

word loaded with an almost languorous relief, "Oh, Johnny. . . . It was awful of me . . . awful . . . but I feel so good. . . . Oh, so good. And Johnny, you've got to believe me. . . . You just have to. . . . I couldn't have done it for anyone else. Only for you because I love you. You know that, don't you, Johnny?"

"Of course I do, Lily darling. And you know I love you too." The words came easily, not simply because, for her self-respect, they were necessary, but because there was a grateful element in him which could refuse her nothing. Truth for him had no further meaning. He had got what he wanted, the last truth about Valda. In return he would act any truth Lily asked.

He put out his arms and drew her towards him and they began to make love again, unencumbered by design, each seeking now the full limit of contentment and union they could find in another.

CHAPTER TWELVE

HE KNEW NOW exactly what he had to do. Before he
satisfied himself, he had to protect Lily's interests. Dilling's
papers had to be found and their sale to the Department had
to be safeguarded. Sir John's brief was to take them and
eliminate all rights in their sale by disposing of Lily. (If Pringle
ever got to the stage of making a claim for his one-seventh, it
would be the stepping stone to his final exit—though he,
Grimster, felt that Pringle would now have the good sense to
disappear before Harrison's people dealt with him. He was
useless to them now and they would quickly write him off if
he gave them a chance.) He was determined that Lily should
get her money and also that she should go on living, free from
all threat. That much he more than owed her, and that much
he meant to obtain for her before he could feel himself free to
deal with Sir John. Everything then rested on his continuing
to work normally for the Department until Lily's future was
secured. When he finally came to deal with Sir John he wanted
no burden other than the obligation to satisfy the now cold,
deep resolution which implacably possessed him and which
now took the place of all passion in him.

The next morning he spoke personally to Sir John on the
telephone and asked for an immediate interview. It was granted
and he drove to Exeter and got the train to Waterloo. The
meeting took place in Sir John's room at the Department high
above the river. The man sat and listened to the story of
Harrison's attempt on his life—which he already knew from
Coppelstone's report—and of Grimster's visit to Pringle. During

169

the detailing of Grimster's love-making with Lily and her hypnotism which had finally restored her memory of the missing Friday, he lit a cigarette and sucked bird-like at it. When he told Sir John about the map in the firecrest ring, he handed him a copy he had made, but which omitted the *Que será será* and the wormlike creature at the bottom. (With Coppelstone in touch with Harrison he could not risk the real map being in the Department.) Sir John heard Grimster's report right through without a single question, and when he had finished he was silent for some time. Grimster waited, watching him, the cold mania in him to kill this man completely under control. He knew better than to make his own suggestions as to the course he wanted to take. Sir John would make them and, in the nature of the facts, there was no course open for the time being except the one which Grimster wanted to take.

Sir John picked up the sketch map. "Has Miss Stevens seen this?"

"Not yet. It may not be necessary to show it to her ever."

Sir John nodded. "Could be. Well, how do you want to handle it?"

"I'd like to make my own arrangements. Go off with Miss Stevens and check the route and see where it gets us. I've a feeling that once we've done that we shall have something to tie in with Dilling's map."

Sir John studied the map for a while and then said, "You've a copy?"

Without hesitation, although it was a lie, Grimster said, "No, I haven't. I'd rather you had it for safe-keeping until I've checked the route." Apart from the lie, which was to cover his own plans, there was a point of protocol involved on which he knew Sir John was testing him. No operator made copies of documents in any case unless he had been ordered to do so, or it was absolutely necessary because of the urgent exigencies of an unforeseen situation. He had to have this man's trust and respect right up until the moment came for the last settlement between them.

Sir John tapped the map. "What do you make of this?"

"It's pure Dilling. A brilliant man with a passion for riddles and mystery—but he always stopped short of inscrutability. He always left some clue, some way in. At the end of Miss Stevens' route I fancy there will be something that will lead to a final solution. Pringle would have understood the map without having to have the route."

"What is there on this that would have given it to Pringle?"

"I don't know."

"Perhaps we should get Pringle."

Grimster smiled. "If the positions were reversed would you let anyone get to Pringle? He's either heading south across Europe at this moment or lying dead in some copse waiting for the police to discover the body. I'd say the latter."

"So would I." Sir John stood up. "All right, you make your own arrangements with Miss Stevens. I'll let Major Cranston know the form and you can call on him for any help you need. As for Miss Stevens, the moment you have followed the route with her, I want her back at High Grange. On no account do I want any hopes raised in her that we may be near to clearing this matter up. This is for her sake, you understand, because I personally still think that Dilling's stuff will turn out to be a lot of nonsense. However, when it's all over we'll pay her handsomely for her trouble and time."

Deliberately, moving in thought and intuition close to Sir John, relishing the solid, well-trained duplicity of the man who had already made all his dispositions for Lily, Grimster said, "Dilling doesn't now come over to me like a crank. We might find ourselves helping Miss Stevens to a handsome fortune."

Sir John gave one of his small smiles and he made it less bleak than usual. "We might indeed. I personally hope so—after the splendid co-operation she's given." He paused and then added without any suggestion of prurience, "It's pleasant to know that there are occasional moments in our profession which are far from distasteful. Very well, Johnny—" It was the ritual dismissal. "—handle it your way and report to me personally."

Grimster nodded and without a word turned and left the room.

Sir John returned to his chair, fingered Dilling's map absently, and his thin lips tightened a little as though there were a sour taste in his mouth. He had once seen Grimster as the one man whom he could have regarded as his rightful successor, but the lines of both their fates had become unexpectedly tangled and only the knife could bring back drastically the order that was needed. At High Grange, when he had lied to Grimster about the nature of Valda's death, it had been, for him, a rare impulse, almost sentimental, to avoid a stupid tragedy. But even as he had lied he had realised the futility of the gesture. For a moment he had acted like a human being, not the head of the Department. But now . . . He sat there and coldly imagined the bedroom of Grimster's suite at the High Grange and, with a clinical self-armouring imagination, saw Grimster moving into bed with Miss Stevens, then saw him as he had been here a few moments ago. The dim outlines of a logical deduction began to clear and take shape in his mind and, for the first time in his life, he began to understand something of the real nature of deep sorrow. He knew, as surely as though Grimster had handed him an affidavit, that Grimster in the near future meant to kill him. The logic was inescapable. While the memory of Valda rested in Grimster's mind and her death had to be accepted as an accident; while, no matter how much suspected, there was no proof of murder by the Department, then Grimster, not even for professional purposes, would so soon have slept with a woman unless he was again truly in love . . . and in love with Miss Stevens he could not be. But he had slept with her because the truth about Valda had become known to him and freed him. Oh, yes, he knew his Grimster. Why should he not since they were both of the same intellectual and emotional mould? In Grimster's place, he would have acted as Grimster must with absolute certainty be planning to act now.

*   *   *   *

Before going back to Devon Grimster telephoned Mrs. Harroway's London house. She was there and he spoke to her. He said that it seemed that the Department's business with Lily would probably be cleared up within a week. When it was would she be prepared to have Lily with her for a while until Lily could make some definite plan for her future? When she said she would he asked her, for the time being, to treat his call as confidential. She gave a small laugh at the other end of the line and said, "Why?"

He said, "I can't tell you that now. But when I bring Lily to you you'll understand that it is not an idle request."

"Very well, Mr. Grimster. If you say so."

He got an early evening train to Exeter and arrived late at High Grange. Cranston was waiting for him and had already had his instructions from Sir John.

Grimster said, "I want a self-drive car laid on for me. I want to pick it up in Exeter at lunchtime tomorrow. You can come in my car and drive it back. I also want you to book a double room in the name of Mr. and Mrs. Jacobs at the Randolph Hotel, Oxford, for tomorrow night and the following night."

Cranston gave him a look but made no comment. He nodded and then said, "This came for you in the afternoon post." He handed him a letter. From the handwriting Grimster saw that it was from Harrison with a London postmark.

Grimster opened the letter. It read—

Dear Johnny,

No one is, of course, more pleased than I that you are still alive since it means that the most interesting human campaign of my life is still very much alive. I under-rated your resourcefulness on the river, and I regret that, having done so, I had the arrogance to make that "inter alia" mistake. I knew—as events have proved—that it would not escape you.

Naturally Pringle must now be considered—and undoubtedly is—

173

hors de combat. You would never be foolish enough to let whatever was in the firecrest ring pass from your hands unless, of course, you have recently suffered a change of heart and head. If you have our offer is very much open still with even larger guarantees of personal safety and financial reward.

I make no apologies, understandably, for the directness of this approach. We have always both been very plain speakers, a virtue our profession has sadly neglected.

If you are interested, get in touch with me. If you are not, I shall nurse my hopes and offer a sincere prayer that you do not put yourself in a position similar to the recent one on the river bank.

Yours affectionately,
Dicky.

Grimster smiled and tossed the letter across to Cranston, saying, "Read it. It'll amuse you. Then let Sir John have it."

He went up to his room, poured himself a brandy and lit a cigar. It was in no way odd to him that he inhabited a world which contained people like Sir John and Harrison. In a sense he had never known any other since the day he had first discovered that his mother was deceiving him with a pathetic and kindly lie. It didn't seem odd to him that Harrison who, more than anyone, he could call a friend, should be prepared to kill him professionally. He would have done the same to Harrison. Sir John could have fifty murders on his hands without forfeiting any respect. They were all advocates of the devil. But Valda had disrupted the pattern from the outside. He, Grimster, had succumbed to a sentiment which no man who had forfeited his soul should have allowed a moment's life. He had fallen in love, known it to be good and right and perhaps sensed that in some doom-marked way it was never going to be complete for him. But no matter that, the death of Valda had, because of his love for her, put him outside any professional category and had made him an outcast and a renegade. He was a professional man no longer. He was simply John Grimster free to indulge himself for the first time in a simple human desire, virtuous to him, because he did not care what self-sacrifice it might demand. He was going to kill Sir John and, after that killing, he was going to live for so long as his own strength and intelligence could sustain him, and—because there was no death wish in him—he saw no reason why his time should not be long and his going when it came a natural one.

He finished his drink and his cigar, went into his bedroom and undressed. Later, in pyjamas and a dressing-gown he went along to Lily's suite. The door was unlocked and in the darkness of the sitting-room he saw the edge of light from under her bedroom door. He knew she would be waiting for him. Neither of them needed the frankness of words to be understood. She had given herself to him, though she could never admit it to herself, to resolve a situation, to make sure that she should inherit her portion from Dilling. But lying in there now he knew that she was well past the point where she needed to make any pretence that she loved him. She *knew* she loved him. For her it had to be like that in order that the slow, rich ease and comfort of her body and mind should not be ruffled. For himself he had to act the part of one who not only received but, too, gave love. The role, because of his new freedom, was an easy one. His body and senses, since she was a desirable woman, needed no forced spur and any words of love he used to her were less lies than a return of thanks for a liberation she had promoted.

When he opened the bedroom door she was sitting up in bed, reading. She dropped the book to the floor and held out her arms to him and said eagerly and without a trace of embarrassment, "Johnny, darling. . . ." She was wearing the green nightdress with black velvet ribbons at cuffs and neck which Mrs. Harroway had bought for her at Florence on her birthday.

The next morning Cranston drove them to Exeter and they picked up the hired car. Grimster drove off with Lily. She was excited and in a good humour. Movement, the sense of doing something, and the fast growth of her feeling for Johnny made her happy. Surely only out of love could a woman have done

175

what she had done? She had risked everything, a rebuff, and possible failure to break Harry's hold on her which, she saw now, was less loving than commanding, often overbearing and selfish. Thank God there was nothing of that in Johnny's love. Except at times like in bed, he was almost shy . . . no, reserved . . . but always loving and courteous. A real gentleman—not like Harry . . . there had been a kind of commonness in Harry; crude almost at times, particularly in making love. And fancy doing that about that Friday! That was something that had come slowly to her; but happily she had caught on to it, and happier still there had been Johnny there with all his love for her, so that, not for one moment, did it have to be . . . well, sort of grasping and selfish to have taken the first step. After all it was her love for Johnny which had shown her the way. . . .

Grimster drove to Taunton and parked the hired car in a garage he knew well. Explaining to Lily that what they were doing was a simple matter of precaution which by now she must realise was a wise one because the Department wanted no risks taken over the Dilling affair, they walked, carrying their cases, to another garage where—by telephone while in London—he had ordered another self-drive car. He had no qualms about this. Sir John he knew would naturally take the simple step of putting a tail on him but he was pretty sure that the tail would begin to operate from the Randolph Hotel at Oxford. But they were not going to the Randolph Hotel at Oxford. From London, too, he had booked a room at the Antrobus Arms at Amesbury which was some thirty miles south of the cottage which Dilling had rented for Lily. Sir John, when he learned that their trail had been lost, would approve. He, Grimster, would only be taking a precaution which any first-class operator would take. If Sir John wanted him followed, then so would Harrison's people. To shake off one was to shake off the other. However, to keep Sir John in a good mood, he stopped at a town en route and posted to him a personal letter which he had written the night before. The letter simply said—

Security reasons, going into the blue. Will report within forty-eight hours. J.G.

(When Sir John received it the next morning, together with the report that Grimster and Miss Stevens had not checked in at the Randolph Hotel, he was not surprised. It was exactly what he had expected. He knew, too, that it would be no good putting a man to watch the Dilling cottage. Although Miss Stevens was going to take Grimster over the route from the cottage which she and Dilling had followed he knew that Grimster would make her begin the retracing at some point well beyond the cottage.)

That night, late, love made, Lily lying in the crook of his left arm, Grimster said, "Will it help you if you drive the car tomorrow?"

"I suppose it might. But I remember most of it pretty clearly, Johnny. I should have thought you'd have asked me about it before."

"No. I want it to come fresh to you as we go along. That way you'll be reminded of things Harry said and did."

"He didn't do anything, not until the end—when he left me."

"How often did you stop?"

"Once, for lunch, that's all. Oh, and for petrol in the afternoon. And then again a bit later."

"Where did you have lunch?"

"At a place in Aylesbury."

"Sure?"

"Yes. We'd been there before."

"No stop before then?"

"No."

"What did Harry take with him from the cottage. Anything?"

"Yes. A small spade, and a brief case thing."

"What kind of brief case?"

"Well . . . it was one of those, you know, slim jobs."

"Leather?"

"No. Sort of lightweight metal."

"You'd seen it before?"

177

"Once or twice. He'd bring it down from London with him."

"What was in it?"

"Search me."

"You never tried to take a look?"

She was silent in the darkness for a moment and then her body stirred against his as she gave a small, guilty laugh. "Well, I did once. But it was locked."

"He didn't bring it back with him?"

"No. He got out with it and the spade, but he only brought the spade back. Not far from home we stopped and he got out and threw the spade into a pond."

"Didn't he give you any explanation of all this?"

"No."

"Didn't you think that odd?"

"From Harry?" she laughed. "No—but he did say something about people being able to tell where you'd been digging from the earth on a spade. But I think it was a kind of joke." She broke off.

He said, "Harry took you pretty much for granted, didn't he, Lily. Why'd you ever let him?"

"I don't know. . . . Because he was good to me. I wasn't really grown-up. He made me see that there were a lot of things in life besides living in a small town and serving behind a counter. . . ." She was silent for a moment and then went on, "I was lazy, too, I suppose. There wouldn't have been any point in standing up against him because he wanted to do so much for me." She moved closer to him and said, "Johnny, you do really love me, don't you? Oh, I know it all began in a funny way with that ring and all and this business of Harry's— but everything has to begin some way, hasn't it?"

Knowing what she wanted, he held her close to him and said, "You know I love you. People can't choose how they come together and meet and fall in love. No matter how it is, you just have to be glad about it."

He felt the physical stir of pleasure through her body and the thought went through his mind that if you keep on telling

178

yourself something long enough you can almost make it become true . . . could make it come true if you were like Lily.

Out of the darkness, her cheek against his warm shoulder, she said suddenly, "Have you got a lot of money, Johnny?"

"Enough. I'm not rich, though."

"Would it matter if I was? I mean, I might get pots from Harry's stuff, mightn't I?"

He laughed and said, "You might. But it's got to happen first. And anyway it wouldn't make any difference. Now come on, it's time you went off to sleep. We've a big day ahead tomorrow."

But he was asleep long before she was. She lay in the darkness and knew that she had been lucky. Perhaps she was going to be that kind. Always falling on her feet. First there had been Harry and now Johnny. Not that you could compare the two. There was a world of difference. There was no feeling ever that Johnny was using her like Harry had sometimes. He was always kind and considerate, made her feel good, a person, and she could tell from the first time they had slept together that it wasn't just her body. He liked her and wanted her for her real self. In a way it was no surprise. A man needed a woman to love as much as a woman needed a man, and ever since he had lost Valda he must, even if he hadn't really known it, have been looking for someone else, just as she had. In that way they were both the same, both looking for and wanting love. Some time, she just knew it, he would tell her all about Valda. She wouldn't have to ask him. He would tell her when he was ready and from that moment on there would be no more sadness in him, no real feeling about Valda at all, just as there was no real feeling in her now for Harry. Memories, yes. But no feeling. Still she had to admit that Harry had been good to her, wanting her to have everything. . . . If she really did get all this money . . . she'd have to be careful at first, having more than Johnny. Men could be funny about that. . . . Like her father who had played up hell when her mother had got a job while he was away. . . .

179

She lay there, planning a future without a flaw in it. There wasn't any other kind of future she could conceive at that moment.

*   *   *   *

The next morning they drove to Aylesbury and had lunch there. When Lily and Harry had made this trip it was February and the light closed in much earlier. From Aylesbury, with Lily driving now, they went north-east towards Leighton Buzzard. She remembered clearly the name of the town, but from Leighton Buzzard onwards she could remember no names.

She said, "There was another place we went on to and then it wasn't far from there. I can't remember the name, but I'll recognise it when I see the signposts in Leighton Buzzard. It wasn't very far from Leighton Buzzard—six or eight miles."

Grimster didn't try to force anything from her. Her memory was good.

He asked, "What time was it when you finally got to wherever it was you went?"

"Oh, it was dark, some time between six and seven. I know just outside Leighton Buzzard Harry made me draw the car up and we just sat there for an hour, maybe more. I know it got very cold in the car so we put the engine on so we could have the heater."

In Leighton Buzzard—it was now about half past three—she picked the name from the town approach signpost at once.

"That's it. That's where we went. Woburn."

As she swung the car off to the left heading north for Woburn, Grimster said, "I'm surprised you didn't remember that name."

"Why, is there something special about it?"

He smiled and said, "You'll see. But forget about it now."

Lily said, "If there was anything special about it, it was too dark to see."

"How far from Woburn did you go?"

"Oh, not far. A mile, perhaps two. I'm pretty sure I can remember the road and we stopped by a cottage place. That had a funny name, too. I'll know it when I see it."

Woburn. That the name meant nothing to Lily really did surprise Grimster. Just outside the town was Woburn Abbey and the extensive estate, parklands and lakes which belonged to the Duke of Bedford, who had developed the whole complex and thrown it open to the public and made it a famous tourist attraction. Surprised or not, he was content to let her drive and see where she would take him. But as she drove, he remembered that Pringle had said that he had once worked for a fencing and road contractor in Bletchley, and Bletchley was only a few miles west of Woburn over the border of Bedfordshire and in Buckinghamshire. And Dilling had been caught for drunken driving in these parts. Grimster sat there, his mind racing ahead. He did what he had so often done before on other cases. Put himself in the place of some other man, trying to make himself think the way that man would have thought with his background, his friends, and his particular characteristics. Already he had a feeling about what he might find. He knew Dilling now. He felt that he knew why Pringle would have needed no more than the sketch map. . . .

They came into Woburn at a crossroads and Lily went over them and within a few moments they were following the public road that ran right through the heart of the Woburn estates.

Grimster said, "You're sure this was the way?"

She nodded. "I remember those gates. Just along here, too, there was sort of water on the left. A kind of lake. I remember the moon shining on it, or maybe it was stars."

Her face was set, eyes all for the road which now held quite a few cars moving along to visit the Abbey. But when they came to the right-hand turn for the Abbey, Lily kept straight on. She said, "I remember those notices now but we kept straight on. What is all that abbey business? Some kind of show place?"

"Something like that."

They climbed up a gentle slope and a few hundred yards farther on the road held a left-hand fork. Cars ahead of them were turning down it. Lily swung left and followed in the evenly strung out queue. A notice said, *Woburn. Wild Animal Kingdom.*

The road curved back to the right and they began to run along a level plateau. To their left the ground fell away from a long run of tall netting which marked the boundary of the Wild Animal Kingdom park. Below Grimster saw the slow movement of cars as they crawled through the various animal enclosures. Then trees blocked his view and Lily without excitement said, "This is it. That sort of lodge house there. That's where we stopped. Just beyond it."

Ahead of them and on the right of the road was a low white-painted gatehouse. As they approached Grimster saw a notice board on the grass. It read—Trusseler's Lodge.

Lily said, "What do you want me to do?"

"Just carry straight on."

Farther along the road a turning to the left marked the entry down to the Wild Animal Kingdom, but Grimster told Lily to carry straight on.

She asked no questions. Whatever he wanted her to do, she would do. She was helping him. All her pleasure lay in doing whatever he said. After a while they hit a larger public road and then, from their map, Grimster directed her back to Woburn by a northern loop of roads.

Half an hour later they were booked into a room at the Bedford Arms in Woburn. Grimster left Lily to have a bath and change for dinner while he went down to the bar. Passing through the hallway he picked up a few brochures which gave details of the various attractions and features of Woburn Abbey and the Wild Animal Kingdom. By the time he had finished his first large brandy he knew conclusively why Pringle would only have needed the sketch map from the firecrest ring to locate where Dilling had buried his brief case, and he knew why Dilling had written *Que será, será* at the head of the map and, far more important, why he had drawn the arched worm-like creature at the bottom. He knew, too, that Dilling's burial of his brief case must have been a far simpler matter than the uncovering of it would be.

182

THE NEXT DAY Grimster told Lily that he had to go off for the morning by himself.

"I can't explain to you yet why I don't want you with me, but when I come back I will. All you need know, as you've probably guessed, is that it's to do with Harry's brief case. I think I can promise you that there's more than a fair chance we're going to get it."

Lily was quite content. He was acting in a way like Harry had. If there was anything she should know she would be told it in his own time. That seemed reasonable to her. After all—quite apart from their private relationship—he was still a government official with his work to do, and you didn't go poking your nose into a man's working life. She would be quite happy reading a magazine or book in the hotel lounge, drifting through the morning to coffee time; or maybe she could go out and get her hair done. But when she suggested this he said it would be better if she kept to the hotel.

Grimster drove the car to the Abbey park and on to the Wild Animal Kingdom. He was early and there were not too many cars making the tour through the various enclosures where the animals roamed free, antelopes, eland and waterbuck, white rhinoceros, and then through the heavily wired cheetah range, the wide spread of lion country and then the forest of monkeys. Notices warned against opening car windows, though—as in all similar reserves—the cars were free to stop so that people could watch the movement of the animals. If you had trouble and the car broke down you sounded your horn and waited for the white hunter patrol to come to your assistance. He made the round trip twice and then drove out on to the near-by M1 road and went down to Luton to do some shopping. Coming back through the park he turned off the public road down to the Abbey itself where he had a cup of coffee in the Flying Duchess cafeteria, which was named after the mother of the present Duke of Bedford. Then he went back to the entrance to the Wild Animal Kingdom and called at the manager's office and, from the selection in his wallet, produced a press card. He explained that he was from a London newspaper and wanted some information for the basis of a feature which his editor was thinking of running. He was given all the information he needed, said that he would let them know when the feature was due to appear, and then made a third tour of the Kingdom before going back to the hotel. Three times now he had passed within twenty yards of the spot where Dilling's brief case was buried. To have had it unearthed officially would have been easy. All that would have been needed was an authorisation from Sir John and a phone call to the Abbey people. But the last thing he wanted was any official move. He had to get the case by himself and without anyone's knowledge.

After lunch, he told Lily that Dilling's case was buried in the lion enclosure of the Wild Animal Kingdom and that official arrangements were being made for its recovery.

She said, "You mean you found that out just by me bringing you here?"

"Chiefly—but we did have some other information you didn't know about. The moment you showed me where Dilling had to stop the car—then everything fitted."

"Clever stuff?" She smiled at him.

"Well, not really. When the two things came together it was obvious. All you have to do now is sit tight here. We should have it by tomorrow and then—if the stuff is as valuable as Harry claimed—it'll just be a case of making a price with the Department. That may take some time, of course, because they'll have to check it thoroughly."

She came over and sat on the arm of his chair. "So I'm going to be a rich woman?"

"It looks like it." He put his hand on her knee and squeezed it.

She said quietly, "Will you mind me being rich?"

With a truth which she could never understand, he said, "It won't make any difference to me. But for the moment, for your sake, I don't think we should look too far ahead."

She laughed. "Cautious Johnny. I don't care what you say. I am looking ahead—and as far as I can see you're there with me. What do you think of that?"

He pulled her off the arm of the chair into his lap, putting his arms around her and kissing the soft underside of her chin. Then he said, "If I didn't have to go out and arrange things right now, I'd show you."

And, while she held him and kissed him, her hand slipping over the breast of his shirt under his jacket, there was no self-disgust in him at the part he was playing. Her happiness was genuine, his only concern was to protect her and make sure that she got what belonged to her. When he left her, and if she ever learned something of the truth, she would merely switch from the luxury of happiness to the luxury of sadness and some grief. Her emotions would be disturbed but not for so long that any real discomfort would be caused. For a while she would enjoy the new role and then facilely slip back into being Lily. At the moment she was playing her part with a warm emotional disregard for truth. What she wanted to be true, she could make true simply by wishing it. She was a child. One day, almost inevitably, she really would fall in love and know its real anguishes and delights. . . . He could almost wish that it would never happen because he felt that her deepest happiness perhaps would always spring from make-believe. Although he was free to love now, he didn't love her, could never grow to love her, but there were moments when, as she gave herself to him and he to her, he knew a need for her, a hunger briefly stilled while he waited to meet Sir John. When darkness and bed closed about them he moved into the warmth and ample passion and comfort she offered so that for a while all thought was washed from him and there was no sensation beyond the rich elemental fusing of their flesh. As he held her now, the need for it rose in him, no matter that there were things he should do in preparation for the night, and he took her and moved her to the bed and they made love, Lily laughing and teasing him at first and then suddenly as hungry and impatient as he.

*   *   *   *

He sat in his parked car. Two hundred yards down the road was Trusseler's Lodge. Along the road to his left a steady stream of visitors' cars passed on their way to the Wild Animal Kingdom. On the far side of the road across a strip of grass about fifteen yards wide ran the tall enclosure netting that formed the north-south boundary of the lion country. He took the small sketch map which had been in the firecrest ring from his pocket and flicked his lighter to it, watched it burn almost to his fingertips and then dropped it into the ashtray. Dilling had loved secrets, but he had always left signs for the properly informed to read, or for the diligent to discover. For Pringle there would have been a direct route—one look at the map would have been enough. For himself, the map had held no clear meaning until he had ousted Dilling from Lily's mind and she had been able to lead him to their stopping spot beyond the lodge. But once there, once in this park, once the names Woburn Abbey and Bedford were forced on him everywhere he turned, then the thing for him, too, had become simple. *Che Sarà Sarà* was the family motto of the Bedfords. In Woburn one couldn't walk the length of a street without seeing it on the Bedford coat of arms. What will be will be. That would have identified the location at once to Pringle, and to pinpoint it there was the blunt-headed arched worm at the bottom of the map which he, Grimster, now knew was the zodiacal sign, clumsily done, for Leo the lion. Pringle would have had no trouble with it and neither had he when Lily brought him here. Beyond the boundary fence he could look from the car down an oak-studded sandy slope to the twisting road that wound through the lion enclosure and pick out the big loop that ran down and around the flanks of a small hill, broken on its westerly side by a large sandpit—the cross-hatched portion on Dilling's map. Standing on its crest were two thorn trees set close together and lower down the slope two more thorn trees almost side by side. North of the top pair of thorns, marking the point of an equilateral triangle, whose base was the thirty-inch distance between the thorns, was the spot where the brief case was buried, probably a couple of feet down in the sandy ground. He knew, too, from questions asked in the manager's office, that the Wild Animal Kingdom had only been opened in the May of this year. In February when Dilling had come to do his burying the high boundary wiring had not been completed and there were no lions in the enclosure. They had been put in just two weeks before the May opening.

Pringle must have worked here on the fencing and road making with his firm and at some time or other he must have brought Dilling along to see the work. They both had a keen interest in animals. Dilling must have made a note of the spot in the lion enclosure where he could bury his brief case. All he had had to do was to come at night with the workmen gone and no guards yet appointed for duty. For Dilling, from where he, Grimster, sat now in the car it had been no more than a two-hundred-yard walk down the slope, over a couple of roads and up to the thorns with nothing to bar his way. Now it was a different matter. There was the outer fence of strong two-inch wire mesh, twelve feet high and with an inwards overhang in addition of two feet six inches. Inside this and about eight feet away was another fence of the same wire about four feet high and topped with a strand of barbed wire, and beyond the fences were the lions, some stretched out lazily in the sun now as the cars crawled their way around, some stalking restlessly across the slopes and through the trees, some moving between the cars on the road with a heavy, padding indifference to the caged creatures moving around their domain. There must have been a small point of pleasure in Dilling that he should hide his treasure among the lions, for his own zodiac sign was that of Leo.

Although the problem of entry was a difficult one, it was not impossible. Each night, after the car visitors had gone, all the lions and lionesses were marshalled and driven by the white hunters in their Land-Rovers to their night pens and shut up. After dark the enclosure was clear of lions, but there was a two- or three-hourly inspection of the perimeter wire from the outside by guards who carried twelve-bore shotguns and .375 Magnum rifles.

Grimster meant to go in that night. There would be no moon, but he needed no light. This was the fourth time he had surveyed the area and every detail was clear in his mind, the slopes and breaks in the ground, the position of each tree, bush and bracken clump between him and the two thorns at the crest of the sandpit hill.

He drove away, out of the park, and found a quiet country lane bordering a patch of heathland. He parked the car on the edge of the heath and took out the purchases he had made in Luton that morning, a hundred yards of thin, strong nylon rope, a tape measure, a length of thick but malleable wire, and a keen-bladed knife. Left in the car was a small pointed trenching spade and a pair of wire clippers. He opened out the coil of rope and began to cut and shape it. As he worked, intent, and in solitude except for the call of birds and the occasional movement of a rabbit in the gorse, he remembered the last time he had done the same thing. It had been at Wellington with Harrison, their knots and loops finally shaped, after much error, to form a long rope ladder they needed to drop over the edge of a local quarry so that they could reach the nest of a kestrel which held young. Although Harrison, even in those days, was a big, heavy boy he had insisted on going down the ladder and Grimster could remember now his friend's language when he had discovered that they had left their attempt too late and the young birds had flown. The whole of Harrison's school life he had had a passion to catch a young kestrel and train it, and all his life, too, he had had a passion for the forbidden and the dangerous . . . mixed-up, self-sufficient Harrison who, even in those days, put a strict limit on their friendship.

The work took him two hours and when he had finished he climbed thirty feet up one of the heath pines and fastened one end of the ladder to a branch so that he could come down it, testing every link, knot and strand. He had long ago learnt the necessity for risking nothing to chance which could be tested in advance. (But no man can live by himself, be sufficient for himself; no matter what his care and caution. No matter how wide-ranging he may question and probe there is always the possible error which comes at the point of contact with other people. Grimster had gone over the ground for the mission he meant to undertake that night, gone over it carefully, lived through it in his imagination, knew in advance every movement he intended to make. He had observed and questioned too. But there is always the one question to which an incomplete answer is given, often in innocence because the answerer has no conception of the real intent behind the inquiry. It was true that each evening the lions were marshalled and driven into their night pens and shelters. It was being done while Grimster and Lily took their coffee in the lounge after dinner at the hotel. But to every routine there is an exception. When a lioness came into her season and the possessiveness of her mate was at its peak, then that lion was never shut up in the night pens because it fought and battled with other lions who came near the lioness. The lion was left out at night to be on its own. And as night darkened the slopes of the lion enclosure there was that night one lion left out. It lay under a tree on the far side of the enclosure, beyond the sandpit hill with its thorns, and close to the row of night pens that were strung out along one of the inner boundary fences.)

At ten o'clock Grimster left the hotel. Under his jacket he wore a dark sweater. He left Lily sitting in the hotel lounge.

He had told her that he had to go out to meet someone in connection with the recovery of the brief case. She was not to wait up for him. He might be very late back.

Lily sat in the lounge reading a book, and debating with herself whether she should order a second liqueur before going to bed. In the end she decided to indulge herself. She felt she had every reason to be good to herself. She had come a long way from the shop counter at Uckfield. That person had been a raw provincial girl. Now she was a woman, experienced, travelled and excitingly involved in an affair which she was sure would have made the eyes of the other people in the lounge pop if they could have known. She had grown up, she had changed. She was a person and life was being good to her and, she had no doubt, would be better still in the future. Harry had started it, and for that she would always have gratitude. But not much else now. Johnny had taken Harry's place and it was without question, she told herself, a change for the better. Where Harry could be unpredictable and unreasonable, Johnny was straightforward and considerate. His body was different too, no flabbiness anywhere. Harry's had been soft, almost womanly, but Johnny's flesh and muscles were hard and firm. . . . She closed her eyes for a moment, fingering her glass of Grand Marnier, thinking of Johnny's body, thinking of their love-making, and then inwardly scolded herself for doing so. Golly, anyone would think she was only interested in that. No, it was Johnny as a man, his character and his niceness, gentleness, and understanding that appealed to her. Unlike Harry, he was a gentleman too. Anyone could see that. Just as you could see that Mrs. Harroway was a lady. No doubt soon he would tell her all about his family, school, university and all that. . . . There was plenty of time. No need to rush things. No need to force him with questions. He wasn't the kind of man to do that to. All in good time. It was something nice to look forward to. She pictured him telling her about Valda . . . paused for a moment to test whether there was any jealousy in her and found none. She would listen, and not have to put on the right face or think of the right things to say. They would come naturally because she loved Johnny and understood him. Really did. No matter how it had all begun with all that hypnotism nonsense, and her not knowing, when she'd guessed what the block was, how to put it into words but having to use her common-sense and plan for the right moment, no matter about that even if it did seem that she'd been a bit fast . . . love had to start somewhere. And anyway, thinking back, she was certain that it had started really when she had first seen him, neat and trim and strong looking, and not a wrinkle on him anywhere like he'd got something about him that wouldn't let dust or dirt settle. Of course, when she got the money from Harry's whatever it was, she'd have to be careful. A man had his pride. He was well off, but she would have more . . . thousands. She'd have to be careful about that. Perhaps he'd like to leave the government service . . . perhaps there was something he secretly longed to do—most men had something. She could set him up in a farm or something. She day-dreamed swiftly of a farm where the sun shone all summer, and of a London flat for when they got bored and wanted a change. Gosh, she was lucky. All the way from Uckfield and those messy, busy-handed boys in cars. That kind of life hadn't been meant for her, that was clear . . . far back she could feel the pull of a fine ancestry. She was coming back to what had always been . . . well, sort of her inheritance, her destiny.

She lit a cigarette, relaxed, and took a sip of the Grand Marnier. Take that, for instance. She knew now how to select and order things. Names which not long ago had meant nothing to her. Grand Marnier, Cointreau, Drambuie, and white wine with fish, red with meat, *sole bonne femme* and *tournedos Rossini*. Tomorrow, she thought, she'd go out and give herself a treat, spend a little something in advance, buy the biggest bottle she could find of Jean Patou's *Joy*. Why not? She was full of joy. Being here with Johnny. Going always to be with Johnny. She closed her eyes as she felt her body contract inwardly with desire for him.

191

*   *   *   *

The night sky had clouded over. The cattle and deer grid at the park gates rattled briefly under the car tyres as he passed. It was not possible to close the parklands off at night because the public road ran right through the heart of them. He drove up the long slope of the road to the crossroads at the top. He went over them, ignoring the left-hand turning which curved away to the plateau above the lion enclosure, and drove on for two hundred yards, then stopped, parking the car just off the road on grass below a clump of trees. He switched the lights off and lit a cigarette. The headlights of a few passing cars picked him out now and then. He had plenty of time. He wanted the traffic to die down before he moved. His car would cause no curiosity. Anyone seeing it would imagine that it held some courting couple. What he had to do would take less than an hour from the moment he left the car. There was no excitement in him. The project was planned and checked. Now he just had to go through the motions. Except in bed with Lily excitement had become a stranger to him. There was no excitement even in the thought that he was going to thwart Sir John first and then kill him. All he was concerned with was the correcting of a balance which had been disturbed. He had loved Valda and Sir John had had her killed. Maybe, in Sir John's place, he would have done the same thing. But that made no difference. The balance had to be corrected. He was going to kill Sir John not to ease any anguish or loss he had suffered but because he had taken Valda's life and because her life was the only one in the whole world whose continuance he would, if the choice had ever been pressed upon him, have bargained for with the loss of his own. There had been earlier moments when he had hated Sir John, felt the warmth in him at the promise of revenge. But now he felt nothing. The man just had to be killed to make the scales swing even again. He had no ethics, no morals. He had killed, himself, before. He had done and seen things done in his professional life which few men would ever have believed possible. That Dilling had mistrusted Sir John and Coppelstone had been entirely justified. That the Department should cheat and kill for any reason deemed good by Sir John and his superiors had never worried him and gave him no worry now. The system had been created long ago and he accepted it, accepted it still, but had decided that he could work for it no longer. Ordinarily he would have accepted, too, the cheating and killing of Lily. It would have meant nothing to him. But Lily was lucky. The dice had fallen in her favour because it was through her that he had come to know the truth about Valda's death. It was a debt which he had to honour before he could deal with Sir John.

He looked at his watch. It was eleven. He stubbed out his cigarette and got out of the car, leaving his jacket behind him. In the darkness he felt the quick wind of a passing bat, swooping low under the trees, touch his cheek. He put the tape measure and the wire cutters in his trouser pocket. He wrapped the rope ladder around the digging spade and the length of wire, and tucked the bundle under his arm. Then he crossed the road to the open parkland on the other side and went across the short cattle-bitten grass, moving slowly, every sense awake now, towards the road three hundred yards ahead of him, the road that ran towards Trusseler's Lodge along the top side of the lion country enclosure. On this side of the road, a few yards back in the grass, was a large oak tree, standing a little short of the place where the boundary fence angled away sharply downhill from the roadside stretch. The bulk of the tree, black against the paler hue of the night sky now that his eyes had become accustomed to the darkness, stood out clearly. He moved into its shelter and lay down behind the great trunk so that he could watch the road running back along the boundary fence towards the lodge. Twenty minutes later a Land-Rover, headlights dipped, came down the road past the lodge. It moved slowly and from it a torchlight beam flicked jerkily up and down the high boundary fencing. It passed the oak tree and he saw it turn on to the rough ground at the angle of the fencing and move downhill. A few minutes later it came back and passed his tree, moving up to the gate at the lodge and then disappearing into the woods beyond. There might or might not be another check that night. He had, anyway, all the time he wanted on his hands.

He stood up, lifted his bundle, flexed his shoulders, stiff from lying motionless, and heard high above the clouds the sound of a passing plane. Calmly, but carefully, alert for any sound or sign of movement, he moved across the road to the point where the fence angled downhill. He moved along it, parallel with the road for a hundred yards and then stopped. Inside the two fences, at the top of the slope, stood another oak tree which he had already marked as the place to cross the fences.

He unrolled the rope ladder and tied the small trenching spade to one end. He fixed the other end to the bottom part of the high fence. Looping the slack of the ladder in his left hand so that it would run out smoothly, he threw the spade-weighted end up and over the top of the fence. It snaked down to the ground on the far side, a few feet away from the inner side of the fence because of the overhang portion at the top. He reached through with his length of hooked wire and drew the free ladder end towards him. In a few seconds he had lashed it firmly to the mesh with a couple of lengths of rope, so that as he climbed his weight would not draw the far side of the ladder back over the fence.

He went up the ladder, twisted himself over the top and found the rope rungs. From half-way down the ladder he dropped free to the ground. For a moment he remained crouching where he had dropped. From somewhere in the distance some animal called, a half-beast half-bird sound. Far away on the main road a car's headlights coming up the hill stroked the dark sky with stiff antennae. He reached out and untied the spade from the end of the rope ladder.

The inner fence provided no difficulty. He cut away the length of barbed wire between two supporting posts and half-rolled, half-vaulted himself over, the spade in his hand, and

194

then moved quickly into the cover of the big oak. Starlight shone briefly on the surface of a rainwater pool in a hollow to his left. Eyes now long accustomed to the darkness of the night, he saw the road, not so long ago heavy with tourist traffic, run away like a pale, grey snake and then loop back and down to curve around the bottom of the sandpit hill. Pressed close against the side of the oak, his nostrils were suddenly full of a sour animal smell and he guessed that the lions used it as a rubbing post. Months ago, he thought, Dilling could have stood here, pressed against this very tree, checking that there were no late night workers about, holding his case, pleased with himself and with all the arcana he was to wrap around his movements, relishing in advance, he was sure, the sex-sated hypnotism of Lily, maybe even at that moment wearing the firecrest ring with its hidden map—never guessing that he had less than a day to live. *Que será, será.*

He moved away from the cover of the oak. Far to his right, back along the road, was the entry gate with its shingle-roofed guard house where the road passed from the cheetah enclosure into the lion country enclosure. If there was a guard there at night he had nothing to fear from him for the guard house was out of sight from behind the crest of the sandhill where the two thorns stood. Tomorrow the tourist cars would come in their hundreds, passing through the main, electrically controlled gates, emblazoned with their two great yellow lions . . . and tomorrow would be the beginning of his freedom from obligation to Lily. . . . Sir John would be waiting for him, and he knew that every step he took towards the man would be dangerous because Sir John knew him and understood him, could read the fast flick of a small signal and was as full of guileful intuition as himself.

He crossed the lower road and, keeping in the lee of the sandpit knoll, moved up to the two thorns. They were thirty inches apart and on that base line Dilling, who would have been precise, had constructed an equilateral triangle with the burial spot of the brief case as the apex.

The ground under the thorns was sandy with a thin covering of grass. Grimster took out his tape measure length and, holding one end against the base of the easterly thorn, drew a large thirty-inch arc around to the north, scoring the dry sand and thin grass with the end of his thumb. He then repeated the process from the westerly thorn. Where the two arcs intercepted one another he drove the spade in lightly.

He stood up and for a while was still, a shadow in the shadow of the thorns, listening. Then he began to dig, going down on his knees to lessen his silhouette, sliding the loose soft sand away down the slope. The digging was easy, there were no stones or obstructions. Two feet down, his spade struck the edge of the brief case. He dropped the spade and cleared the remaining sand away with his hands.

As he stood up, holding the brief case, a lion in one of the night pens on the far side of the enclosure coughed and roared and was briefly answered by another. Leaving the spade where it was, he made his way down the slope to the road, the brief case under his arm. He crossed the road and went up the bracken slope, under the oaks and then out on to the top road. The main fence was now only fifty yards away. The tall mass of the large oak by the inner fence was black and bulky against a sky whose clouds were thinning. Tomorrow the spade, the hole in the ground, and the rope ladder which he meant to leave in place would be found and a mystery would be born. He smiled to himself at the thought of the publicity which the noble duke would wring from that . . . the car queues would grow and the road below the sandpit hill would be blocked, the lions ousted from their prominence in the public eye as the site of the mysterious digging was pointed out.

He was almost at the large oak when a man stepped out from behind it and moved down the slope, stopping a few yards from him. The man stood, facing him, large and still, ponderous in the night whose gloom was not thick enough to mar recognition, not dark enough to kill the starlight gleam on the gun he held in his hand. It was Harrison. Across four yards of grass and bracken, the two men faced one another and Harrison, his voice low and pleasant, said, "Johnny. Clever Johnny. But are you going to be a wise Johnny?"

Grimster made the beginning of a move to drop the case from under his arm to the grip of one hand.

Harrison stopped him with a gesture of the gun. "Keep it under your arm. I want nothing thrown at me this time."

Grimster said easily, "You must have been in need of exercise to come in after me."

"No. But where Johnny goes in he doesn't necessarily come out. This time, no chances taken—and only one given."

"One?"

"Yes, for old times' sake. Just drop the case to the ground and then walk back down the hill and stay there for a few minutes until I'm gone."

"And if I don't?"

"Then I'll have to shoot you and take it. Pity because there's no real need for your death. Just let the case drop and walk away, Johnny."

"How did you get here? Pringle?"

"Don't change the subject, Johnny. Time is not on your side. But I wouldn't have you die curious. That's a bad way for our kind to go." Harrison stirred a little, big shoulders moving inside his jacket. "Pringle. Yes. He had an idea it might be somewhere around here. He worked here. Dilling was interested in the project. Pringle showed him round more than once. You want to hear more?"

"No." It would only be routine detail. Simple, regulation stuff. A willing barman, chambermaid or waiter in every hotel for twenty miles around given a photograph of himself and Lily and a telephone number to ring if either turned up, and then a hundred pounds' bonus added to the retainer already paid. There wasn't a hotel without someone on the staff who couldn't be used. It was a chance which had passed through his mind, but a chance he had had to take. Now his chances were reduced to one simple action, drop the case and move back, but there was nothing in his body or his mind that made that acceptable yet.

"You've had long enough for reflection, Johnny. Drop it and move away—or you are finished." Harrison made a small, stiff gesture with his free hand down the hill.

Grimster let the case drop, but he stood over it.

"Move away," said Harrison.

"There's no need." Grimster touched the case with the toe of his shoe. "I was bringing it to you anyway. They killed Valda. I just wanted to get it first and keep it to help with the bargaining when I came over to you. That's why I didn't cover the chance you might pick us up. Why I stayed right here in Woburn, rather than fifty miles away. All I needed was ¨ust enough leeway to get out of here with the case and—"

"Johnny!" The interruption was little more than a whisper. "Stop talking. Nothing's going to help. We don't want you. You're too hot. But you can walk away and live . . . maybe long enough to get Sir John. Move, Johnny Now."

Only on the last word did his voice rise, and Grimster knew there was little more time left. He had himself killed a man after a given ultimatum. You stood there with the gun and you allowed the grace of a few verbal twists and turns, perhaps out of a feeling that a man should be given some moments of composure before going, and then the point was reached where you knew the shot would have to be fired and in the mind you began to count down from twenty, from ten, from five, from whatever number the cold charity in your heart dictated, and he knew that Harrison was doing that now, and that Harrison would neither be generous nor unduly grudging. Then, as all this flashed through his mind, he saw beyond Harrison, on a path in the brackened slope, the slow movement of a long shape, tawniness turned grey under the night's pale light, blackness shadowing muscled forelegs and mane, the big head held low, the great body, pressing earthwards, moving noiselessly, each forward placing of forepaw and haunch pad a stalking ritual long ordained before killing, always to be observed until the instant of fearful launching through the air.

Keeping his voice low but letting the intenseness stream out with it, praying that Harrison's silent counting would not end, he said, "Dicky, for God's sake listen. Turn fast and be ready to fire—there's a lion twenty yards behind you."

Harrison's big body stirred and he laughed quietly. "It won't work, Johnny. It won't work. Not even though you call me Dicky which you haven't for—"

"Turn, you bloody fool!"

"No good, Johnny."

Harrison's gun hand came up, grey light on the cold steel, as from the pathway behind him the lion from slow stalking moved into a long leap, curving through the air, the great head thrown up and the long forelimbs reaching out with taloned paws. As the beast hit Harrison on the back he fired and then man and animal collapsed into a moving mass of changing shapes. One short, sharp scream of agony from Harrison was matched by the deep, rasping, reverberating roaring snarl from the lion. Loose sand and dead bracken swirled about and above them.

Grimster picked up the case, turned, and ran for the fence, ran from the nightmare behind him, ran knowing it could follow him, but not turning to see, intent only on the fences, waiting for the terror that might overtake him.

He rolled over the inner fence, hitting the ground hard. Fear drove him to the rope ladder and instinct, unrecorded by him, motivated his right arm as he slung the case high and clear over the tall fence, and then he began to scramble up the ladder. He dropped from the top of the fence to safety and, for a few seconds, sprawled face downwards on the ground and felt fear drain from him like a great pain dying. . . . He pulled himself up and looked back into the enclosure. He could see nothing. The space where they had stood close to the big oak was empty, there was no sound, nothing stirred in the bracken. Then on the top road, he saw a movement across its bare, pale surface. The lion, black against the road surface, moved diagonally along it, and its head was held high, neck muscles taut with the burden it dragged, its forelegs straddled wide to accommodate the dragging, limp body of its prey.

He turned away, searched for and found the case and then, as he bent to pick it up, was sick, the body and the mind's distress bowing him to the ground.

Fifteen minutes later, his hands on the car wheel still shaking though he fought to suppress his rebellious muscles, he pulled into a layby a few miles away. He switched off all the lights and reached for the glove compartment. He pulled out his brandy flask, tipped it to his mouth and held it there until he had emptied it. The brandy invaded his body, slowed his tremor and his breathing and smoothed away the worst of remaining horror until finally he sat, his mind cold and bare of all feeling, all imagination, except the fixed picture of Harrison, gun hand raised to kill him and the flying black form of the lion smashing down towards him.

*   *   *   *

He lay in bed, propped against the pillows. The curtains pulled back from the window showed him the slant of steady rain and he could hear the water sounds of the full gutters on the roof. Lily came from the bathroom in her dressing-gown, smiled across at him and flicked on the hotel radio for the news broadcast. She walked back across the room, her dressing-gown swinging apart slightly, her nudity normal before him now and, as he watched her dress, cup of coffee within reach, brush her hair and begin to make up her face, the abbreviated facts came over the radio . . . *an unknown, mutilated man . . . Woburn Wild Animal Kingdom.* Harrison, he thought, calmness melded to the deadness in him, who had fought him on the banks of the Blackwater, shot mallard on the college lake, was gone, and when his end was named with his name many women would remember that they had known him, and the link in the broken chain would be replaced by his employers, and that would be that. For a week or so the publicity and the mystery would

200

persist and then die away. Harrison was gone, but it could have been him. . . . One day his turn would come but for now, he knew with fatalistic certainty, the gods who loved violence were sparing him . . . made magnanimous, maybe even amused, at the small core of violence in him which must be expended. Nothing, the certainty was like a faith in him, could keep him from Sir John.

Lily came over and refilled his breakfast tea cup. "You were very late last night, darling."

"It took longer than we thought."

"Was everything all right?"

"Yes."

"You got it?"

He nodded.

She smiled, handed him his cup and then ran the tip of a finger down his nose. "Then there's no more trouble?"

"None."

She moved away, lighthearted, and he smiled at her blitheness. She made the world what she wanted it to be.

CHAPTER FOURTEEN

BEFORE LEAVING THE hotel he telephoned the Department. Sir John had gone down to Devon for his fishing holiday. Coppelstone was at High Grange. He asked for a message to be sent to Sir John through High Grange that he would be reporting as soon as possible with the Dilling papers.

He drove with Lily to London and dropped her at Mrs. Harroway's flat, saying he would be back in a couple of hours. It had amused him when she had said, "Then there's no more trouble." Just as she had with Dilling she accepted what Grimster told her. She had no real curiosity in men's affairs unless they showed they would welcome it. All the way down she had chatted about trivialities. In their hotel room the news broadcast had passed her by. Her ears were only tuned to what she wanted to hear, her eyes saw only what she wanted to see, and if awkwardness threatened her comfort then she found some way of ignoring or changing it.

He went to his flat and opened Dilling's case. He read the papers through and much of them and their attendant technical drawings meant little to him. But the broad selling outline which Dilling had synopsised at the front of the file was clear. Dilling had invented a new infantry weapon, based on a combined development of radar and the laser beam, which would make night firing as simple as day work and just as accurate. The weapon when swept across an arc at night could locate and register the existence of human and metal targets, lock on to them, follow them if they were moving and automatically establish range, elevation and direction within a matter of seconds. It was compact, easily handled by one man and required only a minimal skill from the operator. There was no doubt in him that the Department would buy. Lily would become rich, and with her wealth, he knew, would come a rapid development of a natural shrewdness which would more than protect her happiness and comfort.

He saw Mrs. Harroway alone after lunch. Lily had gone to her room to rest. Mrs. Harroway, tall, precise, was sitting in a red velvet chair having her coffee. She offered him a cup. He refused and put Dilling's sand-stained case on a table.

She eyed it as though she objected to its incongruity in the richly furnished room.

He said, "The contents of this case belonged to Dilling. He was going to sell them to the Department but they tried to get them without paying. You should lodge them with your bank before they close today. They're valuable. Lily's going to be rich, and she needs you on her side."

Mrs. Harroway nodded. She was a woman who did not have to be told too much. Experience and intuition spoke a silent language to her. She said, "With a little help at the beginning, she'll have no trouble. She tells me she loves you and that you love her."

"Neither is true."

"As I supposed. But you have felt some obligation?" She nodded at the case.

"Yes."

"Professional?"

"The opposite. The Department would have taken the papers, pretended they were useless and found a way of getting rid of Lily to protect their fraud. It is a normal routine where the opportunity offers."

"So my husband often told me. That was a long time ago when the world was just dirty around the edges, Mr. Grimster. Now it is grey-coloured throughout."

"I've got copies of the papers. I shall tell the Department you have the originals and that Lily is with you. You will have no trouble. Once an opportunity like this has passed they make no move to recover it."

"Won't this compromise your professional position?"

"It already has been compromised."

She smiled. "I won't ask what they did to you. It must have been personal and quite outrageous."

"For them it was a matter of routine."

"You would like to say goodbye to Lily?"

"I must."

Mrs. Harroway stood up. "I'll send her in. There's no need, as you know, to be positive with her. She flourishes on half-truths and was born with rose-coloured vision and the luck to go with it. It happens to very few." She paused at the door, considered him, and then went on, "May I ask you a personal question, Mr. Grimster?"

"If you wish."

"How many men have you killed in your life?"

He brushed a grain of sand from the lid of the brief case. "After the first one, the others don't count."

"You're not afraid of death?"

He smiled. "I would like to live a long time."

"You know what I would advise you to do?"

"Yes, but I'm afraid I shouldn't take your advice."

Mrs. Harroway gave a little shrug of her shoulders and went.

A few minutes later Lily came in. She was soft-eyed from her rest. She came to him with a little cry of "Johnny" and put her arms around him, smoothing her cheek against his and then kissing him.

Holding her away, he said, "Darling, I've got to go down to Devon for a few days. You'll be staying here with Mrs. Harroway."

"Well, that'll be a change after the country. But I'll miss you, Johnny—so don't you stay away too long." Over his shoulder she saw Dilling's case on the table. "That's it, isn't it?"

"Yes. Mrs. Harroway is going to look after it until I've arranged things with the Department."

She moved over and put her hand on the case. "It's just like I remembered. They're expensive, this kind, aren't they?"

"Reasonably."

She turned and looked at him frankly. "You do know, Johnny . . . that first time . . . you know, the two of us together. It wasn't because of that." Her eyes slid towards the case. "Behind it all there was the real big thing. You do know that, don't you? I mean you felt that too?"

He smiled and put his hands on her arms, kissed her and said, "Of course I do. You're not that kind of woman."

"No matter what else is involved, there's got to be love first." She smiled and ran on quickly, " 'But love me for love's sake, that evermore thou mayest love on, through love's eternity.' Elizabeth Barrett Browning, 1806–1861. That's true, you know, Johnny, absolutely true. It doesn't matter about anything else. There's just got to be that . . . love for love's sake. Don't you think that's beautiful?"

He let her go on, half listening, and when she had finished, kissed her goodbye. As he went down to the street he knew exactly what she would do with his going. She would go back into the room and stand looking at the brief case and wide awake she would begin to dream . . . rose-coloured dreams. Mrs. Harroway was right. She was one of the lucky ones.

*   *   *   *

From the flat he drove to the Department. He went into Sir John's secretary's room and left with her an envelope which contained the undeveloped roll of film he had made in his own flat of Dilling's papers and with it a letter explaining that Mrs. Harroway had the originals and would be taking charge of all negotiations on Lily's behalf. Then he went to his own room and collected four false passports which he had had made up privately in the past for professional use but which he had never registered with the Department. From his safe he took his reserves of foreign and English currency and his automatic. He had plenty of money banked abroad. Then he called High Grange and spoke to Cranston. He explained that he had been delayed in London and wouldn't be able to leave until early the next morning so that he would not arrive at High Grange until after lunch.

It was now four o'clock. He sat at his desk and began to tie a salmon fly, called the Royal Sovereign which had been graciously accepted by the Queen, following the details of the dressing from a fishing magazine on his desk. But his hands and eyes worked automatically. With his goodbye to Lily and the film and letter already waiting for Sir John's successor— most probably Coppelstone who, despite his genuine loathing of the Department and certain professional drawbacks, was not without ambition—he was now free to think solely of his own plans. Harrison, in the lion enclosure, had refused to accept a genuine warning because it had no appearance of such. To kill a man like Sir John, he knew, meant that he must not put himself into a position where even the shadow of a warning could be overlooked. Sir John and he thought alike, and their instincts ran along the same intricate pathways. So far as he was concerned he knew that Sir John would have always been watching for the smallest sign of a changed intent on his part. He could have given it, too, without knowing. And if the sign had been only the merest flicker, briefer than the small turn of a long grass in an idle zephyr, he knew that Sir John would have given it full value, even though the sigh might prove itself false eventually. Sir John could take no chances. Neither could he. The simple fact that Sir John had gone off on his early autumn fishing trip to Devon instead of being here in London to receive the report on Dilling's papers might mean either nothing or that Sir John was choosing his own ground for a meeting. And what better place than High Grange? Taking meticulous turns of gold oval ribbing around the body of the fly, he knew that he must be the one to choose the ground. Everyone at High Grange expected him now after lunch tomorrow. But he meant to go down that night. Sir John never stayed at High Grange. He always took a room at the Fox and Hounds at Eggesford, farther up the river, and his morning habit was almost inflexible. He would rise early, motor down the Barnstaple road to the pull-in by the railway crossing, leave his car there, walk across to the river and fish for an hour. Then he would come back to his car and drive round and over the river to High Grange where he would breakfast and deal with official work for an hour afterwards. When Sir John pulled into the parking lane by the railway tomorrow morning at half past seven he intended to be waiting for him. With any luck the body would not be found for a couple of hours and he needed no more grace than that. Like most of his professional colleagues, he had contacts and route lines which were never revealed to the Department since a moment of betrayal might come when any known contact or line could be compromised and it was dangerous to be out on one's own. In six hours he could be on his way out of the country. After that it was a complex matter of survival, of disappearing against the background, the spots on the leopard becoming the dappling of sunshine and shadow from the leaves of a forest. . . .

He finished tying the fly, packed his brief case and walked across to the signals office and told the duty officer that if anything came through from High Grange for him to send a messenger round to his flat at half past seven in the morning before he left for Devon.

The man nodded and said, "You knew Harrison, didn't you?"

"Yes."

"A signal's just come through. He's been identified as the man killed by a lion at Woburn last night."

He played surprise. "Harrison? What the hell was he doing there?"

The man laughed. "I don't know. But it wasn't chasing a woman."

Half an hour later Grimster was heading west. Music played softly through the radio. The ashtray was still half full of Lily's lipstick-stained cigarette butts. Now and again he caught a trace of her scent in the warm air of the car. Lily and Harry, and then Lily and Johnny, and in the future Lily and how many others? She would love them all, many or few or perhaps only one. Dilling had he lived would have left her in the end for there must have been the same restlessness in his body as in his mind. Dilling, devious and brilliant, and practical. Trust only the few and make it difficult even for them. He was right. Mrs. Harroway was right. The world was grey right through. He was grey. Cold and grey, touched only with warmth and colour once truly in his life, with Valda. Sir John had made a mistake with Valda. But even the best men made mistakes. In some other context he could have done the same. He was going to kill Sir John. A simple, cold act of revenge. It had to be done because, just as he had now freed himself of Lily, he had to free himself of Sir John, and then move on and let memory's page turn brown and the ink pale to indecipherability.

He stopped at a roadhouse for dinner and was passing through Taunton just before midnight, and it was as he drove through the town, where he had switched hired cars to the one he was driving now, that he found himself thinking of Harrison; living, though this time without emotion, the moment of the lion's great leap. Harrison liked women. Perhaps too much. He wondered if there had ever been any special one in his life. He let his mind wander back over the days at Wellington and the holidays they had spent together. . . . Harrison had known his father and mother and hated them both, rejected and rejecting. He had never known his father, and had long lost all curiosity about him. He and Harrison were a pair, ill-matched fundamentally, but each giving the other something. What? The comfort of their odd relationship, the acknowledgment of each other's self-disgust at the work they did? He smiled wryly as he recalled the excitement he had felt when he had first been called to meet Sir John as a candidate for the Department. . . . Christ, that was one Grimster, but not the one now driving, intent on killing Sir John, the cold intelligent animal. Yes, Sir John had had him trained well . . . made him what he was. . . .

So deep was he in his thoughts that he never saw the police car behind him in his rear mirror. It suddenly swept up on his right-hand side, warning light flashing, passed him with a hand beckoning him to pull in, and then slowly came to a stop ahead of him on the roadside. It was late and there were no other cars about.

Grimster switched off his motor and sat waiting. Two policemen got out of the car and came slowly back to him. One, a tall man, stood by the front of the car for a moment and half bent over, checking the number. The other came to his door. Grimster wound down the window and said, "Good evening."

The policeman smiled and nodded, and said, "Good evening, sir. Just a routine check. Do you mind telling me the number of this car?"

It was the kind of check which had happened before. Grimster noticed that the flap of the man's left-hand top pocket was undone. He gave the policeman the registration number of the car.

"Thank you, sir. Is it your car?"

"No, it's hired."

The tall policeman joined the first and touched his cap with his hand. "Do you mind telling us where you're going, sir?"

"Near Barnstaple. And I've come from London."

The first policeman said, "Did you know one of your rear lights is not working, sir?"

"No, I didn't."

"Better have a look at it, sir. Could be a loose connection or a bulb blown. If you can't do it yourself, there's a garage a little farther on." He put down his hand and opened the car door for Grimster to get out. Grimster slid his legs clear of the seat and out of the door, but the movement to rise to his feet went suddenly dead in him. The two men had stepped a little apart so that he would have to come to his feet between them. Instinctively now, but much too late, he knew that this was no routine check, no polite service to point out a failure in his lighting system, and he knew, too, that, even if he hadn't been day-dreaming, there would have been nothing he could have done about it. Sir John was matching him step for step and now had taken an advantage.

Sitting sideways on the seat, his feet on the road, Grimster said, "This is no routine check."

"No, sir." The tall policeman to his left moved forward, his body now inside the open door so that it could not be closed. A large transport lorry thundered by and, as the noise died, the other policeman said, "Just hold out your hands, sir. I think you understand."

He understood only too well and he knew that for the moment there was nothing he could do. There was no chance to get at his automatic, no chance of escape. There were two of them here and another one sitting up behind the driving wheel of the police car, and the odds were almost certain that they were not police, or, if they were, then police with a special briefing. He'd put the same formula into operation himself many times.

He held out his hands and a pair of handcuffs were placed expertly over his wrists. The action resolved what little tension was left in the two men. The thing was done, their part nearly over, their interest and curiosity cut off at this point.

The shorter of the two men said pleasantly, "Just slip into the back, sir. We've cuffed you in front so you can smoke if you want to."

Grimster got out and the rear door was opened for him and he slid into the back seat. The driving seat was taken by the tall man who had handcuffed him and the other came round and slid into the back alongside him.

The car drove off and as it passed the parked police car the driver raised a hand in greeting. Grimster, through the rear window, saw the police car begin to turn to move away the way it had come.

The man alongside him took off his hat and ran his hand through his hair. He was middle-aged, a brown face cut with deep lines, eyebrows grey as though rimed with hoarfrost, the eyes dark and finely crow-footed with wrinkles.

He said, "Cigarette?"

"No thanks."

The man lit a cigarette. Up ahead the driver took off his peaked cap and dropped it on to the seat alongside him.

Grimster said, "From the Department?"

His companion nodded. "You wouldn't remember me. I went to three lectures you gave once. Four years ago. Sorry, Mr. Grimster."

The driver, eyes on the road, driving fast and well, said, "That goes for me too."

Grimster smiled, but it was only a veil to his thoughts. "But no further?"

His companion said, "I've often wondered what it would take to make me kick over the traces."

The man up front said, "I don't ever want to know." With one hand he unbuttoned the front of his police jacket. "Bloody uncomfortable things."

Grimster said, "There's a brandy flask in the car pocket. I'm not driving now."

His companion moved, reaching forward over the front seat and took the flask from the pocket. He unscrewed the top and handed it to Grimster. He drank and handed it back to the man who screwed the cap back.

He said, "Say when you want it again." He smiled, wrinkles folding around his eyes. "We're just delivering. Not dispatching."

"I knew that. Did the real police help?"

The driver said, "They monitored you down to Taunton. Every county force co-operating and hating every minute. You know what they're like. Very correct. Don't like to have their arms bent. We took over at Taunton. The word is around that you beat Harrison to something."

"Could be."

These men were in his own profession. They knew the rules,

the strains, the disgusts that turned to cold unfeeling acceptance, and over the top of them they played a convincing human role and a little warm dialogue to substantiate it. They had no feeling for him, and very little curiosity. Each was cocooned safely from any weakness that could lead to self-betrayal. At this moment they could have been dispatchers instead of delivery men. It would have made no difference to them. He had a big reputation with their kind. At the moment some of it was lost because they would know that he had made a mistake. Mistakes were unforgivable. His cold design on Sir John had frozen out some small stir of intuition. Sir John no more relished the thought of dying than he did. These men would give him a word or two of sympathy, but they would not feel it.

Echoing his thoughts it seemed, the driver said, "You can't beat the system. Not even if you start near the top."

Grimster's seat mate, ignoring this, said, "I've had a watching brief on Harrison now and again. He was a real sod to keep tabs on. For a big man he moved like a shadow when he wanted. It's no good just having ability. You've got to have talent. He had it."

"But the luck went," said the driver.

Grimster said nothing. He had heard worse epitaphs spoken. None of them ever said the truth. But this one was a little near it.

They drove through the night and it began to rain again. For over a week now each day had been studded with heavy rain showers. It would have kept the river high. Without any self-pity, without any real concern, he thought that he might never fish again, never use the Royal Sovereign in this country or another, never again handle a rod and feel and hear the runout of fast line as a fish went downstream . . . never mark the point of a setter and see the quick flush of a partridge covey. . . . Well, if it went that way it went that way. But he knew that whenever it came Sir John would be gone first. Proof that it would be so wasn't necessary. Cold belief was enough. Everyone made mistakes and he'd made one. That just proved him fallible, which he'd always known. But he still had some reserves left.

The driver switched on the radio. A Continental station was playing Julie Felix. *Judge Jefferies*. The folklore sentiment washed about the car. *Judge Jefferies was a wicked man.* All men were evil. Grey-coloured right through. He meant to kill Sir John.

South Molton came up, the long main street grey with grey houses under the headlamps, the rain a shabby bead curtain. On the radio the voice of Julie Felix switched to *The Space Girl's Song* and the driver tapped his fingers on the wheel to the beat . . . *They said I'd need a blaster and my needle-freezer gun, and I did, I did.* . . . The lines brought Dilling into his mind. The new technology, the new warfare . . . Dilling had served it . . . and because of Dilling, of Dilling through Lily, he was here and he was going to kill Sir John because no movement in life was complete, isolated in a vacuum . . . the chain reaction of digging a two-foot hole in sand went on and on.

He said, "Is Coppelstone at High Grange still?"

The man at his side said, "Yes."

*   *   *   *

Coppelstone was standing on the top step with Cranston as the car drew up, the two of them very still, the portico light above them dwarfing their shadows.

The two men took him from the car, one of them carrying his case, and he went up between them, rain flicking at his face, until he was in the shelter of the doorway.

Coppelstone in a mildly drink-touched voice said, "Evening, Johnny." He took the case from one of the men.

Cranston said to the men, "There's some food and stuff inside for you. But give the car a going over first. I want everything it holds in my office." He looked across at Grimster, fidgeted with his patch and said, "You damned fool, Johnny." The words were heavy with unexpected sorrow.

The two men went back to the car and Grimster was led

inside. The duty man at the desk raised his head sharply, birdlike, and then dropped his eyes to the magazine he was reading. Coppelstone searched him, took all his loose belongings and slipped the firecrest ring from Grimster's finger. "Sir John's instructions." He grinned. "Perhaps he thinks you'll hypnotise us." They went across the hall and down the shallow steps that led to the basement and the shooting range. Grimster knew where they were going. At the far end of the shooting range there was a small room which they called the "brig"; not often used but entirely secure. Their feet echoed on the bare stone slabs. Cranston unlocked the steel door and moved in ahead. The room was windowless. There were gridded lights set in the four ceiling corners. The walls were large granite blocks. Three feet from the doorway a steel grille ran right across the room from ceiling to floor, the bars set so close that no hand or arm could be forced between them. Cranston unlocked the steel-barred door in the centre of the grille and Grimster went in. There was a chair, a table, a small bunk bed with a chamber pot under it, and a narrow wooden shelf on the back wall which held four or five paperbacks which had been there as long as Grimster could remember. There was a glass, a bottle of brandy, a table lighter and a box of cigars on the table. Indicating them Grimster asked, "Compliments of the management?"

Coppelstone nodded. Cranston's face for a moment showed embarrassment which he quickly hid by dropping his head as he locked the grille door. That was why Cranston ran High Grange. He was no good outside, sorrow and embarrassment still came too easily to him.

Coppelstone took the bunch of keys from Cranston and Cranston left without a word, leaving the door to the shooting range wide open. Coppelstone sat himself down on a small stool just inside the door. Grimster stood at the table and lifted the brandy bottle. The cork had already been loosened. He poured himself a drink and sat with it on the bunk, cradling it between his cuffed hands, warming it.

"When's Sir John coming?"

"Tomorrow. His usual time." Coppelstone lifted Grimster's case on to his knees and opened it. He did little more than glance inside, then closed it. "A very comprehensive lot of stuff just for a visit here. What happened to Harrison?"

"He came in after me when I got Dilling's stuff, and wouldn't take a hint."

"Where's Dilling's stuff?"

"The originals are with Mrs. Harroway. I filmed them and left the roll in Sir John's office."

"So we'll have to do a straight deal with Miss Stevens?"

"Yes."

"Chivalrous."

"I wouldn't call it that."

"What pushed you over the line? Proof or nagging conjecture? Valda on your mind so much that it hurt too much and you just had to rid yourself of it?"

"I just made a decision." He smiled and drank large of the brandy.

Coppelstone stood up, holding the case. "You're in trouble, Johnny. But it will be done decently as we understand the word."

"When?"

"Tomorrow. The day after. I don't know. Nothing personal. Just a rearrangement in the Department. You know how it is."

"Of course."

At the door Coppelstone turned and said, "This is the first evening for many a long time that I've cut down hard on the whisky. You've disappointed me, Johnny." He went locking the door behind him.

Grimster finished his brandy and rolled over on the bunk. He was asleep within half an hour.

At seven o'clock the next morning the two policemen, now in mufti, brought him water and washing gear. One, armed, stayed at the main door. Half an hour later they came and cleared his toilet stuff away. The elderly one said, "Wonderful what you can do with your hands together," and the younger one couldn't resist saying, "Like prayer."

Grimster sat and read the *Daily Mail* which they had left with him. There was a picture of a long worm of cars at Woburn crawling round the lion enclosure and another of the two thorns and the vague shadow of the hole he had dug. The noble duke would be overjoyed . . . what showman wouldn't? And there was no incongruity. The nobility had always been the showmen of England, bred for eccentricity and display. Harrison's death had made news. If Sir John had his way there would be no dramatic news of his own going. It was a picture without colour, a thought without emotion. He knew what kind of letter would be written to his mother. There were a dozen carbon copies on the files of those already sent to others . . . *deeply regret . . . long service . . . great loyalty . . . not easily replaced . . . mourned by us all. . . .* Long service would be the only truth in it. His mother would treasure it, mourn him and mould his memory into a comfortable part of her routine. But he was going to kill Sir John first. The mania had long become cold and flintlike in him. Nothing could stop him. He sensed it accurately as inevitable, established, part of the world's will, ignoble but ordained.

Cranston and one of the guards brought him breakfast. Cranston stood at the outer door. There was no embarrassment in him now. He would have gone far in the service if there had never been any at all. Like a kindly nursemaid, he said, "Bacon and sausages, Johnny. We've cut them so you can handle them better. We'd loose you but it was Sir John's orders."

Grimster thanked him. They left him alone to eat. It was awkward but manageable. With the last of his tea he lit a cigar and waited patiently for Sir John to come. He could time him within ten minutes for he knew that the man would not alter his routine. He was on vacation, pleasure came first, the morning fishing ritual; business followed after he had taken his late breakfast. He saw him working the Cliff Pool. It wouldn't be clear enough for a fly. He was a bad fisherman; hasty, impatient, horsing his fish to the bank without finesse, but in the odd way of bad fishermen he caught more than his fair share.

Sir John came within five minutes of his timing. He came alone and shut the outer door without locking it. He sat on the stool and said, "Good morning, Johnny."

He wore dark, chocolate-coloured tweeds, the left lapel of the jacket stuck with flies. The neatly lined, precise face smiled briefly. Sitting low on the stool he looked like some dwarf about to begin cobbling, his legs crossed, his elbows on his knees.

Grimster said, "Did you have a good morning, Sir John?"

"Eight pounder. River's very high. Fairly fresh fish. More fish in the river than last year. Chap from the Fox and Hounds got a twenty pounder yesterday in their Nursery Pool. Beautiful fish. Like a great length of silver. Know the Nursery Pool?"

"I fished it a couple of times. No luck."

Sir John nodded sympathetically and said, "No luck now either, Johnny."

"Seems not, Sir John."

He wasn't deceived by the affability, the use of his name that usually marked the end of an interview. Sir John was not elated, not triumphing. He was simply and with fair grace carrying out an exercise in kindness because the ritual goodbye was demanded by good form. Grimster had been present once before when he had used it on another.

"Understand you've messed up the Dilling deal for us, Johnny?"

"I'm afraid so. The Department will appear honest for once."

"It can't be helped. Nice girl Miss Stevens, I'm told." He fished for his cigarette case and was silent for a while. The cigarette lit he gave it a couple of puffs and held it away from him awkwardly. Every cigarette he smoked was the first of a lifetime with him. Grimster smiled, and Sir John caught it. "Filthy things, but I am addicted." Then with a shuffle and recrossing of his feet he said, "We must talk business for a bit, Johnny."

Not a cobbling dwarf, thought Grimster, but a wise, old thrush, fluffing out feathers, settling to its perch.

"Just as you wish, sir."

"Good. It doesn't matter either at this stage if a little of the confessional creeps in. On my part naturally. Did you get positive proof that we killed Miss Trinberg?"

"Positive enough for me."

"That might mean conjecture, of course. Even so, I knew that you would act some time. I made a bad mistake and I've regretted it ever since. That's why I lied to you once, swore that it was an accident. I wanted to save you, Johnny. There was a time when I saw you taking over."

"Who will when you've gone?"

"Coppelstone, maybe. His drinking is marginal. In our work a man has got to have something he can lock himself away in a room with. For quite a few months now I've spent half an hour every night wondering how, when and where you would do it. Let me say this—I knew that Harrison would never be able to touch you. You'd do it on your own. Pity about Harrison. Likeable, capable. I gave him the chance to come in with us once. He preferred to roam."

"Who was he working for this time?"

"The confessional doesn't go so far as that. Anyway, I'm glad it's not you drawing the crowds at Woburn today."

"All I'll get is a small paragraph in the *Western Morning News*."

"'Fraid so. But you could have avoided it, taken over from me and eventually had a quarter column in *The Times*."

"My mother would have liked that."

"It's all very sad."

"You mean it's all very necessary."

"No, few things are ever absolutely necessary. But many things are sad. More than we are ever permitted to know. Fortunately there's always compromise to avoid stupid situations.

218

I was stupid with you over Valda. When the day came for me to retire I'd got you marked as my successor. That's finished. But, even now, *you* don't have to be."

"You're offering me a deal, Sir John?"

The man smiled bleakly. "If you want it. Professionally you're finished. But there are a lot of things you could still do. You're a man of your word. All you have to promise is that you will give up this idea of killing me, that you will do no more professional work, no matter for whom, and that you will never divulge any of the things you know about the working of the Department. It's a generous offer—and I wouldn't make it to anyone else."

"It would also save your life when I get out of here."

"If you do, yes. But I am not thinking of my life very much. A little, yes, honesty compels me to say that. I'm thinking of your life. Just give me your word and you can walk out of here—"

"And promptly break it and come after you."

"If I thought that, the offer would never have been made. All you have to do is give me your word. Well?"

Grimster shook his head. "The facts are simple, Sir John. You killed someone I loved and I am a revengeful man. I've planned to kill. And I'm going to kill you. It's as straightforward as that. No frills."

"You hate me as much as that?"

"I want you dead. Just that." Clearly pictured, Grimster saw the car come round the hillside curve and the other car sweep by it. He saw the dark peat glitter of the loch far below, saw the blue sky billowing with great cloud shapes, and he watched the car fall, rolling and smashing its way among the heather and the granite boulders.

Sir John stood and went to the door. "I wish it could have been different."

Sir John went, locking the door behind him. Grimster two-handed the brandy bottle and poured himself a drink. The man had given him a chance and he had refused it. There could be

219

no bargaining between him and Sir John. There was nothing the man could offer him. The idea of revenge had become a cold, inflexible passion in him. The debt he owed to Valda. He belonged now to no one and to nowhere. Grace of a kind could only come with Sir John's death. After that he would fashion a form of life for himself that would be adequate and tolerable.

He drank some of the brandy and then lit himself a cigar.

CHAPTER FIFTEEN

At noon Cranston and Coppelstone brought him his lunch and he was freed from his handcuffs. They then locked him in his portion of the cell and Cranston left Coppelstone alone with him.

He had been given cold meat and salad and a half bottle of white wine. He ignored the food for the moment and poured himself some wine. Coppelstone sat on the small stool outside and smoked. Cranston had locked the outer door on him.

Grimster said, "Why are you staying?"

"Sir John's orders. There must be someone with you until we take you out."

"When?"

"This evening."

"How is it going to be done?"

"An accident while fishing. You'll go over from the high rocks at the side of the Cliff Pool. You know the form. You slipped on the wet leaves while looking down into the pool. Body found by a search party late tonight."

"Then a coroner's inquest and accidental death. I know." He did know. There would be nothing for anyone to fault, nothing to make the police or the coroner at all suspicious. He was a top man in the Department. He would go out without a blemish on his professional character.

Coppelstone said, "You're taking it easily. But I'm not surprised."

Grimster drank some wine. "Is this cell bugged or on the television circuit?"

"No. Once a man's in here we know all we want to know about him. You know that."

"Is Sir John going to be present?"

"No. Cranston and I will take you down. He'll get a report of the accident in the morning."

"He's going to be disappointed."

Coppelstone shook his head and then fingered a dry shaving cut on his chin. "No, Johnny, he's not. I'd like to think he might be. But it can't happen. I'd like to think he was going over instead of you."

"So that you could take his place at the head of the Department?"

"It might happen. I hate the Department, but it's all I have. This kind of work is my life and it's killed all normal human feelings in me except one. Ambition. That's something to hang on to, Johnny. Even in our time Sir John has far exceeded his official mandate. All his predecessors did too. That's why the Department became what it is. Power is corrupting. I suppose at the back of my mind is the thought that if I ran the show I might humanize it a little around the fringes."

"Or destroy or finally discredit it?"

Unmoved, Coppelstone said, "That would be overambitious."

"Nevertheless, it's in your mind."

"From time to time."

"We might be able to work something out between us."

"Hope is the last thing to go with ordinary people, Johnny. But I should have thought with a man like you, with all your knowledge, it would be the first. I'm not open to any deals out of friendship or ambition."

"I'm not talking about hope. I'm talking facts."

Coppelstone dropped his cigarette end and screwed a shoe toe on it. "How's the wine, Johnny?"

"Good, but a half bottle is always disappointing. Facts, Coppelstone. Hard facts. You're right about hopes. It's a long time since I dealt in them and they never came to much anyway. The last one went when Valda crashed."

"An accident which you have built into an act of murder. It became murder in your mind not long ago. You began to fly the signals, Johnny, and Sir John saw them. Why shouldn't he? He'd been waiting for them. But you, Johnny, you wanted it to be murder, you made it murder, so that you could have reason to kill Sir John—no matter the consequences to you. You wanted him dead because he represented everything you stood for, everything you'd become. I know because I feel the same. But then I'm not so dedicated as you. I want to be head of the Department, but I couldn't find anything in me strong enough to make me raise my hand to Sir John."

Grimster poured the last of the wine. "I never built anything up in my mind about Valda's death. I know her death was ordered by Sir John. He confirmed it in here a little while ago. I know, too, that you knew it. Without proof it might have taken me a long time to act on conjecture. I might never have acted. But I was given proof."

Coppelstone shook his head. "Only three people knew. One of them is now dead. Sir John and I were the others. A little while ago I called it an accident. But it was murder. I don't mind admitting it either now. It makes no difference."

A fly buzzed over the lunch tray, drawn by the cold meat. Grimster watched it, waited, then swept out a hand and caught and crushed it. "You're not admitting it now, Coppelstone. You told me about it some time ago."

"I did?" Coppelstone looked up, for the first time puzzled, sensing a movement into deeper waters. He was here on orders. Not to have talked would have been boorish and, anyway, he liked Grimster, but so far he had not considered their talk as having any great significance. It was an uncomplicated way of embroidering the passing of time.

"The last night you were down here. Do you remember?"

"Of course, I was pretty drunk. But never as drunk as that, Johnny."

"No. But you were drunk enough to drop some defences.

223

Drunk enough to be in a receptive mood. You remember Dilling's ring?"

"Of course."

"I may want Sir John dead. But I admire him, respect his brain. He gave instructions for it to be taken from me when I was brought here. You know why, don't you?"

"Yes. But it seemed far-fetched."

"Not to Sir John. He never takes chances. He knew what I had done with it to Lily. Simple logic told him that in this cell, who knows, I might try it on someone else. Hypnotise them and make them release me. Far-fetched maybe—but that's why he had it taken from me. But he was too late, Coppelstone. Much too late. I used it on you that night you were drunk. You went off like a baby—and you're not a psycho-passive type. You're psycho-active. But they're the best kind once they decide to drop their defences and co-operate. And you wanted to do that, because at heart you wanted me to have a go at Sir John, to clear the top rung of the ladder for you."

"I don't believe it."

"I can prove it to you. I'm not a bloody fool, Coppelstone. Do you think I didn't know, however clever I might think myself, that once I had proof of Valda's murder I might, unknowingly, fly some signal? Of course, I did—so I felt it wise to keep something up my sleeve. Just in case things went wrong. Which they have."

"You really mean you put me under?"

"Yes. Practically everyone in the world can be put under. We all want to go under and find release for a while. Why the hell else do you think we have to sleep? You went under, Coppelstone, because you wanted release. That's why you drink at night, for release."

Coppelstone shrugged his shoulders. "All right. So I went under and told you that Valda had been murdered, and that set you after Sir John. And now you're sitting there, Johnny— and there's nothing to be done for you."

"Oh, but there is. A lot to be done. And you're going to do

it for me. We didn't only talk about Valda. There were other things."

"What things?"

"That you had a line to Harrison."

"That's a damned lie!"

"No it isn't. You told me. But it was something I'd already seen as a possibility. That's why I asked you about it. Do you think I didn't understand how Harrison worked and thought? He'd always wanted a line to someone in the top of the Department. There was big money waiting for him if he could pull it off, and years ago he'd elected me for the role. He knew it would be tough but that just made it more interesting for him. A challenge. And being me it was rich with irony. He worked carefully. For all I know he might have succeeded. But you and Sir John spoilt it all for him. You had Valda killed. Harrison knew what that would do to me once I knew, and he knew I'd find out some time. He went on playing the game of tempting me, knowing I was reporting everything to Sir John. But I wasn't any good to him. He knew I'd go for Sir John. He wanted someone who would stay in the Department and give his people everything they wanted and, with luck, last for ever without being suspected. So while pretending to be after me, he switched to you and he hooked you fast, didn't he? Because you wanted to be hooked. You wanted to go to the top when I killed Sir John, and you wanted to be there so that you could quietly, secretly, have the Department torn apart and destroyed. I hope for your sake you didn't lie to me when you said this cell wasn't bugged."

"I didn't lie. And I haven't got a line to Harrison."

"It won't work. You've got a line."

"I'm not interested. Anyway, it's only your word. Sir John would write it off as the last throw of a desperate man."

"It's more than my word. All I wanted that night was to find out about Valda. Then I thought I'd follow up this idea I had about Harrison and I questioned you about that because it might be a card up my sleeve—but I had to have real proof.

225

So I slipped back to my room and got a tape recorder and made you go over the whole thing again. The tape still exists. If you want it back you've got to help me."

Coppelstone was silent for a moment. He liked this man, but he had no intention of helping him.

He said, "I'm not helping you, Johnny. I don't care a damn about the tape, because I don't care a damn about myself. You can shout for Sir John and give it to him. But ditching me won't help you. There's no bargain you can make with him in return for the tape. You can only destroy me—and you're not interested in that. All you want in this world is a free hand to get at Sir John—and I'm not giving you that, even though I want him dead. You've got nothing against me, Johnny. That's why you won't hand the tape to Sir John. No, Johnny— you asked for it this way. To be on your own. That's the way you stay. You want me to phone Sir John and say you want to see him again?"

Grimster suddenly laughed. "Don't worry, there's no tape. Only my word."

"It's nice to hear that. I had a suspicion you were bluffing."

"It was worth a try."

"In your position anything is. But nothing is going to help you. You should have accepted Sir John's offer. He told me about it. I can't think of any other man in the world he'd have made it to but you."

Grimster said, "How are you going to do it . . . down there?"

"You'll be handcuffed again and taken down by Cranston and myself. Before we take the cuffs off you'll get a hypodermic injection. You know the stuff. It'll kill you instantly and then we shall drop you in. One of our doctors will sign the certificate. Death from drowning."

*   *   *   *

He waited through the afternoon and the evening. Cranston sat with him for a while, saying little, fiddling nervously now

226

and then with the patch over his eye. The two guards shared the rest of the vigil. They talked little. One said that it had been raining all day but had left off now. He listened to them, chatted sometimes, saw them, but had no interest in them, had interest only for the time that was coming. He had the conviction that sprang from his deep obsession that he was going to get away. He had tried for help from Coppelstone and had been refused it. He had never counted much on it and there was no real disappointment in him. In his obsession, too, there was a stiff pride that it was right that he should have to do it all on his own.

They came for him just after eight o'clock. The evenings were long with light still. It was a time after dinner when any fisherman might go down to catch the fruitful hour before darkness fell. There were the two guards and Coppelstone and Cranston. He was handcuffed with his hands in front and then one of the guards took off his shoes and pulled on his thigh waders. They led him up to the hall and out into the open. The gravel was still wet with recent rain and the sky was washed a pearly grey colour in the east. Westwards the sinking sun was just touching the ridge of far hills beyond the Taw, blackening the slopes with shadow. A lark was singing somewhere. He momentarily thought of Lily and then as quickly forgot her. Sparrows splashed in the rain puddles. His own car waited, and he saw that someone had put up the old Pope rod and fixed it in the rod clips on top of the car. He remembered the day he had come home from Wellington to find it waiting for him, bought second-hand by his mother. The thought of her raised no emotion in him. He owed her little but kindness. These moments now sprang from the moments she had passed as a young girl with the young son of some great house. . . . She had become obsessed with the shame of her love. He was obsessed by the death of his love.

He sat in the back between the two guards. Cranston sat alongside Coppelstone who drove. They left the two guards at the farm with the car and, to stop him running from them on the walk to the woods, Coppelstone tied a short length of rope around his wrists above the cuffs and twisted his hand through a loop at the other end. Cranston took his rod and his fishing bag. Without saying a word the two guards stood by the car, lit cigarettes and watched him go.

Red Devon cattle grazed in the pasture as they went down the path to the woods. The loose tops of his waders flapped against his thighs as he walked and he wondered what Sir John was doing at this moment at the Fox and Hounds Hotel farther up the valley. He came every year at this time and always had the same room. He was probably having dinner alone. His wife always joined him for the last week of his holiday, a plump, friendly woman who nursed a Yorkshire terrier on her lap while she read the papers in the lounge. It was difficult to imagine Sir John with a domestic life, grown-up sons, one in the army and one in the City. . . .

When they came to the edge of the wood, Coppelstone stopped and turned to him. He said, "I've been told by Sir John to say that his offer is still open."

Grimster shook his head.

Cranston said, "Don't be a fool, Johnny. For Christ's sake—none of us want this."

Grimster shook his head again. They went into the woods and down the steep narrow path that ran to the cliff top above the pool and there turned at right angles to run downriver, dropping eventually to the water's level at the tail of the pool.

They stopped, four yards back from the right-angled turn, but they were close enough for Grimster to see and hear the river. The water was high and brown, well covering the beach on the far side where he had stood and played his salmon while Harrison had waited. If Harrison could be seeing this, he thought, he would be relishing it. For a moment the coldness inside him was touched, and he wondered if other people secretly only had such limited moments of love as had come his way . . . Valda's above all, Harrison's, twisted and all sardonic aggression, Lily's compounded of frailties that wouldn't

228

last the length of a severe day. .... Of them all, suddenly, he had a brief, intense moment of anguished longing for Harrison's presence. Then he was feelingless, hard, again.

From behind Cranston suddenly kicked Grimster's feet from under him and he collapsed to the ground in a sitting position.

"Sorry, Johnny, but we want no tricks."

Coppelstone unlooped the rope from his own hand and tossed it to Cranston. "Hold him while I do it."

Cranston dropped to his knees behind Grimster and, before he could move, jerked the handcuff rope back sharply, pulling Grimster's hands up to his throat and began to take a loop with the rope round his neck. As the rope touched his skin Grimster knew that this was his only moment before Cranston would force him backwards, half choking him, for Coppelstone to drop on to his legs, to straddle them, while he got out his hypodermic syringe. He hadn't planned the moment, but his obsessive confidence in himself, his implacable certainty that he was going to kill Sir John, had informed him that there had to be an instant when instinct would operate. He had been content to wait for the moment to come. He was a killing animal now, utterly.

Before Cranston could loop the rope round his neck he smashed his head rearwards viciously and felt the back of his skull crash into the man's face. From the backward movement of head and shoulders he jerked himself forward—the handcuff rope running loose from Cranston's hands—and upwards to his feet. For a fraction of a second he stood face to face with Coppelstone, so close that he felt the man's breath, saw the blood-veined eyes widen. He took a grip on the man's jacket front and rushed him backwards towards the cliff edge. Coppelstone stumbled and began to fall. Grimster let himself fall too and, as they hit the ground, his cuffed hands gripping the jacket front, he rolled and pulled Coppelstone with him down the slight slope to the edge of the cliff.

They went over together, fell fifty feet, and smashed into the racing flood water which took them under in its pull and swept them downstream. Grimster, holding on to Coppelstone, let the water take him. They surfaced and Coppelstone's face was close to his. The man's hands came up, seeking his throat, but he jerked his head forward, smashing his forehead viciously into the wet, red face. They went under again, rolling and twisting in the fast spate.

The current took them into the turbulent stream at the tail of the pool, their bodies swinging and turning in the shallower water. Then they were swept into the deeper run below and the river, slowing a little, drifted them away from the last of the high cliff run and over towards the far side. Grimster felt the rock and boulder strewn river bed beneath his feet and fought, as he still held grimly on to Coppelstone, the thrust of the river and the weight of water in his waders to find a footing. Five yards from the far bank he found a hold and dragged himself upright. Pulling Coppelstone with him, he began to work his way to the bank. And as he went, dragging Coppelstone who was half unconscious from his blow in the face, he had a swift picture of the shadowy form of the lion at Woburn, dragging Harrison across the road.

He reached the bank and hauled his prey up the grass slope and into the field and dropped him. His hands came away from the jacket, stiff and unyielding. Coppelstone lay still on the ground, groaning. Grimster dropped beside him and with his hands clasped together struck him with all his power on the temple. Then he grabbed the wet edge of the man's right-hand jacket pocket and ripped it down. He had seen Coppelstone put the handcuff key there when he had been manacled in the cell. As the side of the jacket pocket came away, the key fell to the grass and with it a small black cardboard box which was only too familiar to him. He took the box and thrust it awkwardly into his own jacket pocket and then picked up the key, clenching it in the palm of his right hand. From away across the river he heard a shout, knew that it was Cranston, but knew, too, that it would take the man some time to find a crossing. Holding the key tight, he rolled over on to his back and lifted his legs high in the air. The water in his waders cascaded over him for a moment and then he was on his feet and running hard and laboriously in the heavy waders towards the far railway line.

He ran, and there was nothing in him of exhilaration or triumph. There was only a cold purpose, so secure that it was an armoured arrogance. He was going to kill Sir John. Nothing could stop him. The picture of the lion dragging Harrison came to him again and he knew, with an icy detachment, that he had become an animal. All he wanted now was to hunt and kill because until he had killed there could be no peace in him, no thought of turning to life again and finding a place for himself.

At the wire fence which flanked the railway line he stopped and looked back, his shoulders heaving and shaking with his hard breathing. The river bank was empty of movement. He slipped through the wire, went over the line and through the fence on the other side. Here, he sat down in the long grass and gave his shaking body a few minutes to quieten down. He put the key into his mouth, holding it firmly between his teeth. Raising his hands, he worked his mouth and wrists to get the key in the lock of the handcuffs. He dropped the key twice before he succeeded, but there was no panic in him.

Free of the handcuffs, he undid the knot of the handcuff rope with his teeth. He stood up and stripped his jacket and shirt off, twisting as much water as he could from them. Then he took off his waders and did the same for his trousers.

A few minutes later he was on the main Exeter to Barnstaple road. The tops of his waders turned down, he clumped his way up the valley road. For the time being he knew that he was safe. Cranston would go across to Coppelstone. It would take time for them to get back to High Grange and then they would telephone Sir John for instructions and Sir John would almost certainly have gone down to the river behind the hotel for an hour's fishing. When they did get in touch with him they would have a problem. If they were going to get police help Sir John would have to do it and that would mean diplomatic explanations to a Chief Constable at least before anything was done. He knew in any case what Sir John would do. The moment he got the call from High Grange he would pack his bag and leave the hotel and move to High Grange. Sir John knew that the hotel would be unsafe with him on the loose. He had only one hope now to finish the matter quickly and that was to get to the hotel before Sir John moved out. If he was unlucky . . . well, then he would have to think again. But luck which had been with him so far, had now hardened to a conviction of success. Sir John on holiday was a creature of habit. Always after dinner he went down to the river. He looked at the sky. There was another half hour of light left yet. Sir John should still be fishing, and would stay until the light went.

Luck stayed with him. Five hundred yards up the road a small van was parked by a field gateway. As he came up to it, he could see a man in the field looking over a flock of sheep. The key was in the ignition switch of the car. Grimster slid into the seat and drove away. The Fox and Hounds Hotel was fifteen minutes up the road.

*   *   *   *

Grimster drove down the long drive into the hotel forecourt. He parked the car alongside the rod room shed and looked at the cars drawn up in front of the hotel. There were half a dozen of them and one of them was Sir John's black Daimler. That meant that the man had not driven to any far beat of the river. He was either in the hotel, or had walked down across the fields at the back of the hotel to the river. Grimster got out of the car and went to the hotel entrance. There was no desk in the hall. The place was run on friendly, easy-going lines. Many of the people at this time of the year were regulars, people who not only came at the same time each year, but also booked the same rooms. There were only two with bathrooms, one downstairs and the other upstairs. They were both double rooms and Sir John always took the upstairs double room overlooking the courtyard because his wife invariably joined him for the last week of the holiday.

Grimster went through the front door and up the stairs. Nobody would think it was odd that he was wearing waders if they saw him. The lounge door on the right of the entrance door was open and there were a few people in there taking coffee. He went up the stairs and along to Sir John's room. There was no difficulty about room keys because the hotel did not issue them. Only if you were inside the rooms could you drop a door catch and secure yourself from interruption. Grimster knew this because he had more than once in the past come over from High Grange to see Sir John.

From outside he had seen that there was no light on in the room. He opened the door and went in. One of the beds had been turned down for the night, but the curtains were undrawn. On the prepared bed was a piece of white notepaper. Grimster picked it up. A message on it read—*Will Sir John please ring High Grange the moment he comes in. Urgent.*

Grimster replaced the message, drew the curtains, and then sat down on a chair in the far corner of the room. He pulled the small cardboard box from his pocket, switched the table lamp on for a moment, and examined the hypodermic syringe. It was full. He put it on the dressing-table at his side. On the window panes he heard the sudden beat of rain as a shower swept up the valley. A car drove into the courtyard and there were the sounds of men's voices, and of a dog barking.

He sat and waited in the darkness, and urgency and fatigue drained from him. He ran a hand over his face which was bruised from smashing it at Coppelstone. He thought now of Coppelstone who had let Harrison ensnare him, who, maybe, had wanted Harrison to ensnare him because he hated the Department so much. Coppelstone, when Sir John died, would become head of the Department, but he would not last long. The odds were too much against him. He would know this and, because of it, would do the maximum damage he could as fast as he could. Coppelstone, like himself, was dedicated to destruction. Both of them when they had gone into the Department had felt and relished the pull of pride that they had become members of a small elite body whose workings had at first attracted and fascinated them, then claimed a cold, inhuman dedication from them, and finally, because they were unable to stifle all human charity, had repelled them so that each in his own way had sought either to destroy it or escape from it. Although Sir John had never even hinted at it, he knew that the man must also share something of the same feeling. But once in it was hard to escape the trap.

Someone came down the passage and stopped at the room door. He heard a man cough briefly and then the door was opened. The light was switched on and Sir John came into the room. He walked straight to the bed, seeing the white note, and reached over to pick it up. He was wearing his brown plus-fours and green gumboots. He turned as Grimster rose and moved behind him.

They faced one another, the younger man with his bruised, blood-marked face, the older man with his lined face, pale, thinly etched with veins, the iron-grey moustache still touched with the dampness of the rain. They were the same height and there had been a time when Sir John's body must have been as hard and strong as Grimster's. Sir John's eyes went briefly to the paper he held in his hand and then came back to Grimster. He crumpled the paper in his fingers, the back of his hand liver-marked, and he said quietly, shaking his head, "What do you expect me to do, Johnny? Plead with you?"

"You won't do that."

"No. So far as you're concerned I forfeited the right long ago. Well, no matter how we would have it differently, all things find their true end." He gave a small shrug of his shoulders and stood there, waiting.

There was nothing in Grimster that could be reached by Sir John, no pity, no anger; there was only his cold obsessive resolution to kill the man because he had had Valda killed and

234

Valda now, over the months, had become a symbol for him of all the things he had wanted all his life, a person to love and to be loved by, a place to return to where comfort and understanding would always be his to give and receive when he reached it.

Without a word he struck the man hard on the side of his thin neck with the edge of an iron-taut hand. A groan exploded softly from Sir John's throat and he fell backwards across the end of the bed and lay still.

Grimster moved over him, pulled back the loose shoulder of Sir John's jacket and thrust the needle of the syringe through the man's shirt and into the upper part of his right arm. He pressed the plunger and held it down and watched the liquid in the container drain away. When it was empty he withdrew it and jerked the front of the man's jacket into place. As he straightened up the picture of Valda's car slid through his imagination, and he knew that it was for the last time. He saw the car somersaulting down the mountain side towards the long shape of the loch below, falling, falling. . . .

He put the syringe back in his pocket, feeling neither relief in the deed done, nor any alteration in himself. There was neither triumph nor disgust.

He picked up Sir John's small suitcase from the stool by the window and dropped it on the other bed. They were much the same height and build and he needed clothes, shoes, and money. He went to the wall cupboard and took what he wanted, jacket, trousers and shirts, socks and a well-worn pair of brown brogues. He worked meticulously, searching and finding all he needed and packing it into the case.

Outside another rain storm beat against the windows. He went to Sir John, searched his pockets and found his car keys, then he reached into his inner pocket for his wallet. It was crocodile skin, well worn, the corners silver-tipped. He emptied its contents on to the bed alongside Sir John's head. There were ten five pound notes, three one pound notes, a driving licence, a Devon River Board fishing licence, made out at the hotel for two weeks, a receipted bill from Hardy's in Pall Mall for some fishing tackle and a small Perspex holder, transparent, of the kind men carry to hold family snapshots.

Grimster put the money into his own pocket and then paused for a moment, looking down at the dead man. Sir John's eyes were open, steely, flinty blue eyes and his mouth had widened in a tiny grimace under the moustache. Grimster without knowing why he did it reached down and closed the man's eyes. The man's face fell sideways, one cheek almost touching the Perspex holder. The movement took Grimster's own eyes to it so that he saw the topmost photograph that showed through the transparent container.

He reached down, picked it up, and studied the top photograph. Then he took all the photographs out and leafed through them. There were half a dozen of them, mostly of Sir John's wife and his two sons. He put all but two back and replaced the container in the wallet with the other stuff and then slid the wallet into Sir John's pocket. He stood then for a moment over the dead man and let the tips of his right-hand fingers just touch the blotched skin of the back of the man's left hand, feeling the warmth in it still and the hardness of the bone under flesh. Suddenly he took the whole hand into his grasp and pressed it firmly, then turned away.

Carrying the case, he left the room and went down the stairs, meeting no one. The door to the lounge was closed and he heard voices inside. He went out into the dark and a swirl of faint rain. There was a light showing through the door of the rod room, and light streaming from the bar windows on the far side of the courtyard. Two Irish setters belonging to the hotel padded up to him out of the gloom as he moved to Sir John's car. One of them nuzzled his free hand.

He unlocked the car door with one of Sir John's keys, slung his case in the back and drove away, up the long uneven slope of the far drive and out on to the Exeter road, then down past the darkened station at Eggesford and up the narrow valley road with the Taw running on his right. He drove without thought or feeling, a cold, grim man who waited for relief to come but until it did wanted neither emotion, nor memory, nor regret to touch him. And because of his mood he drove fast, knowing exactly where he was going, all the lines of possible escape long cleared in his mind, action only now demanded of him. He forced the car beneath him as though it were a living thing to be spurred, its momentum through the dark night along the rain-sheened road giving him perhaps some faint promise of the relief he waited for which, when it came, he knew must either mar the rest of his days with slow anguish and his nights with desperate dreams or else leave him to live on untouched by anything from his barren past.

A mile up the road, his foot hard on the throttle pedal, headlights picking out the beginning of the dark sweep of pine woods to his left, a farm tractor nosed warily, beetle-like, head-lights dim, from out of a woodland cart road on to the main highway. Grimster saw it when it was fifty yards from him, saw it halt with half its length out on the road. He swung the Daimler away from his own left-hand side of the road to pass out and around it. But as he moved out he felt the back wheels slide away in a skid. His hands began to correct the skid. There was no panic or anxiety in him for part of his early training in the Department had demanded long hours on a skid pan. But now, and he was never to know the truth, his hands on the wheel, taking a volition of their own, either faltered in their confident correcting movement, or were stilled by him deliber-ately with the sudden return of thought and feeling, so that some decision was made in him too fast for him to acknowledge it except through his body, the instinct in his flesh welcoming a fate which perhaps a few seconds later his mind, too, would have accepted.

The heavy Daimler slewed into a fast tail slide across the road, swung back, and then half spun round and crashed through a flimsy field gate on the right-hand side of the road. With headlights blazing it raced down the slope of the mole-hill studded pasture. For a moment Grimster saw the gleam of the river through bushes and trees at the bottom of the field, saw the arched shape of a stone bridge farther upstream and then the car crashed into the thick trunk of an oak at the waterside.

He was thrown through the windscreen and slammed into the broad tree trunk with a force that broke his neck and killed him instantly. But in the moments before his death, he saw neither trees nor river nor the end which he could not escape, to which either accident or design had committed him. He was back in Sir John's room, hearing him say, "So far as you're concerned I forfeited the right long ago . . . all things find their true end," and understanding him fully. In that fraction of time left to him he was standing over the man's body, holding the two photographs he had taken from the container. One of them was of himself and Harrison as boys, the two of them on a small river beach, each grinning and holding up a fish. His mother had taken it on an Irish holiday and on the back she had written—*I thought you would like this of our Johnny. (On the right)*. The ink was faded, but her writing was unmistakable. The other was an older photograph, on thicker cardboard, and showed his mother as a young girl of eighteen—there had been a similar one, enlarged, in their sitting-room—her blouse, with puffed sleeves, tight at her throat and caught with a small cameo brooch. On the back in the same but even more faded hand was written—*For my dear John, with all my love for always. Hilda.*

When the body was brought to High Grange, Coppelstone found the photographs and he destroyed them. Grimster had been searched before going down to the river so he knew that he had taken them from Sir John, that Grimster unknowingly had killed his own father; a father who had never acknowledged him but had helped him; brought him as close to him as he could, had planned for him to take his place, had guided and fostered his career, wanting him near but never able to reach or acknowledge him openly.

The Department moved smoothly into action. Sir John had died of heart failure at the age of fifty-nine. Grimster had been killed in a car accident. Sir John got his quarter column in *The Times* and Grimster his paragraph in the *Western Morning News*.

And Lily in Mrs. Harroway's flat wept for her lost love when she heard the news; and through her sorrow saw herself standing in black at the graveside and wondered how soon she could decently talk to Mrs. Harroway about her choice of clothes for the occasion. Her emotion was genuine but not deep. For two nights she cried herself to sleep, knowing she would never love anyone again as she had loved Johnny, and wondered if she should write to his mother . . . and she kept telling herself that despite all, life must go on . . . life must go on because after all it wasn't fair to the dead to live for ever in the past. For two weeks she enjoyed the comforting misery of herself as a tragic figure, and then worried because she had missed her regular period, and then was relieved when it came a week late . . . and then she settled smoothly back again into being Lily—Lily and her ill-starred lovers . . . first Harry and then Johnny . . . poor Johnny . . . no one could ever truly take his place, never, never. . . .